**The torch was behind him
on the wall, leaving his face
cast in shadows.**

As her face tilted up to him, her body
brushing his, awareness grew ever higher,
surging from her breasts down to her loins
with a heat that was startling and embarrassing and . . . tempting.

"Know that if a soldier ever bothers
you—or *any* man—come to me and I will
protect you."

He sounded so sincere that she had to
smile. "Will you strike him with your
crutch?"

He grinned. "It makes a good weapon."

They stood there for a few moments,
trapped in this strange intimacy. How could
she know him for but a day and be so drawn
to him?

She might need to use his assistance, but
she did not deceive herself that that was all
there was between them. . . .

Other **AVON ROMANCES**

Julia Latham

THRILL OF THE KNIGHT

AVON BOOKS

An Imprint of HarperCollinsPublishers

This is a work of fiction. Names, characters, places, and incidents are products of the author's imagination or are used fictitiously and are not to be construed as real. Any resemblance to actual events, locales, organizations, or persons, living or dead, is entirely coincidental.

AVON BOOKS
An Imprint of HarperCollins*Publishers*
10 East 53rd Street
New York, New York 10022-5299

Copyright © 2007 by Gayle Callen
ISBN: 978-0-06-123515-3
ISBN-10: 0-06-123515-6
www.avonromance.com

First Avon Books paperback printing: March 2007

Avon Trademark Reg. U.S. Pat. Off. and in Other Countries, Marca Registrada, Hecho en U.S.A. HarperCollins® is a registered trademark of HarperCollins Publishers.

Printed in the U.S.A.

10 9 8 7 6 5 4 3 2 1

To Lisa Hilleren, fellow Packeteer and writing buddy: You have an incredible gift for figuring out the heart of an idea, and you know how much I have relied on you. You'll always have my gratitude. And now you're starting a new chapter in your life, giving us all a wonderful example of courage and belief in yourself.

THRILL OF THE KNIGHT

Chapter 1

Castle Alderley
Gloucestershire, England, 1486

Lady Elizabeth Hutton lay curled in bed, half asleep, half awake, disturbed by the sound of pounding feet on the winding staircase that led to her tower bedchamber. Frowning, she opened her eyes to see her lady's maid, Anne Kendall, fling open the door and slam it shut behind her. She leaned back against it, breathing rapidly, her face pale.

Elizabeth sat up in bed, the coverlet falling to her waist. "Anne? What is it?"

"Viscount Bannaster."

Elizabeth groaned. "Is he still here? I was hoping

that when I feigned illness yesterday rather than be introduced to him, he would realize the uselessness of his courtship."

"Then you feigned too well. He stayed."

"Does he not care that he looks a fool? I am already betrothed!" Although it didn't feel that way. She hadn't seen her betrothed since he was thirteen years old, and she eleven. And even then, it had been his brother she was first to marry. But William had died being thrown from his horse, the next brother was also dead, and she was down to John Russell. He had spent his adult life in Normandy. Had word even reached him that he was the newest heir of land and wealth—and a bride?

At least being betrothed had been a protection of sorts. Until recently.

Anne came to perch on the edge of the bed. She had black hair and eyes framing the palest skin, and to see her looking even whiter gave Elizabeth the first inkling of fear.

"Elizabeth, his soldiers have apparently been hiding in the forest. They swarmed into the castle just now."

"Oh God, who has been killed?" she cried, flinging back the coverlet and coming to her feet. Her night rail was no protection against the early morning chill.

Anne reached to take her hand. "No one, thank God."

Elizabeth began to shake with relief. Anne handed her her dressing gown and Elizabeth gratefully wrapped it around herself. She could not take any more deaths.

"It was too overwhelming and sudden," Anne continued. "Your men were in the midst of changing duties, and no one anticipated such a maneuver. They are confined to the barracks for now, until Lord Bannaster determines what their next 'duty' should be." She hesitated. "He was still assigning guards to the base of your tower, so I was able to ascend before anyone saw me. I heard him say that he will be up to see you in one hour."

"He thinks he will be admitted to my private chamber?" Elizabeth demanded, trying to force a laugh of disbelief. She had been in command of Castle Alderley since her parents died of a fever six months before. She was not about to relinquish her control.

But Holy God, how she wished her father were here. The ache that never went away was beyond tears now. None of this would have happened if the Earl of Alderley still held the castle, if Elizabeth had any brothers to inherit the earldom. But the only family she had left were two younger sisters, sixteen and fifteen, both being educated with another family, as Elizabeth had been. She had friends and servants, people to help her, but the responsibility for them all was hers alone.

For a moment, she felt disoriented, weak, a woman caught in a situation not of her own making. Her parents were dead, her first betrothed, a man she'd worshiped from childhood on, was dead. She felt passed off to the next brother in line, and now taken advantage of by a nobleman who lusted after the earldom.

But she was not the type of woman to allow herself to feel overwhelmed. She always took matters into her own hands. After her parents' deaths, she had sent a missive to her betrothed alerting him to her situation, telling him that, although he had not planned it, he had to return to marry. She had vague memories of him always in the background being compared to the brilliance that was his eldest brother. But now he was the baron, and she had heard nothing from him. She was considered one of the greatest heiresses in the kingdom—was that not enough to lure him?

"I will let this villain speak, and then I will make whatever decision is necessary," Elizabeth said with determination. "Surely the king will not tolerate such an outrage."

"Lord Bannaster is King Henry's cousin," Anne said bleakly.

Elizabeth straightened her shoulders. "I care not. I am in the right here. He cannot force me to wed him, not when a betrothal is as binding as any marriage ceremony."

"Unless the king decrees otherwise."

Elizabeth threw up her hands. "Anne, I need no more pessimism!"

"Forgive me. I only know what you tell me, that the king is growing impatient with your maidenly status. Your unsettled estate weighs on his mind."

Elizabeth frowned at her.

Anne rose to pour water into a basin. "Let me help you prepare." But as she gathered linen and soap, she suddenly paused. Her expression turned distant, then determined.

"What are you thinking?" Elizabeth asked.

"You have never met Lord Bannaster," the maid said slowly. "Neither have I. You sent word to his lordship about your illness through another maidservant."

"Mayhap he didn't appreciate the slight," Elizabeth said with bitterness.

"Nay, that is not what I mean. I have an idea. If he keeps control of Alderley, you'll be trapped here, at his mercy."

"The king would not allow—"

Anne put up a hand. "It will be some time before the king knows what is going on here. Think you Lord Bannaster will permit someone to inform his mighty cousin? Nay, Lord Bannaster knows what he's doing is illegal. He must be counting on a few days' secrecy to conclude his plan, whatever it is."

"'Tis a good thing you were educated with me," Elizabeth observed wryly. "One of us has to show some intelligence."

"The only way to foil him is to make him think everything is going as he wishes. He'll become overconfident—the servants say he seems quite pleased with himself."

"So you're saying I should let him think he's cowed me?" Elizabeth said, aghast.

"Nay, you'll be long gone, because I shall take your place."

She gaped at her dear friend. "What are you saying?"

"You'll pose as me and slip out of the castle unnoticed. We'll make sure all your servants understand the deception. No one will give you away."

"You want me to leave you all here to submit to his wrath?"

"But he won't know! He's never met you." Anne smiled grimly. "I think I can do a decent job being as stubborn and controlling as you."

In more relaxed times, Elizabeth would have playfully thrown a cushion at her friend. But now she could only shake her head. "I cannot do it, Anne. When Bannaster finds out, think you that I can allow my people to suffer for me?"

"But Elizabeth—"

"Shh, give me a moment." Elizabeth opened the shutters and looked down on the inner ward below. It was strangely quiet. The people who moved about seemed to scurry fearfully. They all depended on her for the necessities of life; she would not abandon them. Calm returned as she realized that she could deal with this situation. She turned to face her maid. "Anne, you are brilliant."

"I do not understand. You just said you would not—"

"I said I would not leave the castle. But aye, you and I will switch places, leaving me free to move about the castle and figure a way out of this dilemma."

Anne blinked. "Oh. I see. And then you could also escape if you need to."

"I won't be escaping."

"But—"

"We have to hurry. Thank God you're tall like me!"

An hour later, Elizabeth and Anne descended the tower stairs one floor, to Elizabeth's private solar. It was the chamber she'd always used for needlework with her mother's ladies. They were all married now with their own households, but Elizabeth was left to defend herself.

Anne looked uncomfortable in Elizabeth's gown— the bodice was a bit tight on Anne's generous figure. But the red embroidered brocade looked stunning with Anne's black hair, which she wore freely hanging as an unmarried maiden.

Elizabeth wore a wimple covering her red-blond hair, with the ends of the fabric draped to disguise her chin and neck. Her gown was a plain brown, with little decoration other than a square neckline to show her white smock up to her neck. It made Elizabeth almost feel invisible wearing it.

This plan would work—as long as she could warn the other servants before they accidentally revealed her identity.

Trying to bolster her own spirits, she smiled at Anne. "You've known me almost a lifetime; you know what I'd say. Perhaps you will be able to talk the viscount back to sanity. He has to realize what he is doing cannot be borne."

"But we are many days' journey from London," Anne cautioned. "He might feel free to do as he pleases."

"You will show him otherwise," Elizabeth said sweetly. "You can do this." She put her arm around the maid's shoulders.

They didn't have to wait long. They heard several heavy footsteps. The viscount was punctual. Remembering herself, Elizabeth shrank back behind Anne, as a proper lady's maid should.

The door opened, and a plainly dressed stranger entered, holding the door wide for another. Viscount Bannaster was surely the second man, for his garments were of the finest fabrics. An embroidered codpiece exaggerated his manly attributes beneath his short doublet. A soft-crown hat perched on his dark brown hair, with a feather curling almost to his shoulder. When he saw Anne, Elizabeth could see his tension replaced by relief. God forbid his captured bride wouldn't be pretty enough for him.

Lord Bannaster swept the hat from his head as he gave Anne an elaborate court bow. "Lady Elizabeth, how good to finally meet you."

Anne said nothing for a moment, and in a panic, Elizabeth tapped her from behind.

In a cool voice, Anne said, "But sir, we have not met. Who are you to invade a lady's private solar?"

Elizabeth almost choked with suppressed glee. Where had this brave, icy Anne come from?

Lord Bannaster's man narrowed his eyes, and his lordship's face reddened. But to his credit, he only revealed a tight smile.

"Lady Elizabeth, I am Thomas, Viscount Bannaster. I have come on behalf of the king to see to your protection."

"The king . . . sent you?" Anne asked.

Lord Bannaster's hesitation was slight. "Nay, but as I am his cousin and was traveling nearby, I took it upon myself to see to his interests. There are factions in this part of the country that have not expressed their clear support of King Henry. He needs this part of Gloucestershire settled. Have your people informed you about the raids on your property?"

Elizabeth held her breath. Had Anne been nearby when Elizabeth had listened to the captain's report about the raids?

Anne inclined her head. "If you mean the theft of several dozen sheep out of thousands, then aye, I know of it. My men are handling it. And how is this your business, my lord?"

"Only that you need a man in charge, so that these things will not happen."

"Sheep are never stolen from men?" she asked wryly.

Oh, well done, Anne! Elizabeth thought.

Lord Bannaster shot Anne a disapproving look. "But suitors don't become embroiled in arguments and fights over men. I am going to petition the king to make me your guardian."

Guardian, Elizabeth thought with reluctant admiration. Lord Bannaster was not stupid enough to boldly demand to wed her. Nay, he was going to sidle his way in by stealth. His motivations could be anything from sudden poverty to simple greed. Alderley was the largest prize in the kingdom. But her betrothal contract was rare, since the earldom was involved. He must be a very ambitious man.

"Your offer is appreciated," Anne said coolly, "but I am not in need of a guardian. My betrothed has been apprised of my situation."

"Forgive me for being cruel, but for all you know, my lady, he doesn't even know he's been named the heir. He might never return from the dangers of Europe. The protection of the castle is too important to ignore."

Anne clutched her hands together behind her back, and to Elizabeth's worry, they were shaking.

"I have my own well-trained army," Anne said.

"But there are thieves in these woods, as you yourself have admitted. Your soldiers will be needed there. My own men will gladly help defend Castle Alderley from your ambitious, dangerous suitors."

And he didn't include himself in such a description?

"I will explain the situation to your men," he continued.

"Am I your prisoner?" Anne asked.

Lord Bannaster gave a rich laugh. "My lady, of course not! But men have begun to quarrel over you. All of this wealth," he waved an arm about the room, "and your husband will inherit the earldom."

Elizabeth had been right about his motives. She leaned forward and whispered quickly, "Only the Russell heir."

Anne drew herself up. "Only the Russell heir will inherit the earldom, as the king decreed."

"King Edward made that document, and he is long since dead. You are a defenseless woman. With you roaming freely about this castle, anyone could seduce you with flattering words, or take you off to compromise you. I feel that you need to remain here in your comfortable suite of rooms until this precarious situation is settled."

"So how long do you plan to keep me a *prisoner*, my lord?"

"That is a harsh word. Once I reach London, it shan't take long to convince my dear royal cousin that I can help him by becoming your guardian. While you wait, you will live in comfortable, familiar surroundings and do whatever you ladies do to keep yourselves amused. Your maidservant will see to your comforts and apprise you of the castle itself." He paused. "As for the man in charge, I regret to inform you that your steward was shocked to see my men peacefully enter your ward this morn. Though I tried to explain, he drew his sword on me. He must have had a weak heart, for he died before we even came to blows. Allow me to express my condolences."

Elizabeth held herself still by sheer will, as their situation suddenly became more perilous. Her steward, her father's dearest friend and servant—dead? He had been a robust hearty man, only just entering his middle years. Bannaster had killed her servant, one of her own people. Who else would die trying to guard Elizabeth?

"He was a good man," Anne whispered.

Lord Bannaster nodded gravely. "Indeed. And I feel responsible. So I am going to offer you the services of my own steward, Master Arthur Milburn."

He nodded toward the other man, who was tall

and lean, dressed in somber colors and wearing an impassive expression. Master Milburn gave a clipped bow.

Elizabeth knew a rising fear. Nothing was going as expected, and her old nightmares about being hunted down dark corridors came back to life. The castle was out of her control—for the time being. It was even more imperative that she discover what was going on down below, see how truly vulnerable they were.

"My lady," Lord Bannaster continued, "I fear even my own soldiers would be tempted to take for themselves the riches that come with marrying you. So I have directed that two of them guard your tower at all times—one of my men, and one of yours."

"Am I forbidden visitors?" Anne asked, for the first time allowing anger in her voice. "Even my priest? How can I not attend mass every day?"

"When I return from London, we shall see how secure your situation is," he said, shrugging apologetically. "Read your bible, Lady Elizabeth. A woman's place is well explained."

Elizabeth flinched.

"Until then, trust Milburn to see to your affairs— and to your safety. A good day to you, my lady." He bowed low. "Until I see you again."

He swept from the room. With another cool look, Milburn followed him and shut the door.

Elizabeth ran to the door and put her ear to it. She could hear nothing but footsteps fading away, and then several male voices speaking from down below, presumably the guards Bannaster had mentioned.

She turned to face Anne grimly. "He had this well planned out. He wants me locked away—and he killed poor Royden, my loyal steward, to ensure that no one would be brave enough to stop him." Though she was livid with anger, tears finally coursed down her face at such a senseless death.

Anne threw her arms around Elizabeth, and they cried together.

Finally Elizabeth backed away and wiped her face. "We have no time for mourning. There are too many people to protect. I'll go see the situation in the great hall."

"But the servants will recognize you! If Lord Bannaster discovers you've deceived him—"

"I vow he won't. I shall go to the kitchens first, and have the cook and her servants spread the news before I enter the great hall. Our people are smart and proud—they won't want such a man deciding our fate."

"And then what?" Anne whispered.

"And then I'll have to think of a plan. I refuse to believe that my betrothed is dead. He's out there somewhere."

Chapter 2

John, Baron Russell, sat angrily on a bench in a decrepit tavern within a day's journey of Castle Alderley, the home of Lady Elizabeth Hutton, the woman he'd only recently discovered was his betrothed. The sounds of drunken men laughing and shouting assailed his ears; the hearth fire sputtered, but he paid attention to none of it, so caught up was he in figuring out a way to solve his problems.

He'd spent these many years pursuing adventure, the youngest son of three, forced to make his own way in the world. He'd gone to Europe at sixteen to be squire to his cousin, growing from a needy boy lost in his eldest brother's shadow, to a man who knew he could rely on himself. He'd been happy in Europe, where his skills on the battlefield had won him the only acclaim he'd thought he would ever need. Tournaments and mercenary work had filled his days, and he'd been proud to support himself, asking for nothing from his family, who'd certainly not expected him to do so well. But the deaths of his older two brothers had made him the baron and given him a noble bride.

He took a sip of weak ale, gripping the handle hard. They were all dead now: his parents, his middle brother, Robert, who'd hoped to be a scholar, and his eldest brother, William, who'd been the epitome of knighthood. Handsome, poetic, and charming, William had won the admiration of dozens of maidens with his flirting ways, even though he'd been promised to Lady Elizabeth. He'd been the measurement that John, overweight and awkward as a child, had always been held to and found lacking by his father.

But now marriage was John's family duty. He'd returned from Normandy several days before, expecting to find Rame Castle ready to accept his leadership. But Rame Castle, the pride of his father, John's new legacy, had been neglected, its fields fallow, most of its soldiers and many tenants long gone. His elder brother had been content to enjoy his life in London, anticipating the marriage that would make him rich, and misusing his own resources.

"I still can't believe what William did to our family name," John muttered into his tankard.

On his right, Sir Philip Clifford, his fellow knight and man-at-arms, turned from contemplating his own ale. "Your brother neglected his birthright. 'Tis not a reflection on you."

"But he is my family, and now I am responsible," John said, slamming down his tankard. Ale sloshed onto his hand. He lowered his voice. "My own brother sucked the life from his estate, leaving me to reclaim it as I can. The steward told everyone that I needed money to live in Europe, that William had to support me." The words choked in his throat.

"Don't let yourself believe that William initiated such a lie, John. The steward was a desperate man who did not want to blame perhaps his own mismanagement, as well as his own lord for the castle's failing."

John wanted to believe that. Would he always wonder? "Regardless, the rest of the country—even King Henry's court—must believe that I am as incapable as my brother." He drained his tankard. "Every coin I have must go to resurrecting Rame Castle."

"You have to eat. After all," Philip added, beginning to smile, "you must keep yourself presentable for your betrothed. Is she lovely?"

"I only received her letter; I did not see a portrait of her face. It has been over ten years since last we met, and she was a child then. She could refuse to marry me. After all, she was to marry my brother, a man who everyone thought fit the ideals of a knight."

"Your parents arranged this marriage long ago, and she won't dishonor them," Philip said firmly. "The king wanted your two families joined when he agreed to give Lady Elizabeth in marriage to the Russell heir. You bring to her a castle that defends the coast of Cornwall. And you bring yourself, a great knight of England, the next Earl of Alderley, as the king wished. What woman wouldn't swoon at your feet? But I ask again, is she lovely?"

"Aye, she was lovely."

The memories flooded back, of watching the pretty young girl with the red and gold of sunset in her hair. But she'd been watching William, whose handsome looks had always drawn every eye. John hadn't expected anything different, not back then. He'd well known how far above him she would always be. Yet still he'd trailed after her, watching her as if she were a rare painting hung in a church. He'd been a foolish, whimsical boy, and the year she'd spent fostering with his family had not improved him.

"I wish you would listen to me," Philip said with a sigh. "This is the perfect time to ask for help from the League of the Blade."

John groaned. "Not that fairy tale again, Philip. Though you may spend every free hour trying to track down each deed attributed to them, what has it gotten you?"

"More clues to work with," Philip said stubbornly.

But his face reddened, and he looked away.

"More myths, more legend. More nothing." John spoke more harshly than he had intended.

Philip glanced at him impassively. "Just because they hide their deeds well, does not mean they don't exist. My own grandmother swore until her dying day that she would have been killed for her money, had not a Bladesman rescued her. I would not even have been born!"

John softened his voice. "I do not doubt your grandmother, Philip. But I will not wish for rescue by a legend when I can solve my own problems. I will prove to Lady Elizabeth that I can be a successful husband."

Philip smiled. "And you've already begun. You left all of your coins to begin the resurrection of your castle's fortunes. The priest will do a good job acting as steward until you appoint someone else. Your parents died six years ago. Even if they watch from heaven above, they would not blame you."

John said nothing. His brother had allowed a mockery to be made of the sum of their parents' lives. John refused to let anyone think that he would make a mockery of his life—of his marriage. He had grown to love his exciting life in Europe, never imagining that he would have the opportunity to make a good match. If he occasionally felt the slightest worry that marriage and nobility might be boring, he always put it out of his head.

There was another burst of laughter from several roughly dressed men gathered at a table near the hearth. They did not soften their voices.

"I don't believe ye." With food caught in his beard, the man speaking leaned back against the wall, almost toppling his bench.

"Whot's not to believe?" another man demanded, getting to his feet, trying to look affronted, but spoiling the effect by swaying. "I just come from there. Her soldiers been sent away, and Castle Alderley is bein' held by Lord Bannaster."

John stiffened. Castle Alderley was the home of his betrothed. It was under attack? He rose to his feet, and Philip followed his lead. With a hand on his sword hilt, he walked to the hearth. The group of laughing men all looked up at him, their smiles fading as they took in the fact that their numbers clearly overpowered John's.

"Mind yer own concerns," Dirty Beard said, spitting into the rushes at John's feet.

John only raised an eyebrow, then ignored him to focus on Swaying Man. "What else do you know about Castle Alderley?"

Swaying Man took another sip of his ale, touching his tankard to John's chest. "And whot be yer interest?"

"You don't need to know my interest. I'm only asking for information you're already freely giving."

Dirty Beard rose suddenly to his feet, pawing at his scabbard. John drew his sword and slashed the man's belt off his waist, dropping his weapon hard to the floor.

Now all six men were on their feet, facing the two swords of John and Philip.

"We want no trouble," John said pleasantly. "Only answers. If you wish to keep your swords—and your lives—you'll respond. Now tell me the news of Castle Alderley."

Dirty Beard and Swaying Man exchanged a

guarded glance, while their four companions shuffled uneasily. They were all drunk, but they seemed to realize that the size disparity between them and John and Philip was not in their favor.

Swaying Man kept a hand on his sword hilt, gave a loud belch, but then grudgingly said, "The viscount is holdin' it for the king."

"And why would it suddenly need to be held?"

"Lady Elizabeth is a maiden yet, and that estate needs a man's guidance."

"Not the way she acts," Dirty Beard grumbled, looking longingly at his sword. "Thinks she's good enough to do it all herself. 'Bout time a man showed her otherwise."

Swaying Man leaned forward as if he and John were suddenly friends. "He's got her locked in a tower, he has. Even now he's gone to London, askin' the king for permission to—"

They all broke into laughter as if each of them understood what the viscount wanted. John's sweat turned cold at the thought of a young woman treated thusly—and because he had not returned in time.

John put up his sword and tossed a coin onto their table. "My thanks for the information."

Swaying Man ignored him as he summoned the tavern owner.

"John," Philip said as they returned to their own table. "I can read your expression. Do not take the blame on yourself. You only just discovered your betrothal."

John raised a hand. "Regardless of whether I believe I could have prevented it, I have to find a way to make this situation right. My castle and lands are in a shambles; I have no army but you, Ogden, and Parker. I will not ask the three of you to follow me into certain death."

"But you're her legal betrothed. We'll go to the king and—"

"Even if I went to London, the false rumors have probably preceded me. And I cannot openly approach Castle Alderley and demand the return of Lady Elizabeth, especially against a viscount who is related to the king. I am a baron without an army. I could lose the right to her."

Though his future might be tenuous, John was no longer that boy who let himself be aimlessly swayed. "I will not permit this to happen."

He pushed his tankard away and rose to his feet. A lone man at another table glanced up at him, then hunched over his own tankard.

John knew that this quest would contain enough excitement and danger to keep him satisfied. "Philip, I will prove that I deserve to marry her. When I convince her of my regrets and my sincerity, she will stand beside me when I go to the king on our behalf."

Philip stood up. As they left the tavern together, Philip asked, "How will we accomplish all this?"

Ogden and Parker, who had remained with the horses, now walked toward them across the tavern yard.

"Milord," Ogden said, chewing on the end of his long mustache, "we heard rumors ye need to know."

"If it concerns Lady Elizabeth, then I already

know. We leave for Castle Alderley immediately. Go inside for your dinner, and be quick."

As the two soldiers hurried away, John glanced at Philip. "You asked how we will accomplish Lady Elizabeth's rescue. We'll need to find her army. Give me some time to think, and I'll come up with the rest. I always do."

They exchanged grins of anticipation.

When the two soldiers returned, the four of them set off. Since there were only so many hours of daylight left, John set a punishing pace. By the time it was full dark, the horses were well lathered and hung their heads in exhaustion.

The party made camp in a copse of trees just off the main road. Around a fire, they ate dried beef and biscuits, and John said little as he contemplated what he could do for Lady Elizabeth. A plan was beginning to take form, but before he could express it, the horses began to neigh with unease. Parker, who'd been on sentinel duty, came through the trees from the direction of the road. He was broad and squat, shorter than most men, but an incredibly skilled warrior. John had taken on him and Ogden when no one else would have them, and he'd never once regretted it.

Parker threw a look over his shoulder back at the road. "I hear nothin', milord, but the horses never lie."

A cloaked man stepped forward out of the shadows, both hands raised in peace.

John's hand dropped to his sword hilt, but he didn't draw it. "Who are you?"

The man slowly lowered his hood so that they could see his face. He was clean-shaven and wore a pleasant smile. "Good evening, gentlemen. Might I share your fire?"

It was hardly a cold evening, John thought, but perhaps a lone man felt safer with others about him. "You may, sir, but I ask your name in return."

The stranger looked chagrined. "And though I regret it, I cannot grant your request, Lord Russell."

John stiffened. "You know me, but I am not permitted to know you?"

"I know *of* you, my lord, and that is a different thing." He glanced at John's men. "Might we speak in private?"

"I will not leave," Philip said tightly.

The stranger considered him. "I know not of you, sir. Lord Russell, do you wish him to remain?"

"I do. He is Sir Philip Clifford." John nodded toward his other two men, and they disappeared into the trees. He motioned to the fire.

The stranger sat down and rubbed his hands together. "The heat feels good to these old bones."

John studied him. "You have no look of age about you, sir."

"Then I hide it well," the man said, smiling softly. "There are days when all of us feel older than time, are there not?" His smile faded. "I come to you representing my brethren, Lord Russell. You came to our attention many years ago, and we have followed your exploits ever since."

John frowned, but to his surprise, Philip leaned forward with intense interest.

"Of what brethren do you speak, sir?" John asked.

With reverence, Philip whispered, "The League of the Blade."

The stranger glanced at Philip with faint amusement, but John was not in the mood for such foolishness.

"Philip wishes for miraculous assistance," John said shortly. "I know better. Whom do you represent, sir?"

"You do not believe in the League?" the man asked in a soft voice.

"As much as any story told to babes," John said. "Only this was told to squires and young knights. I don't believe in encouraging unasked-for hope."

"Skeptical men make good warriors," the man answered.

Philip's grin faltered.

John just shook his head. "Sir, explain yourself or keep quiet so that I can rest."

"You have come a great distance this last month, only to find all not as you'd last left it."

John felt chilled. The story of his neglected castle was already spreading.

"If you know such things," Philip said stiffly, "then you know John is innocent of any wrongdoing."

"There are those who say otherwise," the stranger said.

"Lies spread by his brother's men!" Philip cried.

John held up a hand. "Peace, Philip. Let him speak."

Solemnly, the stranger said, "The judgment on

your family's worthiness has not yet been pronounced."

Through clenched teeth, John said, "And are you and your *brethren* the ones to pass judgment on me?"

"Nay, not us," the stranger answered. "But we do judge where our assistance can be offered."

Philip grinned again and opened his mouth to speak, but the stranger cut him off.

"And that judgment we hold in reserve, for now."

John met the man's stare coolly. "So you tell me of assistance that you will not offer. What purpose does this serve?"

"To alert you to our presence, to have you understand that although we have not yet decided to aid you, we do understand Lady Elizabeth's predicament. She, a woman alone, deserves our help."

"She is my responsibility. She's alone because I did not return from Normandy in time."

The stranger gave a slight shrug. "You bear not all the fault. You could not predict the death of her parents, the death of your brother, or the arrogance of Lord Bannaster."

"I cannot trust in your assistance to Lady Elizabeth," John said. "I know nothing of you or your brethren."

"But John—" Philip began.

"No one is going to control my fate," John continued. He looked at the stranger. "In the morning, go back to your brethren and tell them that I will handle my own problems."

The stranger gave a single nod. "I respect your position, Lord Russell. We will be watching."

"I cannot prevent that," John said. "Sleep well."

John rolled into his blanket and fell asleep. It was Ogden's and Parker's turn at the watch through the night, and John trusted their care. In the morning, the stranger was already gone, though both soldiers swore they'd heard nothing.

As Philip folded his blanket, he said, "Of course they heard nothing, John. The Bladesmen are famous for their ability to appear and disappear in absolute silence."

"Men like you spread rumors that become legends," said John good-naturedly.

"What rumor? 'Tis the truth!"

John only shook his head and continued to pack up their possessions. When the other three were finished, they looked at John expectantly.

"I have a plan," he said calmly. "Without an army, we cannot demand the return of Lady Elizabeth, so Ogden and Parker, you two will be charged with locating the Alderley soldiers. Together we can rescue their mistress. But we need to know her situation, to better understand how. We'll have to disguise ourselves to enter Castle Alderley."

Philip cocked an eyebrow. "And how would we do that, and still be allowed to remain within the castle? After all, Bannaster's men are bound to be suspicious of newcomers, since they have a woman locked in a tower."

"But they also cannot afford to seem at war.

Surely Lord Bannaster wants to show the king that with him in command, Castle Alderley is in good hands."

"Then we would be entering as travelers," Philip continued with a grin. "Wouldn't we be expected to eat a meal, then leave?"

"Aye, so we must make it obvious that we cannot leave."

All three men frowned at him.

John sighed as if disappointed in them. "We'll be suffering injuries from an attack by thieves."

Philip blinked. "An attack?"

"If we're wounded, they cannot in good conscience send as away."

"But—"

John looked at Ogden and Parker. "I'll need the two of you to make camp nearby and locate the Alderley army. If something happens to Philip and me, you will both need to go to the king. You'll be Lady Elizabeth's last hope."

They nodded solemnly.

"And you and I will fake injuries," Philip said skeptically. "How long could that last?"

"You're right," John said, trying not to smile. "We could not fool anyone for long with fake injuries. So they'll have to be real." He again looked at Ogden and Parker. "We'll need to look quite bruised. I think it best to have one leg so swollen that I can claim it broken. But no real broken bones, as we might need to fight."

All three men gaped at him.

John laughed. "Have you not wanted to take out your anger on me? Now is your chance."

"They're not angry at *me*!" Philip protested.

Ogden harrumphed. "So thinks you."

Chapter 3

On the second day of her new identity, Elizabeth awoke wrapped in a blanket, feeling cold and achy and disoriented. She sat up stiffly and heard the crackle of a straw pallet beneath her instead of her soft stuffed mattress. It took her a moment to realize where she had spent the night— in the kitchen, warm before the fire, safe from all of those who slept together in the great hall. It had been Adalia the cook's idea, when Elizabeth had discovered that she wasn't permitted to sleep at Anne's bedside. Frantic with worry, Elizabeth had wanted to sleep at the base of the tower, in case Bannaster tried to get to Anne, but Adalia had insisted that Castle Alderley's soldiers would let no one in the tower without a fight.

Elizabeth drew her knees to her chest and huddled against the wall. For just a moment, fear tried to overcome her, creeping into her mind, poisoning her self-assurance. She felt so very alone. She hadn't even had time to properly mourn her parents or her betrothed. Everything she thought she'd anticipated for her life was gone.

But she still had her own wits to make it through this trial, and she could count on nothing else, not even the next Russell heir, her betrothed. She rose to her feet, smoothing down her skirts and readjusting the wimple to cover her hair. She had to keep going, to remember that her people needed her. Anne needed her. Elizabeth had only been allowed to see her at meals yesterday, and she seemed to be doing well.

Adalia bustled into the kitchens and began to order the maids to work. She was short and thin, frail-looking for a woman who cooked, but she was full of energy and in command of her domain. When the fires were tended and the cauldrons of barley pottage began to heat, Adalia came to Elizabeth and put her arm around her shoulders.

"And you, Mistress Anne," she said with a wink, "did ye sleep well?"

"I did, Adalia, my thanks. It was warm and safe in here." Elizabeth lowered her voice. "Do you think word of my new identity has spread far enough today? I need to be in the great hall, seeing the weaknesses of our enemy."

"The servants have been informed, Anne. That

struttin' viscount already left for London just after mass, so ye need have no fears about him."

"I slept through mass?" Elizabeth said in shock.

"I thought it best not to disturb ye. I told Master Milburn that you were feelin' ill."

Elizabeth nodded her thanks. "Bannaster's steward seems like a man difficult to fool. He wasn't suspicious?"

"He was far too busy seein' his master off," Adalia said. "You let us help ye bear the burden, Anne. Royden, God rest his soul, would want ye safe."

Thinking again of her dead steward made Elizabeth's eyes sting with tears. But as far as she'd been able to tell, the poor man had died just as Bannaster had said—his heart had given out, in front of many witnesses in the great hall. But just because Bannaster hadn't been proved a murderer, didn't mean that he wouldn't stoop to such a heinous crime should someone interfere with his plans.

A young maidservant entered the kitchen at a run and slid to a stop. "The new steward is callin' for Anne, Mistress Adalia." The girl glanced fearfully at Elizabeth, then away. "Two travelers have been brought in. They were attacked on the road nearby."

"Did he say why he needed me?" Elizabeth demanded.

The girl shook her head.

"You'll want to strip the sound of command from your voice, Anne," Adalia warned.

Elizabeth nodded. "Prepare a meal to break Lady Elizabeth's fast. I will return to collect it shortly."

The entire kitchen staff gave her fearful looks as she approached the entrance to the great hall. Yesterday she had skirted the room but once or twice, while her servants had been informed of her new identity. But now their loyalty would be put to the test. She said a brief prayer that no one would be punished should her masquerade be discovered.

She stepped out into the great hall, and as usual, the soaring chamber gave her a sense of awe, a feeling of being part of destiny. Stained glass windows were cut high into the walls. A massive hearth taller than a man filled one wall, and two staircases leading up to private chambers framed the hearth.

Two strangers lay on pallets before the fire. Elizabeth hesitantly walked forward. The new steward was standing above one of the men, questioning him.

"And what is your name?" Milburn asked.

"Sir John Gravesend," the man said in a deep voice, rasping with pain.

Elizabeth could not quite see his face. Though curious, she was reluctant to press forward until the steward told her what he wanted of her.

"I am Master Milburn, steward of Castle Alderley."

He said it as if it had always been so, Elizabeth thought bitterly.

"And your companion—what is his name?" Milburn asked.

"Philip Sutterly, my clerk."

"And why do you have need of a clerk?"

"I am trained as a bailiff, sir, although I am traveling to obtain a new position."

"And you were attacked on the road?"

"Five men jumped on us from the trees. They took all my coin, and left us beaten. It is only through providence that we were able to make our way here. My leg feels broken."

All the while Sir John spoke, Elizabeth had the strangest need to see his face. She took several steps forward and stood behind the soldiers who had brought the wounded men in. A makeshift crutch cut from a tree branch lay discarded beside the pallet. She could see Sir John's body from this new position, though not his face. He was a large man, with the broad shoulders of a knight that his title proclaimed for him. His hands were fisted, white-knuckled with strain. Elizabeth barely stopped herself from ordering Milburn to end the interrogation and see to the man's injuries. She bit her lip, unused to keeping silent, and concentrated on moving to a more advantageous position. For some reason, she had to see Sir John's face.

When it was revealed, he was looking up at Milburn, his brow furrowed in a grimace of pain. Sir John's hair, cut at his mid-neck, was light brown in color. He had the blunt, well-formed face of a man in his prime, marred by a scar from his left temple down to his jaw. It was an old wound, well healed, and rather than make him look fearsome, it gave him a dangerous air. He could not be called handsome, but well formed and masculine. Bruises mottled his face, dried blood led from a cut on his lip, and swelling had begun to distort his profile.

This man was a bailiff, a mere overseer of a lord's manor? It was not unheard of for a knight to hold such a position, but why did he not have his own land?

And what color were his eyes?

When Elizabeth realized the ridiculous path her thoughts were traveling, she silently scolded herself. There were more important things than the appearance of a stranger, one only temporarily passing through Alderley.

"I, too, am new to the castle," Milburn said heavily, "but I have been told of thievery in these woods. We are attempting to correct the situation with a division of soldiers, but I fear too late for you, Sir John. We will see to your injuries." Milburn looked up. "Where is the maid I sent for?"

Elizabeth cleared her throat and threaded past two soldiers, who made way for her. She saw more than one serving maid give her a wide-eyed look and quickly turn away. Oh God, please let her people be cautious. "Master Milburn, I am here. Though I am on my way to see to my lady's meal, how may I help you?"

Milburn turned and scrutinized her. "You are well spoken for a maidservant."

Elizabeth lowered her gaze. Trembling was becoming easier. "I was raised and educated with Lady Elizabeth, sir. I am her companion."

"But not her equal," the steward said. "Your lady-

ship can wait to break her fast. These injured men
need your help."

"But I am no healer, Master Milburn."

"I understand that Castle Alderley does not have
a physician in residence."

"Nay, Master."

"I have sent for the healer from the village. You
may assist her when she arrives."

"But Lady Elizabeth—"

"Can wait," the steward said impassively.

She kept her gaze lowered. It was painfully obvious that Bannaster wanted his heiress to suffer from
loneliness, to be so desperate for companionship
that she would do whatever he wanted. Anne was
made of sterner stuff.

"Wait with the injured men for the healer's arrival,
and assist her as she needs it," Milburn continued.
"Bring them ale, but no food until she allows it."

"Aye, master."

Milburn and the soldiers went back to their duties, and Elizabeth found herself alone next to the
two injured strangers. She glanced at the second
man, the clerk, Philip Sutterly, whose face was as
bruised and swollen as his master's. His brown
hair, tinged red, was drenched with perspiration,
and his tunic was torn at the sleeve. He lay still
with his eyes closed, breathing shallowly as if even
that hurt.

She turned back to Sir John, only to find his gaze
now focused on her. His eyes were a startling blue,
blue as robin's eggs or a summer sky, fringed in
dark lashes, framed with lines etched by sun and

wind—and laughter? His left eye was tugged slightly by the scar, and it gave him the appearance of a man at the beginning of a wink, as if in jest. Something in those eyes inspired a strange feeling of familiarity, but she didn't think she had ever met him before. He was bold with his scrutiny of her, and she would have been affronted—if he'd known who she was, of course. Now, she was only the lady's maid, and any man could stare at her.

"Would you like ale?" Elizabeth asked the men.

Sutterly only nodded tightly, as if he couldn't spare a word.

Sir John said, "My thanks, Mistress . . ."

"Anne, sir. I am lady's maid to Lady Elizabeth."

"Ah, then it is to her that I owe my gratitude," he said. "Would she allow me to thank her?"

"She would, Sir John, were she available to you. But for now, she is secluded in her bedchamber."

"I see." He stirred on the pallet as if he could not get comfortable.

"Let me bring you ale to ease your thirst," Elizabeth said.

In the kitchens, she found Adalia pacing in front of her cauldrons.

"Anne, how are your patients?" the cook asked, wearing a smile.

"They are not my patients, only today's distraction to keep me from the lady's tower." Elizabeth sighed in frustration. "I am to wait on them and assist the healer when she arrives."

"And these men are but travelers?"

"A bailiff and his clerk. Their bodies proclaim

previous training, but five men fell upon them and they succumbed. Have you skins available? That would be easiest for them to drink from."

"Nay, but I have drinking horns."

Elizabeth sighed. "They will do."

She returned to the great hall and went to Sir John. "Can you sit up to drink?"

He came up on one elbow, and the movement must have hurt, but all he did was inhale swiftly, then give her a smile. She felt the force of his personality, his confidence, all shown off with the startling whiteness of his teeth.

Awkwardly, she held out a horn.

He glanced down at it, then back up at her, grinning. "Could you remove the stopper?"

She blushed. "Aye, of course." What was wrong with her? she wondered. Her own betrothed had been more handsome than this man, but there was something so . . . direct about the way that he looked at her. It seemed unusual. And then she realized that as the daughter of an earl, she'd always been treated with distance and respect, even by the men who thought to pursue her should her betrothed not arrive.

But this man looked at her with obvious interest, with frankness, and she felt . . . flustered.

She handed the horn back to him, and as he raised it to his lips, she saw more bruises and swollen fingers. Did he have broken bones?

"Please allow me to help," she said, reaching for the horn.

He eyed her without expression, and then nodded.

She held the horn to his mouth, slowly pouring. She was quite near to him in this position, just above. His keen eyes remained focused on her as he drank.

She watched him, too, the way his mouth pursed to drink, the way his throat moved when he swallowed. A drop of ale escaped and slid across his cheek and down to his neck.

She lowered the horn, and for a moment, they continued to stare at each other. It was the strangest thing—to be in a bustling great hall, sharing a glance that seemed full of . . . intimacy.

"Might I have a drink?" said a deep, amused voice.

Elizabeth broke the shared gaze with Sir John and shook herself from the unwelcome trance. She was blushing, and it somehow seemed a weakness. She hurried to the other pallet on the floor.

"Would you like me to hold the horn for you, Master Sutterly?" she asked.

The man had an open friendly face, but she did not feel as compelled to stare at him as she had at Sir John. She didn't know if that should comfort her—or cause her a deeper worry.

"I am surely not your master, Anne. Please call me Philip."

He took the horn himself, gave Sir John a superior grin, and began to drink. Elizabeth looked between them with amusement, sensing a friendship rather than only the relationship of a master and servant.

She forced her mind back to what was important: her friend imprisoned in the tower in her place.

How had Anne spent the night alone? Was she hungry? Did she think Elizabeth had been discovered? If only Elizabeth could go to reassure her, but all she could do was wait for the healer.

Luckily, the village was not too distant, and soon Rachel arrived, carrying her leather satchel. Elizabeth held her breath as their eyes met, but Rachel only nodded.

"Anne, me thanks for seein' to the wounded men," Rachel said.

Elizabeth found herself nervously fingering the wimple covering her hair, glad to hide beneath it. Her people had been true to their word, and even the villagers knew of her masquerade. But how far would this information spread before it fell into the wrong hands?

Elizabeth stood back as Rachel brought forth jars of ointment and soft cloths. The two men watched her warily, and Elizabeth knew that Rachel's youth and prettiness always surprised people who expected a healer to be a wizened elder. Rachel's mother, the previous healer, had died at far too young an age, leaving Rachel her secrets. The woman had learned them well, and all in the castle and the surrounding countryside trusted her.

Rachel put her hands on her hips and looked down at the men. "I understand that ye both were attacked by thieves."

Sir John nodded, an expression of pain crossing his face at even that small movement. "There were five of them. Philip and I caused an injury or two, but the odds were against us."

"And where be you hurt?"

Elizabeth felt awkward as the men took turns describing their injuries, pointing to their stomachs and faces. Sir John, whose crutch lay beside him, mentioned his concern that his leg was broken. Rachel moved his limb about, and by the whiteness around his mouth, even Elizabeth could see his pain.

"I must see the extent of the injuries," Rachel finally said.

She glanced around and saw Milburn watching them from across the hall. Rachel's eyes met Elizabeth's once more, and Elizabeth thought she saw a faint reluctance.

"Anne, I'll need yer help removin' some of their garments."

Elizabeth swallowed heavily, but other than that, did not betray herself. Of course a lowly maid would be asked such a thing. Perhaps she could yet escape, if they were away from Milburn's brooding watchfulness. "Might I find an empty chamber, so that you could work in privacy?"

Rachel nodded. " 'Tis kind of ye, Anne."

Sir John smiled tightly. "I agree. I did not plan to reveal all to the entire great hall."

With his eyes closed, Philip said, "Speak for yourself."

Elizabeth's eyes widened with amazement, but Sir John only chuckled.

"Forgive my clerk his impertinence," Sir John said. "We grew up together and sometimes he forgets to show respect to the one with the greater education and standing."

Philip opened one eye, muttered, "Hmph," and then closed it again.

After consulting the chamberlain—and being quite subservient to this man who usually consulted *her*—Elizabeth saw to the removal of the patients to an empty bedchamber. A groom from the great hall accompanied them and remained by the door in case the strangers proved unfriendly. Elizabeth fetched lard for Rachel to mix with her herbs, kept herself busy at Rachel's direction, and tried not to stare when the removal of clothing began. Elizabeth, sheltered and protected as a great heiress, had seen little of the manly form, and now found herself far too curious.

Rachel was quite thoughtful, only moving aside one piece of clothing at a time. Elizabeth saw much purple mottling of bruises, but of course she could not help but see the impressive muscle beneath. Though he was a bailiff by trade, Sir John was also a knight, a man at ease with both strength and violence. He must have fought back, as evidenced by the bruises and raw patches on his knuckles.

Rachel was gentle as she rubbed her ointment of lard and agrimony into each injury. There was little blood, except for a cut to Sir John's lip and a scrape along Philip's arm, and the wounds of defense on their hands.

Now that her curiosity was satisfied, Elizabeth

felt a pressing need to go to Anne, to confide their situation. But she could not abandon Rachel, could not risk behaving improperly for a maidservant.

Yet Sir John continued to stare at her, and she found his interest far too distracting.

Chapter 4

John lay back on the bed as each of his bruises was probed, then soothed with ointment. He was glad to be away from the great hall, where so many soldiers had gathered. It had taken all of his will to keep his hand from his sword hilt, as if he might have to defend himself among the enemy. He had to keep remembering that he was a wounded bailiff.

He was appreciative of the ministrations of the young healer—except when she came between him and his view of the maidservant, Anne. A heavy wimple covered Anne's hair and was wrapped about her chin and neck, as if she were an old woman hiding the folds of her neck. But she was not old. Her skin was creamy and looked soft to the touch, without blemishes or pox scars that so many of the women he'd come in contact with had. Her mouth was generous, made for laughter and kisses. She was as fine as any noble lady he had seen from afar, with slim height and regal bearing. As she moved, her curves were occasionally evident beneath the folds of the plain gown. She had the brown eyes of a doe, soft and limpid and so feminine, with their thick lashes that constantly swept downward as if she needed to hide her thoughts.

When he'd first arrived in the great hall of Castle Alderley, the steward Milburn had made no secret of the fact that Anne was Lady Elizabeth's personal maid, and Milburn had wanted her alone to assist the wounded travelers.

Why? The only obvious answer was to keep her from her other duties—seeing to Lady Elizabeth's comfort. Or was Lady Elizabeth being punished? Anne was being kept from bringing her the morning meal, after all. Was she being starved?

But no, he could not jump to conclusions. He had to find the facts. Lady Elizabeth had only been imprisoned a few days, and if she were being starved, Anne would be showing more fear. If Bannaster wanted Lady Elizabeth in marriage, he would be foolish to harm her.

From the moment Anne had been called from the kitchens to tend to him, John had watched her. She was the woman closest to his betrothed. Anne had said that Lady Elizabeth was "secluded," which didn't necessarily mean a prisoner. If Bannaster had meant to keep her status a secret, he wasn't going about it very well. Unless, being the King's cousin, he didn't care who knew his intent. And that could make him a dangerous man.

While John had been in the great hall waiting for the healer, he had noticed the unease that marked every servant's face, the hushed way people went about their work. There were no smiles, no laughter. But there was no open fear, which was a good sign for Lady Elizabeth's well-being.

Anne might be the key, John had realized almost immediately. Was Anne the only one with access to the tower? He would have to discover that as soon as possible.

He winced as Rachel set his leg in a wooden splint and began to wrap strips of cloth about it.

All right, he'd have to hobble around to discover his answers. Ogden and Parker had done a thorough job making him and Philip wounded travelers.

Rachel began to put away her cloths and jars. She glanced at Anne. "I will return on the morrow to see how Sir John and his clerk are doin'. Will ye need me before then?"

A strange thing to ask a maid, but then the whole household had to be feeling uneasy with their mistress "secluded."

Anne shook her head. "I will be fine. Are the men healthy enough to remain alone?"

"You could ask us," John said pleasantly.

Anne gave him a worried look.

Rachel smiled. "You are not badly wounded,

though it'll take time to mend. Stay in here and rest for much of the day, lettin' the servants bring ye what ye need."

"Might they come to supper in the great hall if they're feeling well enough?" Anne asked, blushing.

Did she not want to be alone with two strange men? John couldn't blame her.

Rachel sighed. "If ye feel up to it, Sir John. I will not keep ye prisoner."

When the healer began to talk about the appropriate foods for recovery, John found himself watching the maid again.

As the third son, he had realized early on that he would never attract a noble, refined bride. He'd had to make his own way in the world, learn skills no one thought he'd ever master. And associate with the kind of women who were happy to earn a few coins making a man's night comfortable.

Anne was not like that. Though she was a lady's maid, she had told Milburn she was raised as Lady Elizabeth's companion. But such a woman lived at the discretion of her mistress, and from what John remembered of Lady Elizabeth, she must surely keep Anne busy. Even as a young girl, the lady knew her role in the world, and she'd been confident—though kind—with the servants.

But did she inspire loyalty? Would Alderley's servants want to help him free their mistress? Would *Anne* want to help?

All these things would take time to learn, time he didn't want to waste. He was not a man used to lying about. But he had no choice. He would need allies if he were to rescue Lady Elizabeth. He would have to start with Anne.

To his unease, he almost looked forward to getting to know the maidservant. She was far too attractive. He still wasn't used to thinking of himself as an engaged man.

But *Sir John* wasn't engaged. He was a bailiff who could flirt with a maid. Though John regretted such tactics, they would have to do for now.

After Rachel had gone, Anne said, "I must see to my mistress, but I will have a meal sent in to you."

Philip came up on his elbow where he lay in his pallet. "You are kind to think of us, Anne. But it will be lonely in here all day for two men unused to lying about uselessly. You will come to visit us?"

With obvious reluctance, Anne nodded. "I will do what I can. But all the servants here are cheerful, good people who will be happy to look after you. Someone will come regularly."

"No one seemed very cheerful," John said, turning his head to view her better as she neared the door. "Is all well?"

With her hand on the latch, Anne hesitated. "For now, it is. Rest easy."

The two grooms departed with her, and John and Philip were left alone.

"Well I hope we don't sicken and die," Philip said, smiling, "for all the concern Anne shows."

"She has more to worry about than us," John said. "Listen at the door and see if we are being guarded."

"No wonder you wanted your leg broken."

Philip groaned as he stood up and crossed to the door. He listened for several minutes with his head against it. "I don't think anyone is out there. Should I open it and see?"

"Nay, I wouldn't want to make anyone suspicious. Come speak with me."

Philip pulled up a stool and sat next to John's bed.

With his voice lowered, John said, "What think you of the castle itself? The defenses are such that only a large army can overcome it. Let us hope that when Ogden and Parker locate Alderley's men, they will be willing to work with us."

"They will want to aid their mistress. This is an impressive holding, far larger than your own home. Think you can rule it?"

"Aye." Castle Alderley was the wealthy estate of an earl. If things went as planned, John might be that earl. Once he had been considered inconsequential; everyone had thought he would have to count on the mercy of his brothers for survival. And his oldest brother, William, had shown little mercy, thinking that it was his duty to train John as sternly as possible, to make him a better man.

And now he was Baron Russell, with a bride who needed him and a castle to win.

"Anne called Lady Elizabeth's imprisonment a seclusion," Philip continued. "Is it supposed to be a secret?"

"I know not. But the men in the tavern made it sound like an obvious move on Bannaster's part."

"And the soldiers who carried us to this room

seemed disrespectful of the lady's family, as if they served only Bannaster."

John slowly moved his foot, and he was satisfied when the pain was minor. "Of course he would put his own men in positions of power. I'll assign you to discover if Bannaster sent Alderley's soldiers to a specific place."

"That would certainly make them easier to find," Philip said.

There was a knock on the door, and Philip quickly returned to his pallet.

A young manservant entered, carrying a tray. "I bring this on orders from the kitchen," he said, bowing his head in servitude even as he pulled a small table between them on which to place the tray. "Do ye need help eatin'?" he asked dubiously.

With slow movements, Philip sat up. "Should my master need assistance, I can provide it. Our thanks."

When the groom had gone, Philip removed the cloth from the tray, revealing stew ladled onto bread trenchers and two tankards of ale. He sniffed appreciatively, then helped put cushions behind John's back so that he could sit up. Philip put his own plate on the table, and the tray across John's lap.

They ate in silence for several minutes until John said, "While you find out where Alderley's soldiers are, I'll position myself in the great hall, looking suitably ill, so they won't insist we leave. I'll find out if the steward is the true power while Bannaster is gone. And I'll also see who has access to Lady Elizabeth. We'll need to win their assistance."

"You've already begun with Anne." Philip grinned. "I suspect it will not be difficult for you to sway the young woman to our side."

"She *is* the lady's companion." John wasn't used to feeling embarrassed.

"And she is lovely in her own right."

"That matters not." John dipped a piece of bread in gravy and after popping it into his mouth, chewed and swallowed. "She is allowed to see Lady Elizabeth; that makes her important to us. If she's eventually sympathetic to our cause, she could take messages up for us."

"Risking her own life."

John frowned. "Lady Elizabeth's own life is at risk."

"Are you saying you will tell Anne who we are?"

"Not anytime soon. I will have to be certain of her loyalty first."

"Which means you'll be spending time with her."

John wasn't doing anything to feel guilty for, but thinking of Anne already made him feel that way.

It was past midmorning before Elizabeth approached the base of the round tower, which was guarded by two soldiers, each wearing his own master's colors. Elizabeth wanted to smile with pride at her soldier, Lionel, a young man not yet knighted, obviously chosen by Milburn's soldiers for his inexperience. A man lacking experience would be unlikely to stage an attack, or attempt a rescue alone.

But she knew that Lionel was the youngest of four brothers, all of whom were knights. Lionel had plenty of experience. She wanted to smile at him, but instead she curtsied deferentially, still holding the tray. Lionel gave her a single uneasy look, and then stared impassively at the wall across the corridor.

Bannaster's soldier took the linen off her tray and took a piece of bread for himself. After Elizabeth glared at him, he lifted his hand as if to cuff her. She ducked, hating the subservience, but knowing it was effective with a bully.

"Might I pass?" she asked softly. "My lady has yet to break her fast."

"Go," Lionel said, narrowing his eyes at his fellow soldier as he opened the wooden door.

"Serve her ladyship," Bannaster's soldier said, "and then bring the tray back down. If you delay too much, I'll come to find you myself."

Straightening her shoulders, Elizabeth gave a nod, then walked between them and into the center of the tower. A winding staircase hugged the outer wall, and disappeared up into the wooden floor of the room above. There were no windows this low in the tower, so there were torches to light the darkness. She went up quickly, used to the narrowness of the stone stairs. They had been worn smooth with generations of use, but once it had been only soldiers who tread on these steps. Now, in more modern times, castles were gradually being converted into more luxurious homes. This tower had been her dear father's indulgence to her. She had always liked the solitary feeling, the ability to clear her mind of distractions and concentrate on her art. She would draw elaborate patterns, embroider them, and give them as gifts, sometimes framed, sometimes worked into tapestries or cushions or coverlets.

It was ironic that although she loved solitude, she had now left Anne to endure it. Anne who loved people and conversations and an evening's entertainment, and was bored when she was alone.

Elizabeth quickened her step and passed into the lady's solar. Windows with their shutters thrown back let in the light. There were chairs and stools, cushions piled on the floor, and a worktable covered in fabric and threads.

"Lady Elizabeth?" Elizabeth called loudly, as she shut the door she'd just come through.

Anne descended several stairs from the bedchamber above, and the relief on her face made Elizabeth feel terribly guilty.

"Forgive me for being late, my lady," Elizabeth said, motioning Anne to go back upstairs. Elizabeth hurried to follow her, and then shut this door as well.

The moment Elizabeth set her tray on a table, Anne flung her arms around her.

"What is going on?" Anne demanded in a whisper, pulling back, yet still clutching Elizabeth by the upper arms. "You didn't come to sleep last night. I have been frantic with worry. For a while I thought you were discovered, but then no one came for me. But if those soldiers think you only a maid, they could have—"

When Anne ended her babbling with a sob, Elizabeth knew how deeply frightened Anne had been.

"I am so sorry," Elizabeth said softly. "I am not going to be allowed to see you except for meals. Milburn is obviously under orders to keep you—me as solitary as possible."

"Then where did you sleep?"

"In front of the kitchen hearth."

"Oh Elizabeth!" Anne took her hand and led her to a chair at the table. "Are you exhausted?"

"I was so tired I actually slept well, and I felt safe in Adalia's kitchen. But while we talk, you must eat, because I'm to bring the tray back down, and I'm not to take much time."

Anne sighed as she uncovered the tray. "I had thought we could have a long conversation."

"I did, too. But there truly isn't much to tell. Bannaster left for London this morn, so that is a relief. Adalia agreed to run the household for me, so that none of the servants would forget that I'm now supposed to be you."

"This must be so confusing for everyone," Anne said, and then bit into her buttered bread.

"It is. I finally let myself remain in the great hall for a more extended period of time. All are cautious and quiet, but no one has made a mistake."

"But there are so many others to worry about!"

"I know, but at least I have proof that news of my identity has spread to the villagers. Rachel the healer came up to tend two wounded travelers, and she knew our secret."

"Thank goodness!" Anne said as she began to eat her pottage.

"I can see Milburn's plans for me."

Anne gasped. "But I thought you said—"

"Nothing villainous," Elizabeth hurried to assure her. "But he's finding every reason to keep me from you. That is why I'm so late. He had me tend the travelers, and then assist Rachel."

"Travelers?"

"A bailiff and his clerk." Elizabeth hesitated, and knew she'd made a mistake by the way Anne's eyes sharpened.

"So what is so interesting about these travelers?" Anne asked.

"They were wounded by thieves," Elizabeth answered, trying to sound indifferent. "The bailiff's leg is broken, so they will be with us until Rachel claims them fit to travel."

"I repeat, what is so interesting about these travelers?"

Elizabeth felt a fiery blush sweep over her face. "The bailiff . . . looked at me with interest."

"As if all men don't do that?" Anne said, the hint of a smile turning up the corner of her mouth.

"Nay, it was not the same. Noblemen look at me with a covetous intent—as a prize to win. Hence Lord Bannaster's behavior."

"Elizabeth," Anne began gently.

"It is foolish of me to care, I know. I am already a betrothed woman, and I need not concern myself with such men. But Sir John—" she added.

"He is a knight?"

"Aye, with the body of a warrior."

Anne sat back in her chair. "It is so?"

"I was forced to help Rachel," Elizabeth defended herself. "I tried not to look."

"But he was looking at you," Anne said.

Elizabeth reluctantly nodded. "He watches me as if I'm . . . just a woman, not an heiress, not a prize."

"I have always been worried that some day a man like this would come along to distract you."

"William treated me as a woman," Elizabeth whispered, surprised to find tears so close to the surface. "The romantic letters he wrote me, the way he stared at me whenever we were together. The beauty of his face—"

Anne hesitated. "You only saw him but once a year, Elizabeth. I know he is dead now, and can never prove himself to you, but—"

"He had already done so," Elizabeth insisted. "I will never forget what it was like to be worshiped for my femininity, for my grace. That's not the way this bailiff makes me feel."

"Then how?"

"I feel . . . a strange excitement that is of the flesh." Elizabeth covered her face. "I cannot believe I am speaking of this foolishness. How are *you*, dear Anne?"

Anne looked suspicious of the change in conversation, but she accepted it without complaint. "I am lonely, of course, but that is no terrible thing compared to what can befall a woman."

"Just tell me what I can bring you to ease your day."

"Well, I am taking Lord Bannaster's advice by reading the Bible."

Elizabeth groaned. "Do not let the man hear you say that! His self-confidence already fills every room he enters."

Anne laughed, and Elizabeth was pleased by the return of her friend's good spirits.

"Bring me things from the sewing room to mend," Anne continued. "Though I know you think otherwise, there are only so many hours in the day one can create pictures with embroidery."

"You have your lute," Elizabeth said.

"And no one's voice to accompany."

"I am so sorry," she whispered, taking Anne's hand. "All of this is my fault. If you hadn't been here with me when we were invaded, you would be safe at home."

"On my father's farm, waiting for my parents to find a man they think worthy enough to marry me. The miller was last being discussed, and I guess I should be happy, because he has only one dead wife, two children, and most of his teeth. Nay," she continued, lifting a hand when Elizabeth would have interrupted, "I am content to help you, my friend."

Elizabeth hugged her swiftly. "I will return with your dinner as soon as I can."

Anne gave her a crooked smile. "My thanks. So what will you do until I see you next at dinner?"

"Study how Milburn is running my castle, see how well his soldiers obey him—oh, and take care of two travelers."

"Then I wish you good luck, though you won't need it. You always succeed, Elizabeth. And now that I know Bannaster is gone, I feel much better about your safety."

With the covered tray in her hands, Elizabeth looked back over her shoulder at Anne. "I wish I felt safe. I only feel exposed and vulnerable, and so worried for my people. But I will take your courage with me, Anne."

When Elizabeth walked through the great hall on the way to the kitchens to return the tray, she felt herself being watched. But instead of her own people's sympathetic gazes, she saw several soldiers lounging at a table, leering at her. When they realized she noticed them, they called out to her, beckoning as they crudely laughed. She hurried as quickly as she could, still shocked to find herself feeling frightened within her own castle.

Milburn watched her with a frown. "Come here, Anne," he called, dismissing the soldier he'd been talking to.

Elizabeth approached him and curtsied. "Aye, Master Milburn?"

"Lady Elizabeth is well?"

"She is."

"I imagine she used a woman's tears to try to enlist you to persuade me to release her."

"Nay, she did not," Elizabeth said. "She knows you serve Lord Bannaster and would not disobey him."

Milburn nodded. "Very well. But understand that I will no longer accept *your* disobedience."

Elizabeth gaped at him. "But I didn't—"

"And now you dare to speak back to me."

Milburn took several steps closer, as if to impress on her by his height and scowl that he was her master.

"I ordered you to see to the needs of our guests."

They were "guests" now, not just stranded travelers? Elizabeth thought with suspicion.

"If you cannot see to your mistress in a more timely manner, then I will assign a guard to accompany you to the tower. Do I make myself clear?"

Keeping her eyes lowered, Elizabeth nodded. To her shock, Milburn took the tray from her hands and threw it across the room, where it clattered to the floor, spreading its contents. The few servants stared in shock, while the soldiers guffawed. She felt frightened to be the center of so much attention, so very vulnerable. She had thought the plan to exchange places was smart, but now she saw that, as a maid, she was still at the mercy of others.

Milburn folded his arms over his chest, not even bothering to gloat. Impassively, he said, "Now clean that, and then see to Sir John. As a bailiff, he is a valuable man, one I might find a place for."

"Aye, Master Milburn." Elizabeth saw the threat for what it was. Milburn would use every means possible to keep her busy and away from the tower. What would she do if he assigned someone else to serve Anne in her place? Elizabeth could not afford to anger him again.

Chapter 5

When someone knocked on the door that afternoon, John exchanged a glance with Philip, who quickly got back on his pallet. He'd been observing the inner ward through the window, narrating for John, who felt restless and bored, something he wasn't used to. By lucky coincidence, the tiltyard was within sight, and they could assess the knights training and count their numbers.

When Philip was ready, John called, "Come in."

It was the maid Anne. John watched her walk through the room, admiring the graceful way she moved. She kept her eyes downcast, and he thought a faint blush lingered on her cheeks. He wished even a strand of hair had escaped her wimple, so that he could form a better picture of her, but she was all done up tightly.

She carried two tankards of ale that she set on the table between them. When she finally looked at him, he smiled at her.

Her eyes widened, and then she covered her mouth to hide a laugh.

John blinked in surprise. "Not the greeting I expected."

"If you could see the swelling on your face, Sir John," she said in a melodious voice that struggled to hide amusement, "you would understand."

John frowned at Philip, who shrugged and said, "I wasn't going to tell you."

"And you have two black eyes," John pointed out.

"And your bruises have swollen to interesting shapes as they take on the many hues of a rainbow," Philip said.

Philip glanced at Anne, who gave him back a curious glance.

"You speak very freely to your master," she said.

"I have given him permission," John explained. "We have always traveled much together, and the constant politeness and reserve grew boring."

"He can be reserved?" Anne asked, wearing a faint smile.

"I am quite a serious fellow," Philip insisted.

John sensed that he had captured her amusement for only a very brief time as already her thoughts were turning to the dilemma that faced her mistress. She was glancing at the door in worry.

"You are forced to be here with us?" John asked.

Her gaze darted back to him in surprise—and then anger, with a trace of fear.

"Forgive me, Anne," he said before she could speak. "I did not mean you to think that I would ever consider reporting anything you did to the steward. It is Alderley's steward you fear, is it not?"

"He's not our steward." Her face paled, as she seemed to realize what she'd said.

She glanced at Philip, who excused himself and left the bedchamber. John was alone with Anne now, and much as it felt very intimate, he wanted to use that intimacy to uncover more of what was happening at Castle Alderley.

John frowned. "Master Milburn is not your steward?"

She sighed. "Our steward, Royden, suddenly fell ill and died."

"I am sorry."

"It is not your fault."

"Whose fault is it?"

She opened her mouth as if she would speak, then she merely sighed and shook her head. "Lord Bannaster gave us the use of his steward."

"Out of guilt?" John asked.

She shrugged.

"But you wish to be with your mistress."

"It is my place."

"And someone is forbidding it."

She watched him with consideration. He saw a keen intelligence in her eyes, and recognized that he could not sway her so easily. The women he was used to treated a man with subservience for the coin it would bring them.

John added, "Because Lady Elizabeth is in seclusion."

Anne nodded, her impatience evident.

"Then I guess today I can understand how your mistress feels," he said.

Anne's eyes flared to life. "You are only here because of infirmity, not the will of others." She bit her lip as if in regret, backing away. "Excuse me, I have duties."

John decided to push a little harder. "You're not saying anything that has not already spread by rumor to places nearby."

She halted, and the surprise showed on her face. "People are talking about . . . my mistress?"

"We heard of Lady Elizabeth's imprisonment yesterday morn."

"And that is why you came here?" she asked in bewilderment.

"Nay." He wasn't ready to tell anyone his real identity. But these words were common knowledge. He smiled and pointed to his injured leg. "*This* is why I came here. After all, I am not a man of influence with an army to command. I will admit that I did not believe the rumor. I thought it far too bold for a man to attempt on the daughter of an earl."

"He is the king's cousin," she said softly.

"And this gives him the right to imprison an heiress?"

"He thinks so." She stiffened. "But this is not your concern, Sir John."

"It is obvious I will be unable to travel anytime soon, so I thought it best to understand what was happening."

"And you think you know?" she said, with slight mockery.

She was not a woman used to being under the authority of a man. Was she like Philip, treated as an equal?

"Nay, I freely confess my ignorance," John said.

When she made to leave, he knew he should not push her any further.

"Wait, Anne. I know that it is not my place to offer advice, but should you ever need someone to confide in—"

But he had miscalculated. Her eyes hardened and all emotion faded.

"I met you this morn, Sir John," she said impassively. "The fact that you are interested in so personal a matter as Lady Elizabeth—"

"Does she not want aid?"

"And how is she supposed to know whom she can trust?" Anne demanded. "After all, the cousin of the king himself felt free to abuse his privileges as a guest. Are you trying to do the same?"

He knew he could not earn her trust in only a span of hours, but there was something about her that made him feel as if he knew her already. She was too proud to show him her fear, had learned too well the lesson that men could not be trusted. He would have to start all over again.

"Forgive me, Anne," he said. "It has always been my nature to try to help."

"That is not something I find trustworthy," she answered, lifting her chin. "Already Master Milburn says he might find a place for you here. Think you that that should inspire my trust? Perhaps you are only another dependent of the viscount's."

"Anne, that's not true."

But she'd already turned about and was striding to the door, impressive in her cool anger and contempt. When the door shut, it opened again almost immediately, but John knew better than to be hopeful.

Philip closed the door behind him. "By the expression on her face, that did not go well."

"I am farther away from earning her trust than I was this morn as a complete stranger." He flopped back on his cushion in disgust, feeling the pain in his leg flare to life.

"Why do you push so hard?"

"Because we don't know how much time we have before Bannaster returns, perhaps with an agreement from the king. And because—" John found himself staring at the door uneasily. "There is something about her that makes me want to befriend her."

Philip snorted. " 'Befriend'? So that's what you call it?"

John frowned.

Elizabeth was so angry, she had to force herself to slow down and walk tentatively into the great hall as a servant might. She had lost her temper; she had lost control of her masquerade as Anne. She had argued with a man she knew nothing about, risking discovery.

What did it matter that Sir John knew of her imprisonment in the tower? With an estate this size, it would only be natural that people would hear of it.

But then wouldn't someone come to help? she thought, her stomach tightening, her eyes tearing. Had she no neighbors willing to confront Lord Bannaster?

It was still early, she told herself. Less than two days had gone by, and just because the news had traveled among a few men at a tavern, did not mean it would reach her nearest wealthy neighbor, Lord Selby, who was a half day's journey away. If Parliament was in session, he might even be in London with the rest of the county's noblemen.

Elizabeth lowered her gaze to hide her watery eyes. Luckily, only a young groom tended the fire, and a maidservant laid out tablecloths on the trestle tables that had been set up for the coming meal. After one brief glance, both of them studiously ignored her, and she was grateful. She wondered where Milburn was, if he was inspecting her property and cataloguing its worth.

Elizabeth sat down before the hearth and hugged herself, feeling like she could never be warm again. Nay, Lord Selby would not be quick to help her. His son had been one of her recent foolish suitors. For all she knew, Lord Selby had stolen her sheep to try to force her to accept his son's protection.

Maybe her neighbors thought she was too sure of

herself, that maybe a man's guardianship was the best thing to happen to her.

This self-pity had to end, she told herself, wiping her eyes furiously. She was down here among her people to take stock of her situation, not whine over how she wished things were different. She would go for a walk through the ward, see how her people were being treated by Bannaster's soldiers.

She would not think of the sympathy in Sir John's eyes. He was a simple bailiff, with nothing of his own. He could not help her; she sensed he might only be trying because he wanted to be closer to her.

And she wasn't in the mood to be courted as the future wife of a bailiff. She was the future wife of a baron, a man destined to be earl. She barely remembered John Russell except for his awkward body, and the way she'd occasionally caught him staring at her.

Was he as dead as his brothers? Could she really be a woman any man with an army could take for his own?

The death of her dreams ached within her heart. She had always thought she'd have a life like her parents, who were friends since childhood, then had a marriage of love and understanding. But her father hadn't been granted the earldom during those years; there was no great fortune to protect.

With William, she had thought she could have the same happiness. But she would now have to settle for security—if she was lucky enough to have that.

After making sure her wimple still covered her

hair completely, Elizabeth crossed the great hall and allowed the usher to open one of the double doors for her. She stood on the top step and tried to take satisfaction in the normal comings and goings of her people. She could hear a hammer striking an anvil from the blacksmith's shop; one dairymaid called to another from the buttery; and dogs chased chickens across the hard-packed earth. Soldiers left the barracks heading for the tiltyard, shoving each other and boasting of their prowess. That was when her fantasy of her old life was shattered. They weren't *her* soldiers. Hers were out in the forest somewhere, ordered to look for thieves—ordered not to return?

Bannaster's soldiers eyed her people and her property with a lasciviousness that frightened her. As she walked down the stairs to the ground, she again drew the regard of more than one of them and wished she'd brought a cloak to wrap about herself, as if she needed protection. When her parents and first betrothed had died, she'd felt vulnerable, but nothing like this. There was no protection when she was masquerading as a simple maid. Where Sir John had looked at her with interest, these soldiers looked . . . lustful. She shivered. She'd thought to control her life by taking on Anne's role, but the vulnerability of it stunned her.

She wanted to escape back into the castle, but if she showed fear, they might consider her even more a target. So she forced herself to walk toward the lady's garden, her private retreat with trees and flowers and walkways, fenced off from the rest of the ward.

As she walked, she glanced up at the window of the bedchamber Sir John and his clerk had been given. Someone stood there, looking down on the ward below. Surely it was Philip the clerk, but somehow, just the sight of him gave her resolve. She was not going to allow fear to rule her. She had handled the bailiff and his clerk—she would handle these soldiers.

Her presence here would prove to her people that she had not forgotten them, that she would prevail. Even if no outsiders came to help them in time.

As the great hall was beginning to fill for supper that night, Elizabeth went to Sir John's chamber to inquire whether he wanted a tray sent up. When she heard the summons to enter, she did so, and then came up short. Philip was absent, and Sir John was on his feet, propped up with a new wooden crutch rather than the makeshift branch. She had not realized how very tall he was, how he dwarfed the small chamber. When he saw her, he smiled, and the effect once again flustered her. She would have thought that a man with a narrow scar down the side of his face would be ugly, but it only made him appear even more a man. He had not gotten such a thing hunched over his account books. Even the bruises on his face did not bother her. He was wearing a tunic that covered him to his knees, probably to hide the fact that he couldn't wear hose over his splint. His boots were laced all the way up his calf, though she imagined that when he sat down, his bare knees would show.

Why was she thinking about that? She had to remember her anger, the way he suspiciously questioned her too closely about things that were not his business.

Elizabeth cleared her throat and tried to appear distant, though pleasant. She did not want to encourage any more intimacy. "Sir John, I was going to ask if you wanted a supper tray, but it seems you wish to venture out of this chamber."

"The hours have seemed long today, Anne," he said, limping forward. "I sent Philip to find you, but you must have missed each other."

"The corridors can be confusing at first."

She eyed him with growing trepidation as he came closer and closer. The width of his chest was as great as any knight in training; surely he still wielded a sword in practice.

But she was so distracted by his physical being that she failed to notice his eyes widening as the crutch caught on the bed.

"Move aside!" he commanded.

The power in his voice was so great that she almost obeyed him. But how could she let an injured man fall to the floor? His hand flailed for a bedpost, but it was too late. Elizabeth stepped forward and grabbed his upper arms, trying to brace him. His chest hit her hard in the shoulder, but she was a strong woman, and bore his weight until he was able to get his good leg back under him. She felt the warmth of his body against hers. The muscles in his arms were thick and as hard as marble. When he righted himself, he stood far too close, looking down on her as she looked up. His gaze was intense, curious, and she wondered how she had felt to him.

Oh bother, she thought, backing away several steps. "Are you all right?" she asked.

He smiled. "I will be when I learn to use this crutch. Please forgive my clumsiness."

"I'm glad the chamberlain found you a bedchamber on the first floor, so you could come to the great hall without using stairs. But you'll need to use them to go outside."

"Sending me away already?" he asked softly. "Did I so offend you this afternoon?"

She hesitated. "Nay, I was not offended."

"You were."

She bit her lip and met his gaze. "Aye, I was. I've since thought on it, and I know you were only trying to help. But I know you not, and I could never trust you."

He nodded. "Trust takes time to flourish. I am patient."

"Why do you want my trust?" she asked suspiciously.

"I worry for you and your mistress."

She looked away. "Come, they will not hold supper for us."

Elizabeth walked slowly at his side down the long corridor, relaxing as he limped with more and more confidence. She tried to imagine being able to rely on Sir John, but she couldn't. How could a mere bailiff—and injured at that—help her? He and his clerk were alone in the world.

The trestle tables in the great hall were filling up with household servants, as well as those whose duties were out in the ward. Elizabeth was worried about the slight hush that occurred at her entrance, but immediately someone had laughed loudly, and the normal hum of conversation resumed. Trying to relax, she remained at Sir John's side, keeping her eyes on his progress through the clean rushes on the floor, rather than on her people. Philip waved his arm, and they joined him at a free table.

Just as Elizabeth was about to leave Sir John and take a tray up to Anne, she heard Milburn call her name. He was seated at the head table on the raised dais, as if he'd become the earl of Alderley.

Elizabeth approached him. "Aye, Master Milburn?"

"You were not thinking of leaving the great hall," he said reprovingly.

"I was going up to my mistress to eat with her."

His jaws clenched together. "Nay, I have been studying the efficiency of the servants at meals and more help is needed. Go to the kitchen and help serve."

Elizabeth nodded and turned away, but she could not miss the wide-eyed gazes that stared back at her in shock. She smiled pleasantly at her people, hoping they understood that this did not bother her, that they must keep calm. But after taking a serving tray from Adalia and beginning to offer slices of roast lamb to the nearest table, the muttering grew worse. Laughter died. When she could, she tried to reassure stable grooms and dairymaids alike with quiet whispers, but the looks cast at the steward grew in ferocity.

Elizabeth did not want to be discovered. She smiled and encouraged people to help themselves from her tray. She saw Sir John frowning as he looked all around him, then back at her. Even Milburn seemed mildly surprised by the reaction.

She neared a table of Bannaster's soldiers, and one grabbed her arm. He had a thick beard and long hair, which seemed to merge together at his shoulders.

"Ye passed me by," he said angrily.

She tried to shake off his grip, but he held on. "I was returning to the kitchens for more lamb. Would you not rather have fresh, hot meat?"

"Aye, I would," he said, sharing a raucous laugh with his tablemates.

He pulled her closer, until she was forced to lean over him, or lose the use of her arm. Did this fool not hear the angry silence that had greeted his treatment of her? Or mayhap he did not care.

"You are not an old hag to be wearing the likes of that," the soldier said, gesturing at her wimple. "Take it off, so I can see the color of yer hair."

Several of the stable grooms had risen to their feet, as well as the blacksmith, who flexed his enormous arms in preparation for a fight. A soldier behind her assailant stood as well, his face ferocious with anticipation.

And then someone touched her shoulder from behind, and she screamed. Were they coming at her from all sides?

Chapter 6

❧ ⸙ ❧

John felt Anne's cry reverberate through her tense body where they touched. She struggled against the man still holding her arm, even as she glanced over her shoulder. When she saw John, some relief showed through her fear.

"Release the maid," John said coldly.

The bearded soldier rose to his feet and tugged even harder on Anne. The tray fell from her hands to spill into the rushes, and she stumbled into him.

John could not allow her to be mauled. He slid his arm around her waist from behind to steady her. He wished he could wield a sword—or even the crutch— but he must not draw more suspicion on himself.

Anne was warm and soft, trembling violently. Yet still the soldier gripped her arm. John balanced on his crutch and used his free hand to draw his dagger.

"Are you goin' to prick me with that little thorn?" the soldier called, roaring with laughter. "I'll go through you before I get to the maid."

The hall had grown so quiet that this boast rang out, drawing the attention of the steward.

"Enough," Milburn called in his usual clipped tones. "Anne, sit down and amuse our guest. He does not know anyone here but you and his clerk."

The bearded soldier released her slowly and let his fingers trail hard down the length of her arm. "Another time," he growled, low enough that only she and John heard him.

As she pulled away, the man's grip lingered too long. John felt a rush of uncommon rage that threatened to overrule his good sense. He envisioned the damage he could do to the soldier's face with one thrust of the dagger.

But at last Anne was free of threat, and John reluctantly stepped away from her. With her head held high, she turned and headed for his table. She was a brave woman, obviously unused to such poor treatment, especially having been raised with an earl's daughter.

John gazed into the eyes of her attacker as he slowly sheathed his dagger. And then with a deliberate insult, John gave his back and limped away. There were whistles and hisses behind him, but he did not turn around. He would have felt it, had the soldier come at him. He had made an enemy this day.

Anne sat down on a bench, looking back to give

John a smile that tried for polite and came across as grim. "My thanks, Sir John. But you should not have endangered yourself when you are ill."

He took his seat opposite her, frustrated at having to back down. With a rough voice, he said, "You thought I should watch that son of a—"

"Anne," Philip interrupted, "might I fill your plate for you?"

John stifled his anger.

Though her eyes were narrowed as she studied him, she said to Philip, "The servants will come to me eventually."

Within minutes, she was being offered trays of meats and cheeses and cut fruits. Her face grew redder with each increase in attention.

"You need not be embarrassed," John said, having recovered his calmness. " 'Tis obvious the residents of the castle are devoted to you."

Surprisingly, her blush worsened. "Nay, it is my lady they honor, not me. They are concerned for her. Never before has she been so removed from them."

He was surprised that she brought up the subject after her anger with him only hours earlier. She was probably still so flustered.

"They worry about her," Philip said.

Her voice was a murmur. "As do I."

John allowed her to eat for several minutes as others talked all around them. He noticed how she picked through the food, as if her appetite were lacking. He realized he would not soon tire of looking at her. He had always thought a woman's hair was one of the most glorious parts of her, but Anne proved that true beauty went beyond that. She had long-fingered, graceful hands that held a piece of bread as if it were the wand of a magician. Her lips were delicate bows, rounded, made to fit—

Philip kicked him beneath the table, but too late. Anne had already noticed that he was staring.

Why could he not remember that she was only a means to an end to him? He didn't want to hurt her—God's Blood, he wanted to rescue the woman who was obviously her dearest friend!

Yet when he looked on her beauty, even though she now frowned at him with suspicion, he could only think about kissing her.

To distract her, he said, "Anne, have you lived at Castle Alderley all your life?"

She slowly shook her head. He would have to ask questions that needed a deliberate answer.

"Where are you from?"

She swallowed a piece of cheese. "A prosperous farm a few hours' journey from here."

"And you are one of the ladies attending Lady Elizabeth?"

Her eyes widened, and her smile relaxed just a bit. "Nay, I am not of noble birth. I am her lady's maid, not her lady in waiting. As a bailiff, you must have worked closely with noble families. How could you not know the difference?"

He heard Philip choke, and gave him a hard pat on the back. But Anne wasn't distracted. He could hardly tell her that the women he most associated with were far too common to even be maidservants in a castle. It had been many years since he'd lived in a noble household, and even then, the memories were hazy, full of disquiet and awkwardness.

"You are so gracious and educated," John said, "that I simply forgot your status."

"Others haven't," she answered shortly, glancing over her shoulder at the soldiers.

They were drinking more than eating, and it did not bode well for the evening. He had thought it best to leave his sword in their chamber, but now he wished otherwise.

"Lady Elizabeth did have several ladies living here with us for a time," Anne said, as her eyes seemed to focus on the past. "But all of them gradually married."

"But not your mistress, which is why she is in such danger today."

With a sigh, Anne nodded.

John had never paid attention to the betrothal contract between his family and Lady Elizabeth's. He had only thirteen years at the time, and it had had nothing to do with him. Calculating quickly in his head, he knew his betrothed was twenty-two now.

"Lady Elizabeth is surely betrothed," he said, "being the daughter of an earl."

She was showing more interest in dessert, a custard, than she had for the meal. But she nodded.

"Why is she not married? Surely that would have solved this problem long before Lord Bannaster took an interest."

She glanced swiftly at him, and the anger in her eyes on behalf of her mistress impressed him with her loyalty. She looked around as if to leave him because of his presumption, but the soldiers were standing in a group now, distracting the serving maids and valets who were trying to clean their tables.

He hated to see her afraid. She seemed like too strong of a woman to have experienced it much.

With a sigh, she rested her chin on her hand. "My lady's long maidenhood was . . . a combination of faults," she said slowly. "The earl and countess enjoyed their eldest daughter, and did not want to lose her so soon. I will admit that Lady Elizabeth . . . flourished under the attention. Everyone thought there was plenty of time to marry. Her betrothed enjoyed life in London, and was also in no hurry. But now they're all dead," she said, her voice full of grief and even bitterness.

"I am sorry to hear that," John said. He glanced at Philip to see his reaction, but his friend was showing deep interest in his meal, giving her some measure of privacy.

Although John knew the rest of the story, he pretended otherwise. "So your mistress no longer has the protection of a betrothal?"

"Nay, the two families planned well." She spoke tiredly now, as if it no longer mattered. "Lady Elizabeth is to marry the heir—whichever brother it is."

"But surely she is sad at losing the man she thought she'd marry for so many years."

With a sigh, she murmured, "I was often their chaperone. He was a romantic, handsome man, and his poetry made my lady happy."

"Poetry?" John repeated, wondering how he was going to compete with such a memory. He already knew that his visage would never be as pleasing as William's, especially now with the scar. But poetry? He was a man of armor and horse, of a traveling life since he had sixteen years. What did he know of the wants of noblewomen?

"The last brother of three is all that is left," Anne continued. "He is in Normandy somewhere, and probably did not receive the letter she sent him months ago. He might not even know that he is betrothed!"

"Surely travel back to England takes time," he said, hoping to comfort her. "He might very well be on his way."

"There is that fear, too," she said forlornly.

John stiffened. "What do you mean?"

"If he comes with an army, there might be bloodshed. Lady Elizabeth could not live if her people were hurt in defense of her."

"How would she expect her betrothed to rescue her?"

"By marrying her, of course! By proving before all who he is. The Russell name is an old and honored one."

Not anymore, he thought bitterly. Obviously no one here had yet heard of the neglect of Rame Castle. Once again, he remembered how betrayed he still felt by his elder brother. William had been the one who could do no wrong in the eyes of his parents. And now John was going to be tainted by his brother's deeds. He had to make things right. How could he come to Lady Elizabeth only as a poor husband? His pride would not stand for it. King Henry would need proof that John would be capable of ruling such a vast estate.

And the proof would be in gathering Alderley's soldiers and convincing them to follow him to aid their mistress, should it come to that. He was a man who knew how to command; he could lead men—but what if that turned Lady Elizabeth against him?

"Perhaps John Russell does not have the same honor as his elder brother had," Anne said sadly. "After all, he hasn't returned to England in many years. It is as if he forgot his family."

John took a deep breath and tried to control his fury. This maid was ignorant of all that had occurred—as was poor Lady Elizabeth, trapped in her tower.

"Remember that Lord Russell is a third son," John said, "who probably had no hopes for family property or wealth. Perhaps he had to earn it all on his own."

She frowned, appearing undecided. Finally she stood up. "I will tell my mistress your words. Excuse me while I see to her."

"Of course."

When she had gone, Philip leaned toward him and whispered, "It sounds like Lady Elizabeth is ripe for rescue. At least you don't have to worry about being unwelcome."

"If only I could speak to Lady Elizabeth directly, to gauge the kind of woman she is."

"Perhaps you should confide in her maid?"

John frowned in disbelief. "A woman I have only known for one day? She is already trapped in a dangerous situation. I will not give her knowledge that might endanger her—or us—further."

John watched Anne leave the hall for the kitchens, and he noticed that he wasn't the only one doing so. The bearded soldier would have to be dealt with.

Philip looked around the hall, wearing an expression of anticipation. "You know, the League could already be here."

John rolled his eyes. "If there really *is* a League, rather than a few men who think themselves important."

Philip gaped at him. "How can you doubt it?"

"Please don't bring up your grandmother's rescue again."

"I don't need to," Philip answered, offended. "You know of the smuggling raid. You are from Cornwall, after all."

"Aye, the League supposedly helped a small group of smugglers get out from under the fist of a tyrant."

"Who was using them as slaves."

"So I've heard."

Philip shook his head. "And yet you doubt. Christ himself could appear and you would still . . ."

John let Philip talk on.

Philip finally frowned. "You're not even listening. Those soldiers playing dice look like they need a jovial companion."

John glanced at him with interest. "I cannot wait to hear everything you discover."

Philip stood up, smiling. "Perhaps I'll tell you; perhaps not. You'd doubt me anyway."

John grinned and shook his head. He was glad to have a friend such as Philip, who could certainly be off on his own adventures instead of helping him. By tomorrow, John would have to send Philip into the forest to meet up with Ogden and Parker, to exchange information. Perhaps luck had been with them, and they had already found Alderley's army.

John remained in the great hall throughout the evening, observing both the castle residents and Bannaster's soldiers. Musicians played for several hours, and even a traveling jester performed. But the merriment seemed forced—except for the soldiers, who grew more boisterous throughout the evening.

And Philip was right in the middle of it. If he was only pretending to be drunk, it wasn't evident. He grew just as red-faced with laughter as the next man.

Strangely enough, Anne's departure seemed to signal a relaxation amongst the castle's residents. Though their conversations were muted, and they glanced suspiciously at the soldiers, they didn't find their pallets quickly. It was as if without Anne, it was easier to forget the plight of Lady Elizabeth, trapped in her tower. Several people came and introduced themselves to John, and he encouraged their friendship. He needed to know as many people as he could, in hopes of earning their loyalty if he needed to rely on them to help rescue their lady.

When John was alone again, Philip staggered back to him and sat down on the same bench, almost knocking both of them to the floor. John caught the table and held on, glaring at Philip, who looked apologetic.

"Any ale left?" Philip asked, his words slightly slurred.

John silently passed Philip his tankard.

Across the hall, a game of Tables was growing boisterous, as two soldiers hunched over the game board, and more gathered around.

In a soft voice, Philip said, "They're all Bannaster's men, at least the ones in here tonight."

"So 'tis true that Alderley's soldiers were sent away. Are any left on the grounds?"

"Not many." Philip tipped his tankard back and drank, spilling some down his cheek to his neck. "Most were sent out into the forest to hunt for thieves. It seems the castle residents would have been more upset, but the attack on us showed them they really had a problem."

"So Bannaster wants them gone indefinitely."

"But he didn't kill them," Philip pointed out.

"But they're not here to do their duty."

"Four soldiers remained behind to take turns guarding the base of Lady Elizabeth's tower."

John glanced at his friend incredulously. "Milburn allows *Alderley* soldiers to guard his captive?"

"There is one Bannaster soldier and one Alderley soldier guarding the tower at all times." Philip halted, and gave a bleary grin as two young maidens walked by. When they were far enough away, he continued. "It seems Lord Bannaster did not want to trust even his own men with his prize."

"And did you discover whom they allow to see Lady Elizabeth?"

"Didn't get to that," Philip said, hiccuping. "Too many questions. And 'tis your assignment, isn't it?"

John smiled. "Aye, it is. I'll start to walk the corridors to keep up my strength. Strangely enough, that tower will be my frequent destination."

"So I am finished with the soldiers?"

"I think not. Who knows what you can discover."

Philip sighed. "When one is pretending to be drunk, yet still must appear to keep drinking . . . it is difficult."

"You are succeeding admirably."

"My thanks." Philip pushed himself to his feet and went over to watch the Tables tournament.

Anne eventually returned by the same door she'd left, and John knew that that was where he'd first start exploring on the morrow. She sat down near the hearth, looking tired and lonely. His first instinct was to go to her, but he knew that that would be too much pressure in one day. She had to think that he would not force her into revealing what she didn't want to.

He watched her covertly. Not many people spoke to her, which surprised him. Why wouldn't people want to distract her from her worries? Or perhaps she spent so much time with Lady Elizabeth that she didn't really know anyone else. Could his betrothed be so demanding? Anne's solitude did not bode well for Lady Elizabeth's disposition. When the cook finally came and sat down beside Anne, John relaxed.

Elizabeth looked up with a smile as Adalia sat down beside her. She was glad for the company, for the distraction.

"And how is our mistress tonight?" Adalia asked.

Elizabeth sighed. "She is well. The tedium is beginning to annoy her, but I brought her some mending to do, so she is happy."

"Happy to mend? The girl who loves to talk?"

Elizabeth shrugged. "She has no one but me to talk to." She looked about, but with the Tables game distracting most of the residents, she and the cook were truly alone. "Anne and I came up with a plan," she said softly.

Adalia scooted closer on the bench. "What is it?"

"I'm going to send a missive to the king and tell him what his cousin has been up to."

The cook gave her a doubtful look. "But Lord Bannaster will be in London before yer missive."

"But do you think he'll tell the truth, that he's kept a lady prisoner?"

"I'm sure he'll make it seem like he's protectin' ye."

"But we both know he's protecting his own interests. I can tell the king that my betrothed is surely on his way by now—"

"But ye don't know that."

"It has to be true," Elizabeth said stubbornly.

"What if the king decides that ye're causin' too much trouble? Maybe 'twill be easy for him to give ye to his cousin. Then he'll be able to trust the next earl to support him."

"But he has to hear my side," Elizabeth whispered, her hands fisted. "How will he know if I don't tell him? I have to take the risk. Otherwise, I'm just sitting here waiting."

"But who will take the missive, Anne?"

" 'Tis a dangerous journey for a man alone. I wouldn't want to take a man away from his farm, or choose someone too visible, whose absence Milburn would notice."

"What about the miller's son, Harold? And he's even been to London before."

"Perfect! I'll write it when I'm in the tower in the morning, and I'll make sure to seal the wax with my father's crest."

"Surely the ring is in your father's private solar," Adalia warned. "Milburn uses the room more than the steward's chamber."

"I'll keep watch on the chamber and wait for him to leave. It shouldn't take me long."

"Anne, if ye feel ye must do this, I can send word to Harold that I need a shipment of grain from the mill."

"I'll let you know when I need him."

There was a shout and sudden laughter, and the two women looked up to see a little boy running toward them, his face alight. A scullery maid was chasing him.

"Mama!" the boy called to Adalia.

Adalia surged to her feet. "Holy Mary, I told that girl to keep him away from the hall."

Elizabeth tried to shrink back, but it was too late—Joseph had seen her. He had but four years, and would not understand that he couldn't shout her name to earn his hug.

The boy began, "Lady—"

"She's not here, Joseph," Adalia said, swinging the boy into the air and tickling him as he came back into her arms.

He giggled and squirmed and threw himself backward until she caught him, a favorite pastime of theirs. Elizabeth watched fondly, her heart still pounding even as Adalia took her son back to the kitchens.

Elizabeth risked a glance around the great hall. The soldiers were still preoccupied with their game, and more servants had gone to find their beds, or were already wrapping themselves in blankets to sleep in the great hall for the night.

But Sir John was still awake, and he was watching her. How much had he seen—or heard? She knew she should look away, pretend a casualness she didn't feel. But she couldn't. His eyes, deep and blue, still showed her compassion and interest. She could not ignore him and hope for the best. With a sigh, she rose to her feet and crossed the hall to stand near him.

"Sir John, I did not expect to find you still awake," she said, trying to sound pleasant.

He studied her face, but all he did was smile and say, "I was waiting for Philip, but he seems to be winning at Tables."

Elizabeth glanced at the group of soldiers, but

she couldn't see the clerk in the crowd. "It seems he might be a while."

Sir John nodded.

"Would you like me to accompany you back to your bedchamber?"

He didn't even hesitate. "If it would not be an inconvenience for you." He rose slowly to his feet, as if his bruises pained him.

"Nay, I was about to find my pallet as well."

"Do you sleep in your mistress's chamber?"

"I am not permitted to," she answered with regret.

He frowned. "She is alone, then?"

"Except when I bring her meals."

"It must be difficult for her."

She shrugged. "She is a strong woman."

"I am glad to hear that. I pray that things are resolved quickly."

"As do I, Sir John."

They walked in silence from the great hall and through the torchlit corridors. There was a comfort and strength in his presence. Since her father's death, no man had made her feel safe.

And no man had ever made her so aware of him. He exuded masculinity, raw and potent, making it hard to ignore him.

She felt guilty, since she was sworn to another. But if eventually Sir John proved trustworthy, she might need his help. How could she reject him now, just because of her own fears? She had to trust herself to be able to keep temptation at bay. She would be the one to control this situation.

As they neared his door, to her surprise he wheeled clumsily and blocked her path. She came up short, her face tilted up to him, her body just brushing his.

And the awareness grew ever higher, surging from her breasts down to her loins with a heat that was startling and embarrassing and . . . tempting.

The torch was behind him on the wall, leaving his face cast in shadows but for the gleam of his eyes and teeth. He wasn't smiling, but his lips were parted, and she realized hers were, too.

He was the one to take a step back, farther into the light, and she was grateful and disappointed at the same time. Why had she not seen the danger and moved first?

"Anne, I am still not used to this crutch. Forgive me."

She could only nod as she licked her suddenly dry lips.

And he watched her do it, his brows lowered, his gaze intense, sending a strange thrill through her body.

"Know that if a soldier ever bothers you—or *any* man—come to me and I will protect you."

He sounded so sincere that she had to smile. "Will you strike him with your crutch?"

He grinned. "It makes a good weapon."

They stood there for a few moments, trapped in this strange intimacy. How could she know him for but a day and be so drawn to him? She might need to use his assistance, but she did not deceive herself that that was all there was between them.

Backing away, she murmured, "A good night to you, Sir John."

"Pleasant dreams, Anne."

She turned and walked swiftly away, knowing he watched her until she turned the corner.

Chapter 7

J ohn's sleep was restless and filled with dreams of darkness and warmth and the touch of a woman's soft skin. When he awoke at dawn, he cursed himself for his weakness. He had to remember that he would be married soon enough, that he could have his wife whenever he wanted her in his bed.

But he didn't know Lady Elizabeth; Anne was the one he saw, the one he dreamed of, the one he followed like a sheep to his shepherd.

He saw her at mass that morning, then breaking her fast, but he came no closer, determined not to frighten her into avoiding him. She smiled at him once, hesitantly, and that would have to be enough for now.

The healer returned and pronounced Philip and he improving, though she said their facial bruises could frighten children. John received her approval to begin walking about more, and he took to the corridors in relief, while Philip went out to watch the knights and soldiers train. John needed to learn the layout of the castle, and he was certainly not used to sitting still.

He lost his way more than once, and servants pointed him in the right direction. As luck would have it, just when he decided to explore the base of Lady Elizabeth's tower, Milburn was there, conversing with the two guards. The steward gave John an arched brow of curiosity.

John smiled and continued on past, speaking over his shoulder. "Just trying to get used to the crutch."

But at least now he knew where the tower was. It would be getting Lady Elizabeth out of the castle that would prove most difficult.

When Elizabeth brought a tray up to the tower bedchamber, she found Anne munching on a piece of bread, reading a book.

Anne looked up and smiled. "I don't know how you did it, but I am so thankful!"

Elizabeth frowned. "Did what? Bring you a meal?"

"But you already sent me a meal. Who did you get to climb to the top of the tower? Tell me you didn't risk it yourself!"

Elizabeth set the tray on the table. Only then did she notice the unfamiliar basket. Inside were several more books, choice cheeses, dried fruit, and a stoppered bottle of wine. A parchment note read, "Patience."

"I'm practicing my patience," Anne said almost defensively as she lifted the linen that covered the tray. "But how can I be patient when this smells so good?"

"I didn't send the basket," Elizabeth said, her stomach clutching with anxiety. "How did it get here?"

Wide-eyed, Anne said, "It was lowered by rope from the top of the tower. It wasn't ordered by you?"

Elizabeth shook her head. "You didn't lean out and see who it was?"

"I tried! Looking up made me dizzy, but I don't think I saw anyone. Wouldn't they have signed the note if they wanted me to know?"

With a surge of terror, Elizabeth asked, "Do you feel well?" She put her hand on Anne's forehead. "Do you feel hot or clammy? Is your stomach starting to cramp?"

"Nay!" Anne cried, pushing Elizabeth away. Her face paled. "It cannot be—poisoned! I have been eating it for over an hour."

Elizabeth nodded, her breath coming too fast in relief. She closed her eyes. "Surely you would have been suffering by now. Thank the lord."

She heard Anne flop onto the bed.

"What a fright!" Anne said with a groan. "And it was delicious food."

"I should have known you wouldn't pass up a meal."

Anne threw a cushion at her. "I'll share this second meal with you."

"I have no time to eat. There's so much to do! But first, it seems we have someone who wants to help. Mayhap if the person does it again, you can pass up a note asking his identity."

Anne giggled. "I can't tell you how startled I was to hear the basket clunk against the closed shutters. It happened when you were all at mass in the chapel."

"That makes sense."

"Who else would want to help you? The castle residents know you're masquerading as me."

"Not everyone," Elizabeth said thoughtfully, thinking of Sir John. But surely the man was too injured to lower baskets from the top of a tall tower. And why would he, when he knew that Elizabeth was bringing food at every meal?

"*Bannaster's* soldiers want to give me food?" Anne said in disbelief. Then she studied Elizabeth more closely. "You think it might be the bailiff and his clerk. Why would he—unless you've been telling him, a stranger, about our troubles? And why ever would you be doing that?"

"Because he . . . wants to help," Elizabeth said, wincing. "But it could not have been him. He is too injured."

"Wants to help?" Anne said incredulously.

"I find myself telling him things about our situation, but he is far too intelligent not to figure it all out for himself."

"So he's intelligent, as well as handsome."

"I never called him handsome!"

Anne grinned. "You didn't have to."

"He's certainly not as handsome as William was. If William were alive—"

"If William were alive, you'd be married to him by now."

Elizabeth sighed, feeling sadness creep over her again, making everything seem futile.

"Forgive me," Anne said, sitting down beside her on the bench and putting her arm around Elizabeth's shoulders.

"Nay, there is nothing to forgive. I have been full of self-pity of late."

"I would think if anyone deserved to feel that way, it should be you."

"It's difficult to be down below, to see everyone . . . going on with their duties, with their lives, without me."

"You're right there with them!"

"I'm something they have to avoid, so that they don't accidentally reveal my identity. Milburn and Adalia are running the castle adequately now. I think I make things harder on the servants. Perhaps it would be easier if I just—"

"Accepted your fate? Married a man who has stolen you, who wants you for your wealth, for this castle and a title, so that he can control *your* people, and subvert what your father intended?"

Elizabeth gave a small smile. "You have a very persuasive way of making me forget about pitying myself."

"Good."

"Let me make you feel better. I warned the guards that you had been without your bath for several days, and that I would need the help of servants to carry hot water up to you. I'll try for tonight."

"How thoughtful of you. Have you been able to bathe?"

"Once in these past two nights, in Adalia's chamber off the kitchen. It was a hurried affair."

"You must miss your bedchamber," Anne said, looking about the luxurious surroundings with guilt.

"Nay, I am grateful you are accepting the solitude for me. Let us write this letter and hope we can end your imprisonment." Elizabeth pulled out a sheet of parchment and her quill pen.

It didn't take long; she'd been thinking of the wording all night. She did not call Bannaster a thief outright, but she made it clear to the king that he was behaving illegally, and that she wished to wait for her betrothed.

As the ink was drying, Elizabeth said, "I sent several of the older stable boys out into the forest yesterday to look for my knights and soldiers. They returned this morning with no news. It is as if they vanished."

Anne paled. "You don't think—"

"Nay, even Bannaster would not kill an entire army of a hundred men without suffering the king's wrath. I shall wait a few more days and send someone else. They could just have gone farther away." Now that the ink was dry, she rolled the parchment carefully, and then tucked it into her bodice, just above her girdle. "I must leave. I'll let you know what happens."

"Do be careful, Elizabeth," Anne said, following her down to the solar.

"You be careful, my lady. Remember to find out who sent you the basket."

"If they even send another."

Elizabeth took the tray and gave a nod as Anne shut the door behind her. She passed the soldiers without uttering a word, and after turning a corner, left the tray beneath a set of stairs, then hurried toward her father's solar. She listened outside the door for several long minutes, and after hearing nothing, she slipped inside.

Only one shutter was open to let in light, but she didn't need much. She knew the coffer that housed her father's personal items; she'd had to use the ring more than once since her father's death to seal her official correspondence to the king. But she wouldn't remain here to heat the wax. She would return to Adalia's chamber and—

The latch on the door lifted so suddenly that Elizabeth was caught standing in the center of the room as the door was thrown wide.

Milburn came up short when he saw her. "What are you doing here?"

"I was sent to clean, master." She was grateful when the lie came to her.

"I see no rags or pail. What do you have in your hand?"

Her heart sank. There was no point forcing him to wrestle the items from her; he would win. She silently showed the wax. He came forward, frowning, then grabbed her other hand, which was fisted.

"Open it."

She reluctantly displayed the ring. His fingers tightened on her wrist until she gasped with the pain. Why did he not name her a thief and call the guards? Scenarios flashed through her mind of imprisonment, and her people trying to rescue her. Deaths all attributed to her—

Instead, Milburn took both the ring and the wax and stared at them. "No one who wants to steal the priceless ring of an earl also steals wax."

As he studied her face, he let go of her arm, and Elizabeth rubbed her bruised wrist.

"You wanted to seal something with the proof of the earl's ring."

"Nay, Master Milburn. My lady was worried that the ring would be stolen. She wanted it safe."

"Show me what you have concealed."

He spoke so impassively, without anger or inflection, that Elizabeth knew he would do whatever was necessary.

"I have nothing, master."

"Your bodice is loose. What do you have hidden there?"

She flushed with anger and humiliation, and then removed the missive, knowing he would have stripped her until he found it.

Milburn unrolled it and read without expression. When he looked back up at her, he said, "Your mistress is a fool. All this has done is earn her a day without food. It has earned you—"

There was a knock on the door, and he gave it an impatient glance. "Who is it?"

The door opened, and in limped Sir John, leaning heavily on his crutch. He came up short when he saw Elizabeth. She was grateful for the interruption, glad that there would be a witness to her whereabouts. Milburn could so easily put her somewhere to keep her out of the way.

Sir John nodded. "Forgive me for the intrusion, Master Milburn. You had told me to come discuss a business opportunity with you."

"I also told you to come in the afternoon."

Sir John shrugged his shoulders. "I was walking by and thought I'd see if you were here."

"Aye, you have been walking much today," Milburn said musingly.

Elizabeth looked between the men, trying not to show her interest. She had known Milburn had some sort of plan for Sir John. She hoped they would discuss it and forget about her.

But Milburn gave her a speculative glance. "Sir John, you have come at an opportune moment. I was going to ask your help with a nearby manor whose bailiff has become ill."

Elizabeth was bursting with the need to ask who the ill man was, but she remained silent. She had no idea why Milburn needed to discuss this now, when she waited anxiously for her own punishment.

"I cannot offer a permanent position at the moment, but would you consider supervising this manor on a temporary basis?"

Sir John smiled. "Master Milburn, I would be

happy to accept. Even if only temporarily, it will give me a chance to replace some of the earnings that were stolen from me."

"Good. We will discuss your payment at another time. You will need an assistant."

"Philip Sutterly—"

"Will be busy. I am assigning him to be the clerk to the captain of the guard. He needs someone to keep the account book as he supplies his troop. The captain informs me that your clerk has become familiar to the soldiers and should work well with them. And to you," Milburn said, allowing a trace of sarcasm to enter his voice, "I offer the assistance of the maid Anne."

Elizabeth stared at Sir John in confusion. Her punishment was to act as a clerk?

Nay, it was to keep her from the tower as much as possible. It was an effective punishment.

"Master Milburn," she began, "my lady needs—"

"Your lady's needs will be met. But she does not need someone who will help her in rebellion."

"But I didn't—I don't even know what the missive says!"

"I know you are not to blame, girl," Milburn said gruffly. "Your mistress has to learn to accept the consequences of her actions. Her punishment is greater, do you not think?"

"Might I tell her what has happened?"

"Nay, I think we shall let her wonder for today. Sir John, the manor is at Hillesley, a small village several miles from here."

As Milburn told Sir John what he'd been able to

glean from the servants, Elizabeth tried to remember who the bailiff of that particular property was. And then it came to her—Master Wilden. He was an older man, whose wife had died and whose children were grown and married. He used to give Elizabeth apples from his orchard whenever she visited with her father.

"I just need an accounting of what is going on at Hillesley," Milburn was saying.

"Master Milburn," Elizabeth interrupted, "do you know if the bailiff will live?"

"The healer has been to see him, and he will be unable to work," Milburn said shortly. "That is all I needed to know."

"Thank you for the opportunity," Sir John said. "I will let you know what I discover." He opened the door. "Anne?"

She hesitated. Milburn would hide her father's ring in a new place, and she might never see it again. Had Bannaster been looking for it? Had she just made things easier for him?

Milburn arched a brow at her, his lips thinning. There was nothing she could do. She curtsied, preceded Sir John out of the chamber, and turned toward the tower with determination.

"Anne," Sir John said from behind.

She ignored him and started to walk.

To her surprise, he caught her arm.

"Let me go," she said angrily, trying to pull away. "He hasn't told the guards yet. They'll let me up to see my mistress. I can explain—"

His arm slipped around her waist from behind

and she sucked in her breath in shock as he pulled her against him.

Against her ear, he murmured, "Cease this foolishness. You will only bring more trouble down on yourself and your mistress."

"But he's not going to allow me to feed her!"

"For how long?"

"Today."

"Will she starve?"

Reluctantly, she breathed, "Nay."

"Then leave it be. Your mistress will understand."

"She'll be frightened and worried," Elizabeth whispered, tears stinging her eyes.

He squeezed her waist gently and released her. She was left with the impression of warmth and now solitary cold. She hugged herself.

"Mayhap, but she would rather you, her dear friend, be safe."

She turned around and looked up at him. "How do you know she considers me her friend?"

"Because of the way you speak of her. You were raised together. How could I not tell?"

He looked at her with so much sympathy that she wanted to cry. She wanted to break down and tell him everything, to lean on him for comfort and assistance.

And this shocked her, because she knew nothing about him. She stiffened and gave him a suspicious glare. "And why did you happen to enter the solar at just that moment?"

He grinned. "I was following you."

"Following me?" She took a step back.

"I was practicing with my crutch, getting to know the layout of the castle. You walked by a corridor I was in and set down your tray in a corner, instead of taking it to the kitchens." He shrugged. "I was curious."

"And what else did your curiosity prompt you to do?" she asked with sarcasm.

"I listened at the door and overheard why you're being punished. Your loyalty to your mistress is commendable, but—"

"Your opinion does not interest me." She whirled around and started to march away.

She could hear him following, his heavy step alternating with the sound of his crutch hitting the wooden floor. He kept up very easily.

"You'll become used to how freely I offer my opinion," he said. "We'll be spending much time together."

She gritted her teeth and said nothing.

"It will not be a terrible punishment, I assure you. I am not an evil master."

Whirling to face him, she said, "You are not my master. And this is not a punishment for me so much as it is for Lady Elizabeth. They want her so lonely and desperate that she'll accept anything, not simply the guardianship proposed, but even marriage with that—that—"

"I would keep your voice down, now that the *viscount* is temporarily in control of Alderley."

She let out a heavy sigh and folded her arms across her chest.

"It is not marriage the viscount says he wants?" Sir John asked, his head tilted.

"There is a binding betrothal contract with the Russell heir. For now, the viscount is petitioning for guardianship, but my lady sees his method for what it is: just the first step. Once he has guardianship, he has legal control of my lady and her assets. If Lord Russell does not return soon, Bannaster will use his absence as proof of his death, as proof that the instability that King Henry hates still exists in this part of England. He'll bribe an archbishop and—"

"The betrothal will be overturned," Sir John said softly.

He gave her a measuring look, and she felt confused. He took a breath, opened his mouth, and then shook his head.

"I wish I could help your mistress solve all of these problems," he said with a sigh.

"One man alone cannot."

"And your mistress thought a missive would help?"

"It would at least alert the king to the danger," Elizabeth said with determination.

"Instead she has alerted Milburn that she is not as meek as he had hoped."

With a groan, she stalked away from him.

"Be ready to leave after the midday meal," Sir John called. "I need to see Hillesley."

Elizabeth was furious with herself—her own stupidity had led to her banishment from the castle a good part of each day. What if someone tried to get into the tower while she was gone?

She could hardly delude herself that her presence was any protection against such an occurrence. Nay, what she was really worried about was being alone with Sir John. He was far too interested in her, and she in him. She would use him if she had to, but already she felt her control of the situation slipping away. Every time he touched her, she thought about *him,* not her mission to save herself and her people. Now she was going to be spending even more time in his company. She had to prove stronger than the lure of a man treating her simply as a woman. She was not destined for that sort of life. The legacy her father had begun and strengthened now rested with her; she would not cheapen it by pretending she could be a normal woman.

Even if such feelings made her understand for the first time what it felt like to be desired for herself.

Chapter 8

Elizabeth spent the rest of the morning feeling restless and useless. She'd meant to take Anne's soiled garments to the laundry maids, but had forgotten to bring them down in her excitement over the letter. Elizabeth wasn't used to having nothing to do. Finally Adalia had allowed her to chop carrots.

When Elizabeth entered the great hall for the midday meal, she was greeted with fearful, wide-eyed looks from several valets and maidservants. She came to a stop, frightened and confused—until she saw one of her suitors, Sir Charles. He was already seated at the high table next to Milburn. Elizabeth whirled about and tried to retreat to the kitchens.

"Anne, come sit beside me," Sir John called from one of the far tables. "We have much to discuss."

Elizabeth pretended to have a coughing fit as she walked toward the far side of the hall, keeping her head lowered and turned away. Thank God for the wimple. She was about to seat herself across from Sir John, but he slid down the bench and gestured for her to come nearer. Since she couldn't call any more attention to herself, she sat down beside him, keeping as close to the edge as possible. She knew that her rational mind turned to mush when he touched her.

He leaned nearer. "Coming under Bannaster's influence solved one problem for your mistress."

"What is that?" She kept her gaze fixed on her empty plate, trying to pretend that she did not feel the brush of his sleeve against hers.

"That is one of Lady Elizabeth's suitors, is it not?"

"Aye. He is Sir Charles, son of Lord Selby."

"I overheard Milburn telling him in no uncertain terms that Bannaster will be named her guardian soon, and not to return until then."

"Though my lady will be glad to know that there is one less man fighting over her, she is still locked away, starving."

"Is she truly starving?" he asked with concern. "She has no food or drink in the tower?"

She hesitated, remembering the basket. "I guess she has enough to get by today."

"Then I guess you had better not get into any more trouble, eh?" he asked, smiling.

She didn't smile back.

"I was attempting a jest," he said, elbowing her.

"I guess it wasn't funny," she told him.

"When this crisis is over, I promise to give you more pleasant memories."

She stared at him in confusion.

His smile returned. "Ah. Have you been kept so sheltered with your lady that no men have played with you?"

"*Played* with me?" she asked faintly.

"The play of words between men and women." He grinned. "I know that it is not the time for teasing, but when I look at you, it is easy to forget that I mustn't talk about 'pleasant memories.' You are a beautiful woman; you should be used to men forgetting themselves with you."

She knew she was blushing, and she despised herself for it. When men forgot themselves with *Lady Elizabeth*, it was with a poem too romantic, or holding her hand for too long when a dance was done. There were no remarks hinting at unsuitable intimacies.

But she had heard that unmarried men never waited for the marriage bed, so it was with maidservants that they had . . . experiences.

And Elizabeth was a maidservant now. She had to make Sir John understand that she wasn't interested in a dalliance with him.

"Sir John, I am not a woman you can tease," she said softly, hoping no one overheard. "I have a duty to my lady and this castle, and that is all I can think about."

He leaned closer. "I am simply enjoying your

company. Your prettiness and your ability to flirt simply make me forget—"

"Now you're blaming me for your behavior?" she whispered.

He laughed, drawing the gaze of many people around them. Adalia gave the two of them a surprised look.

"Anne, it is far too enjoyable to tease you, but I will do my best to restrain myself."

"Please do," she said between clenched teeth.

During the meal, she spoke to him as little as possible. Philip came in from the tiltyard briefly to join them. He must have sensed the tension, because soon he was looking between them in confusion. But he shook his head and remained silent.

When Philip got up to leave, Sir John said, "You seem to be enjoying your duties as the captain's clerk."

Philip grinned. "I was doing inventory in the armory when someone insisted that a mere clerk could not hold his own amidst trained soldiers."

"And you showed them otherwise."

"I am in the process of it. Have a good afternoon, Anne."

She frowned and said nothing.

Philip glanced at his master. "I don't seem to know what is going on today."

"I have been assigned *your* duties," Elizabeth finally said.

"And I have been assigned to my own," Sir John said. "I will be able to earn wages while I recover."

"That is a good thing." Philip studied Elizabeth.

"I think. Anne, have you good writing skills? Sir John is a demanding master."

Before Elizabeth could speak, Sir John said, "Oh, she will be quick to assure you that I am not her master. We are only temporarily working together."

She could not take their laughter for another moment. She rose to her feet to leave.

"Anne, come out to the stables when you are ready," John said.

"And you will be able to ride with your leg broken?" she asked.

"Nay, I plan to ask for the use of a cart. You can ride at my side."

"Not behind you, like a good maidservant?" she asked sweetly.

"At my side will do," he said softly. "Someday I'd like to show you other ways to ride."

When they both started laughing, Elizabeth looked between them in confusion. She guessed he had said something lewd that she did not understand. In a huff she turned away and almost strode right toward the head table, where Sir Charles lounged like the lord of the castle, a position he obviously coveted. She ducked down the first corridor she came to, and wished she could escape from all men.

When Anne left them, John's smile faded.

"Whatever you're doing," Philip said, "I don't think 'tis working."

"I'm not so certain about that."

"She seems angry."

"I think she's angry because she likes me too much."

"And you're angry because . . . you like her too much?"

"When I rescue Lady Elizabeth, how can I allow Anne to remain as her servant, after the way I've treated her, after how she makes me feel? Anne will never be able to trust me."

" 'Tis not she who needs to trust you, it is Lady Elizabeth. And she'll be so grateful for the rescue, that she'll forgive your methods."

"But Anne will be hurt," John said quietly, looking at the empty doorway through which she'd disappeared. "I fear flirting with her is becoming far too easy. But I cannot stop."

Elizabeth perched on the seat of the small cart as Sir John guided it beneath the portcullis in the gatehouse and out into the countryside. The sun was warm on her face, and for a moment, she reveled in it, closing her eyes and letting the heat soothe her after the never-ending damp chill of the castle. The road jarred them repeatedly, and she had to catch hold of the crutch so that it wouldn't bounce right out of the cart. She kept it between them, like a line neither of them should cross.

Sir John glanced at her occasionally, his eyes inquisitive and amused. The sun glinted off his light brown hair and sparkled in his blue eyes, and she found herself feeling . . . breathless. She told herself that the scar represented a man scarred within as well, but she couldn't believe that.

He was taking her away from prison and into freedom, and for only a moment, she imagined being a simple maid, courted by a handsome knight. But even simple maids often weren't free to choose their own destiny, and if she ran away with her handsome knight, Anne might be killed when the deception was discovered. Nay, the burden of Castle Alderley was Elizabeth's. She would bear it and free her people.

As the road curved and the castle disappeared from view, she leaned back, cupped her hands around one knee, and glanced at Sir John. "By your title, you are a knight," she said, hoping that by keeping him talking, she could distract them both from other things.

His lips curved in a small smile that she found mischievous.

He flicked the reins. "Aye."

"You have no land of your own?"

"None. I am the youngest son—like your lady's betrothed."

"Ah, so you feel you understand him."

"Nay, I only know my own situation. My father had but one estate, and it went to my brother."

His voice and eyes were serious, and she sensed there was much he did not say. He kept his gaze on the road ahead, and she was able to study his profile.

"But you think you could have done better than your brother?" she asked.

"Aye, there is no doubt of that, but it is useless to talk of the past as if one could change it."

"So you studied to be a bailiff while you were training as a knight?"

"Before. It was my father's suggestion that I learn a trade, and I always had a good head for numbers. I was a small, awkward child, and it did not look as if I would ever make a useful knight. So I followed our bailiffs from estate to estate, learning."

"And you were content in your father's plan?"

He grinned at her. "Nay, I was furious. But it was better than the priesthood, which I refused outright. I knew I would do well as a knight, and it angered me that he could not see that I would grow into my body. But my brother had been active and good at everything almost from the moment he was born."

"So it was difficult to follow him."

"Difficult, but also the challenge I needed, mayhap. I learned about account books and farming methods, enough to know if we were being cheated by our own bailiff. But then I took up a sword."

"And you were good at it."

He arched a brow. "It is so easy for you to believe that of me?"

She eyed the width of his shoulders and blushed. "You simply look . . . like you carry a sword well."

"But I didn't then. Even a blunted training sword was too unwieldy for me." He sighed. "My father despaired, and then he died before I could prove to him that I would succeed."

"But you proved it to your brother."

"Nay, not even that. He had little interest in my achievements. And though I earned knighthood, it is expensive to keep armor and a well-trained horse for combat."

The lack of money had stopped his dreams, she realized, finding herself feeling sorry for him.

"It is lucky my father insisted on my learning a trade," he added.

"Mine did, too," she said, speaking as Anne.

"And you succeeded."

"I'm going to marry well—then I will have succeeded."

"And who does a maid aspire to marry?"

She opened her mouth, but found herself hesitating. "A maid aspires to marry a yeoman, a man with his own property, and the chance to rise higher."

"That is quite the aspiration."

She glanced at him quickly, wondering if he was teasing her, but he was not. "And who does a bailiff aspire to marry?"

She held her breath, hoping he would not say, "a maid."

He laughed. "I am a poor bailiff. Until I earn enough wages to deserve a bride, I fear I am destined to remain a lonely man."

"I cannot imagine a man such as you is ever lonely," she said dryly, thinking of her own quick attraction to him.

"A man such as me?" he echoed, smiling.

She cleared her throat and stared at the road again. Thankfully, the small village of Hillesley was coming into sight on the edge of a low hill. "A man who flirts with every maid he meets. Surely some woman eventually agrees to be the recipient."

"Have you seen me flirting with every maid I

meet?" he asked with interest. "Are my movements of such interest to you?"

She felt flustered and out of her element. Men did not treat her so familiarly, and she could easily fall under the spell of this . . . flirting. "I just assumed you flirted with every maid, Sir John, since you flirt with me."

"And think you that I don't find you worthy of all my attention?"

She frowned at him. "I don't know what to think about your motivations. We're here."

He looked at her, his blue eyes probing, but then he pulled on the reins and brought the cart to a halt near a small village green. A well dominated the center, and several sheep and cows grazed nearby. Stone buildings clustered where the crossroads met, and off in the distance, Hillesley Manor, made of yellow Cotswold stone, sat on a hill. She wondered if Master Wilden, the ill bailiff, was being cared for there.

After Sir John climbed awkwardly out of the cart with his splinted leg, he was introduced to Master Wilden's assistant, Hugh, the village reeve. Hugh commiserated with Sir John about the bruises on his face. Elizabeth tried to remain in the background, pretending that she had little to say. That was easy enough when Sir John seemed so very interested and asked intelligent questions. She fell behind the group and admired the peacefulness of the village. She'd been here before, of course, but always on the way somewhere else, as if her life had so much more meaning than did the lives of these villagers.

But now she watched a husband and wife working

together in the kitchen garden behind their small two-room stone cottage. A child crawled in the dirt row behind them. They had little, but they shared all, including the work. There was a fondness in their shared gazes that spoke of love and loyalty. This man did not consider his wife above him, an object of supreme devotion, as so many of the romantic poems implied. Elizabeth knew that that was how William would have treated her. She still longed for the comfort and familiarity of that. But there was something about the way that this simple farmer looked at his wife . . .

As the afternoon went by, John found that, when he could forget about his growing attraction to Anne, he enjoyed having her at his side. She was knowledgeable about the village and the manor itself, although at first he had to coax her into speaking. She kept shyly ducking her head and looking at the villagers from beneath her lashes, as if taking her out of the castle made her unsure of herself. And Anne was one woman he would have sworn had confidence in any situation.

Hugh spoke with John about the service owed by each of the villagers, and assured them that no one was causing trouble. They met with the hayward about the hedges that kept the sheep from wandering too far. Even the crops were doing well.

At last, John paused, balancing with the aid of his crutch, and looked up at the manor. "And how is Master Wilden?"

Hugh, pale and blond, ran his forearm across his damp forehead and frowned. "Master Wilden suffered from the fever for many days, yet the healer believes he will recover. But he is old, and it will take him a long time."

John nodded, relieved that the man would live—and relieved that he himself could continue to do the bailiff's work for a while longer. "Do you know if he would like to speak with me?"

Hugh shook his head. "He sleeps much of the day yet, milord. The next time ye're here, perhaps. Would ye care to stay for supper?"

This time Anne showed more emotion—in fact she looked worried.

"It is a kind offer, Hugh," John said, still watching Anne, "but we want to return before dark. Our cook sent along food for the journey."

She looked away, although he could have sworn she sighed with relief.

When they were once again riding in the cart, headed back to the castle, several villagers waved at them as they came in from the fields, a day's labor done. Anne showed more enthusiasm now, waving in return. When she faced forward again, she sighed and closed her eyes.

"That was difficult for you?" he asked.

She shook her head. "I am just uncomfortable as your assistant. They all know who I am."

"Uncomfortable? I didn't even ask you to write in an account book, yet. There was little for you to do but listen and learn."

"Then I fulfilled your expectations," she said.

She seemed a little too pleased with herself. John let the silence build for half a mile, and then he said,

"Ah, there is the small stream I remember. We'll stop here."

Her eyes opened in a hurry. "Stop? But we need to return before dark."

"But we have to eat. Adalia packed the satchel in the back of the cart."

"I can eat and ride."

"Well, I cannot. The food will bounce out of my hand. We'll stop here."

He guided the cart beneath a small cluster of trees. Once again, getting down from the cart proved a delicate, dangerous act, but when he was safely on the ground, he looked back up at Anne. She was still seated on the bench, and she was frowning at him.

Chapter 9

E lizabeth remained perched on the bench of the cart, looking down on a confused Sir John. It was too secluded here. Trees grew protectively around a small stream, and she could hear its gentle babble.

They were alone. Truly and completely alone, no one within calling distance, no one to stop him should he try—

What? What did she think he would do to her? After all, she'd known him only days, and this fragile feeling of friendship that had formed between them could be an illusion. Perhaps it was part of a wicked plot.

A plot to seduce a maidservant? Why would he

bother, when with his face and good nature, he could have any woman he wanted?

"Anne?" Sir John said, reaching up a hand. "May I help you down?"

He was the one injured, a splint on his leg. She meant to turn and put her foot on the wheel, but he caught her about the waist and lifted her off her feet. Startled, she clutched his shoulders as she was lowered easily to the ground. For a moment they stood thusly, their hands on each other while they stared. She had felt the strength in him, the way the muscles in his shoulders bunched and moved. His hands were large on her waist, making her feel delicate. And for a woman who was considered tall, she didn't even reach his shoulders.

She took a step away, looking anywhere but in his eyes. "So you brought us a meal?"

"Of course." He reached down within the cart and brought forth a stuffed satchel.

"We could eat right here," she said, looking about the grass clearing.

He smiled knowingly. "I suggest beneath the trees, by the stream. We'll be thirsty. And we wouldn't want your fair skin to redden. You unpack the satchel, and I'll see to the horse."

Elizabeth gritted her teeth and turned away from him, striding toward the water.

"You look as if you're marching off to battle," he called, amusement in his voice.

She ignored him. It was cooler back beneath the trees. The stream flowed over a tumble of rocks,

then wound down a hillside away from them. Wild-
flowers peaked from beneath ferns and from within
the stand of trees. It was a peaceful place, and she
felt her anger cooling, her dismay being replaced
by resolve. They would eat and leave. There were
still plenty of hours of daylight left for the journey
home.

Adalia had thought of everything when she
packed the satchel. There was a cloth to sit upon,
and Elizabeth spread it wide and knelt down. She
set out a round loaf of bread, cheese, almonds, and
strawberries. There were two horns with ale in them.
Simple fare, but she found her mouth watering as
she looked at the feast.

She heard Sir John's uneven gait and looked up
in time to see him coming toward her. She almost
thought she saw resolve on his face, but then he was
smiling, and she forgot the strange thought.

"You set a fine blanket, Anne," he said, as he
dropped his crutch.

He bent forward, braced his hands on the cloth,
then turned and seated himself right beside her,
rather than across the cloth, where she'd intended.
Nothing about this day was going as she'd planned,
and she feared it could only get worse.

"Almonds?" he said, surprised. "Your cook thinks
highly of you to spare such a luxury."

She nodded, hiding a wince. Perhaps that had
been foolish of Adalia. She broke apart the bread
and handed him a piece, only to see that her fingers
were trembling.

He noticed it, too, for his smile faded, and he

glanced up at her. "Anne? Is there something you fear, some cause for nervousness? Tell me it is not because of me."

"Of course not," she scoffed, keeping her hands busy by ripping the bread into even smaller pieces. "I have not been away from my mistress since she was held captive, and I worry what is going on at Alderley."

"If it eases your mind, I told Philip to pay attention to the tower as much as possible. He's already befriending the soldiers, so I'm sure he'll be able to prevent anything from happening."

"But . . . why would he form friendships, and then risk that to antagonize the soldiers?"

Sir John shrugged, and seemed to attack a piece of cheese with too much eagerness.

"Is he doing this . . . for my lady?" she asked softly.

"Until both your bailiff and I are recovered, Philip and I will remain at Castle Alderley. It only makes sense to help where we can." Then his blue eyes focused on her. "Because your mistress only has you to help her. Bannaster seems determined to keep her alone and desperate."

She nodded, shredding a piece of bread in her fingers. "And did you find another way to help?" she blurted out.

He stiffened. "What do you mean?"

"Someone lowered a basket of food to the window from the top of the tower."

Wearing a frown, he said, "It was not me, nor my clerk."

She was almost disappointed, because at least if it was him, she would have known who their benefactor was. But now . . .

"You look so sad," he murmured.

When she glanced up, he dropped back on one elbow, his head a little below hers.

And too close.

He reached up, and she froze in shock as he touched her cheek, letting his fingers skim it gently. Instead of feeling soothed, it ignited a fire beneath her skin, as if it burned where he touched, but not with pain. Something more focused and dangerous. She shuddered, her breath caught on a gasp. His gaze suddenly focused with clarity on her as he cupped her cheek, cradling it for a moment. His skin was so warm against hers, his palm rough, but that somehow made him more attractive to her.

With just the pressure of his fingers sliding onto her neck, he slowly pulled her forward, her face over his, until she was forced to brace her hand on his chest or fall into him. Her world had narrowed until it was only him—his blue eyes, his parted lips, his hand holding her in place. Her resistance was token, fleeting, and then gone. She wanted to know how this felt, to be desired as a woman. It was a heady, strange, intoxicating feeling.

She closed her eyes as their lips touched. She kissed him gently, tasting strawberries and a heat that was all his. His lips were surprisingly soft, surprisingly in command, moving against hers in a way that made her insides seem to heat and melt and coalesce into something new. His hand on her neck held her in place, yet she did not resent the control; indeed, it was thrilling and wicked, allowing her to feel seduced.

When his tongue boldly threaded between her lips, she was so startled she granted it entrance without a thought, and the deepening of pleasure was a surprise she welcomed. He turned her head so their mouths could widen and mate. With only the slightest hesitation, she met his tongue with her own, and a battle of supremacy was joined. He groaned into her mouth, pulling her closer. Her hand on his body gave way, and her chest fell against his. It was a pleasure-pain that made her breasts ache. Somewhere inside she thought only he could give her what she needed.

And with that, her doubts began a slow bubble back to the surface.

When his fingers slid from her neck and up against her wimple, she pulled back, breaking the kiss. His head was still beneath her, his mouth wet, his breathing as labored as hers.

"I have never seen the beauty of your hair," he whispered.

She pushed away from him and sat back on her heels. Contemplating uncovering her hair reminded her of all the secrets that she also kept covered. "Nay, what was I thinking to allow such familiarity?"

He took a deep breath, eyes closed, his face pained. "You will not kiss me again?"

"The day grows long," she said firmly, pointing to the west. "I did not wish to stop for a meal, let alone—" She broke off, embarrassed. "Do not ask me for such intimacy again."

John stared at Anne, stunned by the vehemence of her reaction. Hastily, she began to pack away the remains of their meal. He had never met a maid who did not want his kiss, although he admitted that many were motivated by the promise of payment. Sex had always been a part of it—whenever a virgin had caught his eye, the lure of adventure and the road had drawn him away before he could become entangled.

Anne's anger puzzled him. She had even said her parents wanted to see her married soon—would not a bailiff be more prestigious than a common farmer? He had thought she would respond to his seduction happily, which of course would hurt her more in the end.

But this anger seemed . . . wrong, and it made him think about the other unusual things about her. For a maidservant who had grown up in Castle Alderley, she seemed surprisingly remote from its people, as if everyone went out of their way to avoid her.

Anne herself seemed a good-hearted woman; he could only conclude that her treatment by others was due to her mistress. More and more it made him wary of the woman he was supposed to marry—the woman he was betraying by kissing her maid.

Nay, he was rescuing Lady Elizabeth. Only Anne had access to the tower. Anne, with the luscious mouth, with the heavy breasts that had pressed against him so fleetingly. He felt a kinship with her, perhaps because she was as common as he'd been before his elevation to the title.

Mayhap it was *time to tell her the truth,* he thought. Only then would he be able to cease his flirtation with her. She was heroic, after all, the only person between her mistress and Bannaster. She'd braved Milburn's wrath to try to send a missive to the king.

But she was so angry with him right now. After washing her face and hands in the stream, she patted water on the back of her neck as if she were over-heated. Was she angry with him—or with herself, for forgetting her mistress in a moment of pleasure?

And how could he know if he could trust her with his secrets, when her own people shied away from her?

He could not think of an answer now; he would talk to Philip for a rational opinion, because John feared he himself was no longer objective where Anne was concerned.

He came up on his good knee, his splinted leg out to the side. The leg itself barely ached anymore, but he could not remove the splint without looking sus-picious. He braced the crutch under his arm and maneuvered himself to his feet. When he'd moved off the cloth, she knelt down to fold it up and stuff it in the satchel. Though he knew he shouldn't, he re-mained near her, watching her below him, wishing he could push her down into the grass and—

He had to get this desire under control, before its wildness turned back upon him and ruined every-thing.

* * *

Elizabeth resisted all of Sir John's efforts to engage her in conversation on the way home. She was angry with him, but mostly angry with herself and the way she'd just let him seduce her senses, seduce her lips. She had to force her mind not to think of his heart thudding beneath her hand. And the taste of his mouth—

Oh, she was furious with herself. He could not remain bailiff here, whomever she married. How could she look at him every day, knowing what they'd done together?

When the cart rolled into the inner ward, she didn't even wait to see if Sir John needed help getting down. She simply grabbed the satchel and ran inside. Supper was over, and already the soldiers were beginning their nightly indulgence in ale. One or two of them grabbed for her as she hurried by, but she ducked away and headed for the kitchens. Adalia wasn't there, only several scullion boys cleaning spits and firedogs. Adalia was probably with her son, and Elizabeth didn't want to disturb her. The cook was a widow, and only had so much time to spare for her child.

Elizabeth desperately needed to talk to another woman. She was fixated on her first kiss. She kept trying to imagine what it would have been like with William, such a gentle, sensitive poet. William would never have thrust his tongue into her mouth. It was wrong—indecent!

Then why had it felt so good?

With a groan, she fled the kitchens and found

herself heading for the tower. Surely they would allow her entrance even if she didn't bring food with her.

Elizabeth curtsied to both soldiers. Young Lionel, Alderley's representative, flushed as if she shouldn't have to debase herself for him.

"Lionel, might I see Lady Elizabeth this evening?"

Bannaster's soldier leaned his staff across the door, barring her way.

Lionel winced. "M—Anne, Master Milburn gave explicit orders that you were not to be allowed up today."

"But Lady Elizabeth won't know that!" Anne cried. "She will be so frightened. I only want to tell her—"

"She knows," Bannaster's soldier said impassively.

Elizabeth beseeched Lionel with her wide-eyed gaze.

"She was down here not an hour ago," Lionel said. "Worried about ye, o' course. We told her through the door that you'd been ordered to stay away today, but that you'd be back up in the mornin'."

She leaned back against the far wall in relief and closed her eyes. "So my lady will rest easy," she murmured. If she couldn't talk to Anne on her own, at least she could be comforted by that. "My thanks, Lionel."

She turned and walked away, not paying attention to where she went. She was tired and sad and distraught, and all she had were her thoughts to comfort her, not the wise words of a friend. Her plan to send for help had turned upside down, punishing Anne, the poor girl who suffered the most in this terrible affair. Elizabeth's punishment had only given Sir John greater access to her, and she'd responded to his kiss like—

A hand suddenly covered her mouth, and her scream was only a muffled thing. An arm snaked around her waist, pulling hard until her breath left her lungs.

"Told ye I'd find ye another time," rasped a voice in her ear.

His beard moved against her neck as he spoke, and she knew at once who it was. It was the soldier who'd grabbed her in the great hall at supper last night.

She struggled against him, but her arms were held tight to her sides. She kicked, and he only laughed and lifted her off the ground. Wildly, she looked around—she had no idea where she was.

When his free hand squeezed her breast hard, she cried out. She sank her teeth into his hand, and it was his turn to moan in pain. She kicked harder, bending her knees to reach up behind. To her surprise, he gave a muffled "oof" and doubled over her back. Her feet touched the floor, but he still gripped her hard. With one hand, he yanked at her neckline and pulled. There was sickening rip of fabric, air wafted against her breasts, and her fear rose so fast she felt dizzy with it.

"Release her!"

She almost didn't recognize Sir John's voice; it had deepened and roughened and sounded dangerous.

The bearded soldier turned around to face this new threat, keeping her back to his front. He had her wrists pinned together with the same hand that held her body firmly to his.

Sir John loomed out of the dark corridor, the crutch in his hand like a weapon, and in the other a small dagger. His damp hair fell across his forehead; his day's growth of beard made him look menacing— and the scar completed the effect. He was no longer a bailiff, but a warrior—a warrior with a broken leg, she realized in dismay.

The soldier guffawed. "I seen you watchin' her, cripple, but I got here first."

"Let her go, and I will leave you unharmed," Sir John said, limping forward step by step, closing the distance between them.

The bearded soldier didn't retreat; he only held Elizabeth up like a prize. "Unharmed? Think ye I cannot kill ye easily?"

"Not while you're holding a hostage."

Sir John didn't even look at her. All his attention was focused on his opponent. Even when the soldier pulled her hands lower, and she realized her bare breasts peaked between ripped fabric, Sir John never looked at the display.

"Don't ye want to see what I won?" the soldier said gleefully.

As the crutch swung over Elizabeth's head, she ducked and heard the crack against her assailant's skull. He let go of her as he stumbled back, and she darted beneath Sir John's arm. Falling onto her hands and knees, she rolled onto her back in time to see the bearded soldier draw his sword. She gasped, but he was already staggering from the first blow. He raised his sword high, but Sir John bent and elbowed him hard in the stomach. The soldier stumbled about, roaring his outrage, thrusting his sword wildly as Sir John danced between the blows.

Sir John swung the crutch again, catching him beneath the jaw. His body arched backward, feet coming off the floor, before he slammed onto his back and lay still.

"The cripple won," Sir John said with satisfaction, standing over the body.

Elizabeth propped herself up on her hands, then caught the bodice of her gown as it sagged forward. Her head spun as a flicker of black dots danced before her eyes.

"I didn't need you to rescue me!" she cried, falling backward, as the floor rushed up to greet her.

Chapter 10

⌒◝◜⌒

Elizabeth suddenly realized that Sir John was carrying her, and she didn't remember him lifting her from the floor.

And that made her even angrier.

"Sir John!" she cried, outraged.

"Shh!" he looked behind him, then back down at her sternly. "Do you want someone to see you like this?"

She felt his arms warm and hard behind her back and beneath her knees. If anyone saw him carrying her—and then she saw her bodice, and realized that the scraps left revealed a dangerous amount of cleavage. With a gasp she grabbed the fabric and tugged.

"Where are you taking me?" she whispered.

"To my bedchamber, where we won't be disturbed."

She opened her mouth to protest, but then it dawned on her that his arms were around her, and he wasn't using the crutch. It was tucked beneath his arm, rubbing against her legs with each stride.

He wasn't even limping.

She glared at him in suspicion, knowing he couldn't have healed in just a day. But then he was shouldering a door open, and they were in his bedchamber. Philip was not there.

He put her down on his bed, and she scrambled back to her feet, holding her bodice closed.

Sir John arched a brow at her. "For someone who just swooned, you're remarkably agile."

"I did not swoon!"

"Your eyes were closed and you didn't respond to your name." He put his hand on her shoulder and said, "I was quite concerned."

The warmth and sympathy in his eyes was touching her too deeply. She felt scattered and helpless, and hated feeling at the mercy of men. She had kicked her assailant—she would have gotten away on her own. But Sir John had once again risked himself to help her.

"I do thank you for your assistance," she forced herself to say. "I was not paying attention to where I was going."

"I know. I was following you."

"Again!" she cried, her anger stirring back to life.

"I felt the need. You were distraught when you left me, and I worried about what you'd do. But I don't need thanks for my rescue efforts, only your silence."

"My silence?" she asked, beginning to frown.

And then he tossed the crutch onto the bed and started to pace.

Without a limp, just as he'd walked through the corridors.

Unease was a dark heaviness in her belly. "You lied about your broken leg?"

"I had to. I had to make sure that Bannaster—and now Milburn—could not force me to leave."

She found herself more intrigued than frightened. It was crazy to still feel so trusting of him. "If you want me to be silent about your false injury, you have to tell me why. It was obvious you were beaten."

He gave her a wry grin. "I had my own men do it."

She frowned in disbelief, but he held up a hand.

"I hope, when you hear the whole story—and when you explain it all to your mistress—you will both accept what I've done, knowing it has been for the right reasons."

"And what have you done?" she demanded.

"My name is not John Gravesend. It's John Russell, and I've come to rescue Lady Elizabeth, my betrothed."

Elizabeth didn't remember sitting down on the bed, but she found herself there, feeling stunned and overwhelmed. Her mind only seemed capable of considering the silliest part of this—that this man was nothing like the boy she remembered, who was short and round and under his mother's rule. And hadn't his hair been lighter?

"I . . . don't know whether I can believe you," she finally whispered, staring at the body of a strong— and strong willed—man. "You are nothing like . . . my lady described."

"She saw me when I was thirteen," he answered. "As I told you this afternoon—and most of it was the truth—my father despaired of me."

So he had come to her . . . at last? She had thought she was helping herself, and instead she was being rescued—by her own betrothed.

Her betrothed—who was kissing her when he thought she was a lady's maid?

Elizabeth felt the simmer of anger beneath her bewilderment boil over into fury. She had been about to blurt out her own identity, but now she thought better of it. How could she trust such a man? The entire story might be a lie—after all, she was the greatest heiress in England, and men would do much for her fortune and the earldom.

He grimaced at whatever expression he saw on her face. "I know what you're thinking—I have not treated you well since I arrived. But you have to understand that I did not know whom I could trust here. I saw you as the person closest to my lady, the way for me to reach her the easiest."

He thought it was *easy* to use her? "Why did you not arrive as yourself and demand your right to speak with your betrothed?" she asked in a tight voice.

"And therein lies the problem," he said, beginning to pace again. "When I received Lady Elizabeth's letter about the death of her parents, I was in Normandy. I had not even known of my brothers' deaths until she told me. To go from being the youngest son on his own, to the baron with a bride waiting for me—I was stunned."

"I am sorry you did not know about your brother's accident," she said stiffly, trying to make excuses for his behavior in her mind—if he even *was* John Russell.

"There is a lot I didn't know about my brother," he said bitterly.

She felt defensive on behalf of the man she'd loved her whole life. "I do not understand your tone of voice."

"He is the reason I had to come to Lady Elizabeth this way. I returned to Rame Castle almost a fortnight ago, only to discover that it had been grievously neglected. Most of the tenants were gone, their fields unplanted. The sheep and cattle had been sold, and the soldiers—they were off to seek a master who would pay them. My contingent consists of myself and three men-at-arms. Not exactly an army capable of winning and defending Castle Alderley," he added with sarcasm.

Such cruel words about William could not possibly be true. "You make no sense. I had met Lord Russell, who was a charming, sincere man. He would not deliberately abuse his own people."

"I tried to think that," he said quietly.

When he sat down on the bed beside her, she jumped to her feet to put distance between them, holding her arms over her ruined gown.

"But the proof is Rame Castle," he continued. "More than one servant swore to me that William preferred London to his own estate. And living at court requires money to keep up the correct appearances—according to my brother, anyway. I wouldn't be surprised if he just assumed that soon he'd be earl, with all the money he needed to return our home to its former glory. But our people . . ." He ran a hand down his face, his dark whiskers shadowing his cheeks.

"So you have no money," she said slowly, avoiding the way he slurred his own brother, "no army, no way to prove that you are Lady Elizabeth's betrothed."

"Oh, I have proof, for all the good it will do me. I have the ring."

But he didn't produce it, and she realized just in time that she was only a maid, and could not ask such things of him. She remembered the ring well enough from her childhood. It had been the insignia used to seal her betrothal contract. She had been so young, so innocent; she had thought it meant freedom for her. At the time, the ring had freed her from men trying to take advantage of her. It had promised her a future with a handsome, smiling man who would someday wear it—

Now the ring tied her to another man—a liar, a user of women. A man who would betray his own brother's memory.

She stared at him and realized to her dismay that the blue of his eyes had always attracted her—because it had been the same color as William's.

No wonder he had seemed familiar when first she'd seen him lying wounded in the great hall. He did not have William's handsome looks, but his hair was the same shade as their other brother, Robert.

Could he really be John Russell?

She had thought this day would be one of rejoicing. Instead all she wanted to do was cry as her last dreams of a romantic, happy marriage died. This man did not hold women with the reverence they deserved.

"Do you believe me?" he asked.

"It is not for me to believe or disbelieve," she said without expression. "It is my lady you must convince."

"Nay, it is you, too, I must convince, Anne."

His voice rang with the tones of truth and sincerity, but she could believe none of it.

"I have treated you poorly, and only because I had to. I could see no other way to reach Lady Elizabeth than to send a message through you. I didn't know you; I couldn't trust that you would believe me."

"So you felt the need to . . . play with my emotions?"

He stiffened. "I did not mean it to go so far. Milburn kept us together, and I thought I could control everything. I am used to that."

He was used to being in control, she thought bitterly. Hadn't she wanted a husband *she* could control, so that she could live as she wished? Instead here was John Russell, manipulating her into doing things she had never thought she would be capable of doing. What had happened to the malleable boy she remembered?

"You must forgive my behavior," he continued.

"Must I forgive that kiss?" she whispered. "Must I forgive the actions of a man who would deliberately hurt me?"

"Anne, I cannot explain—I never meant—" He sighed. "I have never met anyone like you, not in all of my years of wandering. The women I knew only wanted pleasure, and the coin with which I paid for it. I am not used to women raised as you and Lady Elizabeth were, free and intelligent, who act because it is right, not because they will be rewarded. But you have suffered because of my actions, so please tell your mistress whatever you need to. I will not ask for your silence for my indiscretion." He gave her a measured stare. "But I am here to help; tell her that. I vow that I will make things right—for the both of you."

Her eyes were burning now—she could listen no more. "I—I will tell my lady your words and give you her response."

She tried to move past him, and he touched her arm.

"Anne—"

"Do not ever touch me again!" she whispered, mortified to feel tears escape her eyes. She ran from his chamber and shut the door behind her.

John bent over and rested his hands on his knees. That had gone just as he'd expected—badly. When the door opened, he looked up with relief, but it was only Philip.

"I saw her running down the corridor," Philip

said. "She turned her face away when she saw who I was. I think she was crying."

John nodded. He ached inside for the misery he'd caused, for how he'd made Anne feel. "I told her the truth."

Philip sat down on his own pallet across from him. "What made you decide to do that?"

"I must obviously trust her, because I kissed her this afternoon."

His eyes widened. "You *kissed* her? How did flirtation lead to that?"

John shrugged. "It wasn't supposed to. Yet . . . I couldn't help myself."

"And now she's running to tell Lady Elizabeth."

"I apologized, told her things had gone too far. I know not what she's going to tell her mistress. It is only fair that she make that decision."

"Now Lady Elizabeth has much to hold against you, including the lie told about the estate supporting you in Europe."

"I didn't tell Anne that. She didn't want to believe that my brother could have neglected the estate—how could I make him look worse?"

Philip groaned.

"We know that lie is untrue," John continued. "It might not even have spread beyond Rame Castle, since I explained the truth to my people."

"If they believe you over your brother's steward."

"How could they not? He took all their goods and rent, where I gave all the money I had to begin repairs."

"That could look like guilt."

"I intend to explain it all to Lady Elizabeth when we meet. I want nothing to stand between us."

"Anne already does," Philip said, shaking his head.

John sat down on the bed and faced his friend. "Let us put this aside for now. Tell me what you heard from Ogden and Parker."

"There is no good news. They've spent the past night and day searching for Alderley's soldiers, and have not found them yet. They're going to start asking questions in the villages for at least a direction to expand their search, but you know how long that can take when one doesn't want to arouse suspicion."

John cursed, but it didn't help his feeling of frustration. "There is little we can do until we have an army behind us."

"And that is assuming, once we find them, that they trust us."

"Believe me, I will make them see the wisdom," John said grimly. "Did you make arrangements to meet with Ogden and Parker again?"

"Nay, because they'll be roaming farther afield. They promised to come to us when they have the news you need."

John nodded silently, already finding his thoughts on Anne again. "When I saw that soldier attack her," he murmured, "it was like a part of me was glad that I could fight him. Have you found yourself . . . itching to train, to pick up a sword?"

"What do you think I've been doing to help you keep an eye on the soldiers?"

"Then you've been lucky. I've been feeling restless, as if my skills are fading away with every moment I remain on a bench because of this supposed broken leg." He gave Philip a worried look. "What if it's the adventure I need? I never thought I'd marry. Perhaps I won't be good at being a husband, leading a life of leadership while others do the physical work that I've always enjoyed."

"I've heard of many a man who worried about such things. They made it work."

"How?"

"Maybe getting into their wives' beds was the true challenge?"

Philip chuckled to himself, but John couldn't see the humor. What if when he saw Lady Elizabeth, he wasn't as attracted to her as he was to her maid?

Chapter 11

‹‹——∽◦∽——››

Elizabeth spent the night wrapped in a blanket in front of the kitchen hearth, wearing a gown from Adalia, feeling like she would never be warm again. She'd cried so much that her eyes were raw and fuzzy, and her brain seemed to be merely floating. She'd made it through mass, keeping her head down in prayer, having no idea if Sir John—Lord Russell was even in the chapel. She hadn't even asked the true name of his friend, who'd seen her run by crying last night.

But now she could finally go to see Anne. She held a tray in her shaking hands, realizing she hadn't even broken her own fast. Food didn't seem to matter this morn. The soldiers stepped aside for her, and she sighed in relief and practically ran up the tower stairs.

Anne must have heard her, because she flung open the door to the solar. Elizabeth slid the tray onto the table, then turned and threw her arms around her friend. She wouldn't have thought she had any more tears, but she found herself crying again.

" 'Tis all right," Anne said, patting her back. "The soldiers told me you were forbidden to bring me food for a day. Milburn discovered the letter?"

Elizabeth could only nod and hold her tighter. "You—you were not too hungry?"

"Nay, although another basket did not come, the first had enough to keep me fed for the day. It was you I was concerned about. I am an heiress," she said sarcastically, "so he could hardly punish me too severely. But you—"

Elizabeth backed away, accepting a handkerchief to mop her face and blow her nose. "I was not beaten, or even denied food." She related how Milburn had caught her.

"What did he do to you? Surely it had to be *something*. Come sit down and tell me. You look pale as a ghost. Have you eaten yet this morn?"

Elizabeth gave a shaky laugh and shook her head. "Food is unappetizing today," she said, sitting down on a cushioned chair before the bare hearth.

Anne sat in the other one and took her hand. "So tell me."

"He obviously wants to keep me away from you, so he assigned me to act as Sir John's clerk."

"Ah, Sir John, the one who looks at you with interest," Anne said, wiggling her eyebrows.

Elizabeth sighed, her chest aching from crying. "I discovered yesterday that he's not who he said he was."

Anne straightened in surprise. "He's not Sir John, a bailiff?"

"Nay," she whispered. "He's John, Lord Russell, my betrothed."

Anne's mouth fell open. "Are you certain?"

"He says he has the ring," she answered dully, "although as a maid, I could not demand to see it. He has William's eyes and Robert's hair."

"Well, I . . . I know not what to say. This is a good thing, is it not? You've been telling him our problems."

"Well it might have been all right," Elizabeth said, her voice rising, "if he hadn't kissed me yesterday, hours before telling me the truth!"

"Oh my," she breathed. Tugging on Elizabeth's hand, she said, "Upstairs."

Elizabeth followed dispiritedly and allowed Anne to close the door behind her.

Anne looked at her with worry as she guided her to another chair. "But he likes you; surely that is a good thing between two people who are going to marry."

"Do you not understand?" Elizabeth cried. "He kissed me, the maid, knowing that I was not his betrothed, knowing that he was lying to me."

"But you are his betrothed, and you're lying to him, too," Anne said, her expression confused.

"But I didn't kiss him! Well, all right, I kissed him back, and I felt terribly guilty. But he admitted he's been using me to get to you."

"You mean using you to get to yourself."

"Anne, stop! You know what I'm saying. He deliberately targeted me because I am your maid."

"He has been trying to rescue me—you?"

"So he says."

"You are the only one with access to the tower. Doesn't his reasoning make sense?"

"All he had to do was befriend me, Anne," Elizabeth whispered. "Teach me to trust him and then tell me the truth. Instead he flirted and he teased and he . . ."

"He kissed you."

She nodded. "He said he hadn't meant to go so far, that he couldn't help himself."

"Again, I insist that you see this in a good light. Surely he must be happy now that he knows who you are."

"I didn't tell him."

Anne groaned and sank back in her chair.

"How could I, after what he revealed? He used me, Anne! If I were a mere maid, I would have thought he had feelings for me, and my own feelings would have been crushed. And don't say he was desperate. I care not. He is nothing like William, who treated me with reverence, with love; John uses women. He even admitted that the women he's usually with are *paid* to be with him!"

"Well, I've heard that men—"

"And he has no money, no army!" Elizabeth

interrupted. "He tried to claim that his own brother neglected Rame Castle, and that all the soldiers are gone, and the people poor!"

"Do you think he lies?" she asked cautiously.

"I know not if he's lying or someone lied to him, but that cannot possibly be true. William would never harm his own people."

"But Lord Russell has no army."

"Only three men-at-arms, one of whom is Philip Sutterly—or whatever his real name is. I didn't ask where the other men are. So he has no show of force to win my release."

"I thought you didn't want him to bring an army. You were worried our people would be hurt or killed."

"I know!" Elizabeth jumped to her feet, unable to sit still a moment longer. "I wanted my husband to be respectable. But John . . . needs me for my money," she whispered brokenly, hugging herself. "It makes me feel . . . worthless as a woman."

"Any man you married would receive your dowry," Anne insisted. "It is the way of things. For you to take that personally is foolish. So his estate has become poor, however it happened. Would you feel the same way were it William coming to you, needing your money?"

"Aye, nay—I don't know! William is dead. The life I had hoped to lead has died along with him. And the worst thing is . . . though I'd felt guilty, for once I had felt desired as a woman. But that wasn't true; John was using me to get to you. To me. Oh!" She dropped back into her chair.

"And did he feel guilty for kissing you?"

"He said he did, but what does that prove? I have no idea what is a lie, or what is the truth. Perhaps he stole the ring!" she said shrilly.

"You said he looks like his brothers."

In a sullen voice, Elizabeth said, "Only a bit."

"So what are you going to do?"

Elizabeth glanced at her desperately. "What do you think I should do?"

Anne put up her hands. "Nay, this is not for me to decide. This is your life, your future. I have not met Lord Russell, so I cannot give you my opinion."

"You would tell me to confess the truth, that I am his betrothed."

Anne shrugged.

"Well, I cannot, not until I can trust him. That would be putting too much power into his hands. I'm alone with him constantly—he could abuse that like he did yesterday."

"His kiss was an abuse?" she asked hesitantly.

"I don't want to remember it."

"But . . . you enjoyed it."

Elizabeth groaned. "Aye, I enjoyed it, but that matters not! He could compromise me, and then my choices would be lost."

"But if he's your betrothed—"

"*If.* King Edward thought he was uniting two powerful families—it sounds as if John's family has fallen in the world. Perhaps that nullifies the contract."

"You would go against your father's wishes? Was not your mother dear friends with Lord Russell's mother? And wouldn't that leave you vulnerable to Lord Bannaster, or whomever the king chooses?"

"Oh, Anne, my head is spinning! I don't know what I'm going to do about the betrothal. I only know that right now, I need to find out if I can trust this man. He might be our only chance to put things right. Or he might be the worst thing to happen to me. I have to find out."

"All right, I understand, and I even agree. But you cannot withhold the truth from him for too long. It would be as unfair as what he did to you."

"But he will have deserved it, whereas I didn't."

"Oh, Elizabeth, I hope you can make all of this work. It seems like a dangerous undertaking."

"Mayhap. But I have to know the truth. Maybe I can eventually persuade him to show me the ring."

"What will you tell him that I—you—said about his revelation?"

"That I don't know whether I can trust him. That I'm confused, and worried about my people. And all of that is the truth."

"Why don't you ask him what ideas he has for your rescue?"

Elizabeth took a deep breath. She had to remember what was important here, and not concentrate on how everything affected her. "You're right. I shall listen to his thoughts, but I don't think I can yet trust him to carry them out. I don't know what he's been doing in Europe, why he has so little money of his own—"

"Youngest son?" Anne helpfully supplied.

"Besides that. I guess . . . I'll just have to keep

spending time with him. When we are better ac-
quainted, perhaps I'll reveal myself."

"Perhaps?"

When Elizabeth glared at her, Anne smiled. "I'm
sorry. I do not mean to tease you. This is a serious
dilemma and I don't envy you your decisions."

"Are you still all right up here?" Elizabeth asked
with concern.

"I am, although I hope we're rescued in weeks
rather than months." Anne stood up. "Break me off
a piece of bread, and I'll tell you all about the book
I'm reading. Oh, and I'll need more mending. In fact,
I have some thoughts on your latest embroidery de-
sign."

"Can we not just eat?"

John ate his morning meal very slowly, waiting
for Anne. Lady Elizabeth's reaction to the truth of
his identity might well mean success or failure. He
could be judged on William's flaws—or on his own,
and those were numerous as well.

Anne finally appeared from the kitchens, and
John stood up awkwardly, cursing his splint. Several people around him snickered when they looked
between him and the maidservant. Surely it was
because they were finally realizing that their newest bailiff was courting their mistress's maid.

When Anne was near him, he gave her a smile of
welcome, as if nothing was wrong in Sir John's
world. Anne frowned her suspicion, then seemed to
remember their roles and gave him a small, nervous
smile.

"I tried to wait to break my fast with you, Anne," he said, "but I was hungry."

She eyed his chest. "You must need a lot of sustenance."

He grinned. "Sometimes it never seems enough. Would you like to eat with me?"

When she tried to sit opposite him, he took her hand and pulled her to his side. He felt the stiffness of her fingers, sensed her struggle. He hated hurting her, but they both had to keep up the masquerade.

"Forgive me," he whispered, leaning close to her. The wimple brushed his face, and he found himself wishing it were her hair. How was he ever going to learn to control his desire for her, when he had to pretend to court her? "We must keep up the pretense."

He saw her slight nod, and she took a piece of bread from his plate and began to pick it apart again, just as she'd done yesterday when she was nervous.

"I ate with Lady Elizabeth," she said awkwardly.

"I guessed you might. You must have had much to talk about."

She only nodded. He wished he could ask her the results outright, but there were still too many people in the hall, mostly servants cleaning up after the meal. And to his surprise, they didn't seem to want to leave. Were these people, who seemed to ignore Anne most of the time, now playing chaperone?

"We have to return to Hillesley today," he said. "Master Milburn told me it was time to collect the rents."

"He could not possibly trust you, when he's known you so short a time," she said impassively.

Was she also speaking for her mistress?

"That's why he's sending soldiers with us today," John continued. "He told me it was to provide protection against theft."

"You do need money," she said dryly.

She'd landed a particularly accurate blow, he thought. His lack of fortune must not have impressed Lady Elizabeth. "Come walk with me outside."

To his surprise, she leaned toward him, and even touched his arm. His body responded far too quickly.

In a low, intimate whisper, she said, "Still courting me?"

"I must."

"I won't make it easy."

"I know."

And she didn't. Outside, she offered to help him down the stairs from the great hall to the ground, but he declined. She waited patiently at the bottom for him, looking up with a deferential interest that made him even more suspicious. They walked side by side across the inner ward, past the soldiers' barracks and the stables, and he knew that they were the objects of curiosity. How would these people feel when they discovered that he was their future lord, not a bailiff courting a maidservant?

But as if Anne knew what he was thinking, she took his free hand, as a friend would, but still too intimately. They stopped at the tiltyard to watch

Bannaster's knights and soldiers train. One young soldier was bearing the brunt of two men attacking him.

"Is that necessary?" Anne asked in dismay.

"It is a normal training procedure."

"Their swords aren't blunted."

"I noticed," he said tightly.

"That poor young soldier is one of Alderley's own."

That explained the vehemence of what should be a training exercise.

"There are only four of our men left," she continued. "Are they to bear the brunt of this *training*?"

John saw Philip leave a sturdy building next to the barracks. John knew he'd been working in the armory. Today he wore a battered chest and back plate, though he still carried an account book. When he saw them, he strode over.

"Sir John," Philip said, nodding. "Good day, Anne."

Philip could not have missed the way Anne stiffened and regarded him warily. Apparently Philip was the enemy now, too.

But Philip only continued to smile at her.

Anne pointed to the training exercise. "Philip, there are two of Bannaster's men against one of Alderley's."

John was relieved that she'd let go of his hand.

Philip looked over his shoulder, and they all saw Alderley's soldier drop to his knees, though his shield was still raised, and his sword absorbed the blows.

"Hmm," Philip said, frowning. He glanced at John. "Shall I see to that?"

"If you can," John said, thinking that Philip would use his judgment about whether too much interference would harm their masquerade.

But Philip must have taken it as a challenge, because he pulled his sword from the scabbard. "Never fear, Mistress Anne. I will right this wrong for you."

John saw Anne bite her lip, almost as if she wanted to smile. With a laugh, Philip threw himself between the combatants, and gave Alderley's soldier a chance to recover.

Elizabeth watched John's man fight, and wondered if John was that much better. It was easier to concentrate on Philip—or whomever he was—than think of John. Philip was amusing and obviously compassionate. And he wasn't the one who'd come up with the pretense of courting her to get to the tower.

Several soldiers had gathered to watch this new battle, and suddenly she remembered her attacker, though she didn't see him. Would he want revenge now? Had John made everything worse by defeating him so easily while posing as an injured man?

"Do you think the bearded soldier is here?" she asked. The hesitation in her voice bothered her.

"The man who attacked you last night? I had a discussion with him this morn."

"And?"

"I convinced him that you did not want his attentions, that I had your interest. And that I had Master Milburn's ear."

"Ah, I see." He had remembered to protect her, without her reminding him. She could not bring herself to thank him. She gave him a sideways glance. "So you have my interest."

"It must appear so."

"A man who shares my interest would wish to be alone with me. So come."

She took his hand again, felt the way he stiffened, though he remained silent. Her anger was ruling her, and she didn't seem to be able to stop it, though a rational part of her urged caution. She led John to the lady's garden. There was a half-wall cutting it off from the rest of the ward, and inside it was a welcome respite of plants and flowers. A gravel path wound through it, and she followed it deeper in, until the trees and shrubs hid them from passersby.

When they reached a secluded stone bench, she said, "Please sit down and rest your leg, Sir John."

"You know I don't need—"

But she gave him a hard push, and short of grabbing her for balance, he was forced to sit down.

"So we're courting," she began, considering him. "Shouldn't I be sitting in your lap?"

With her knees pressed together, she sat down on his legs, her hip against his stomach, her shoulder against his chest. He leaned away from her, his hands bracing himself on the back of the bench, his eyes narrowed.

"Why are you doing this?" he demanded. His breath was coming harder than a moment before, and his narrowed eyes burned into her.

"Isn't this what you've been doing to me, deliberately courting me?"

"I was not so"—his gaze dropped down her body—"so intimate with you."

In outrage, she leaned in closer and tried to ignore the heat emanating from him. Having nowhere to brace herself but his chest, she laid a fist there. "And what do you call that kiss?"

"A mistake I've already apologized for." He looked at her lips. "I don't think you're going to want to have to apologize to me."

For a heartbeat she stared into his eyes, and finally realized that her treacherous body was enjoying having his beneath her. She swept to her feet. "Never."

He stood up. "You have every reason to be angry with me, Anne."

Just hearing her maid's name made her vaguely uneasy. How ridiculous! He had not yet proved that he deserved to be trusted with the truth of her identity.

Chapter 12

John felt frustrated and guilty and angry when they were finally sitting in the cart, driving toward Hillesley. In front of them rode two mounted soldiers, who conversed with each other and ignored the cart and its occupants behind them. The sky was overcast, and a light mist had begun to fall, but it didn't even begin to touch the fever that heated John's blood.

How could he continue to be so drawn to Anne? She was angry and hurt, and had every right to punish him. For all he knew, Lady Elizabeth had *told* Anne to torment him, as if he had to prove himself.

He'd passed the first test, at least as far as Anne was concerned. He hadn't touched her, hadn't kissed her.

But inside, where it most counted, he'd failed. His

fingers had itched to caress her; his cock had been so hard, he wasn't sure how he'd managed to keep the proof of it from her. Leaning away as she'd sat atop him had helped.

He'd had the faint hope that things would be easier once Anne knew the truth, but it wasn't so. He still wanted her. If only he could see Lady Elizabeth again. Her beauty as a child had been enough to make him follow her like a puppy, until she'd laughingly chased him away. But that image was fading now under the onslaught of Anne's creamy skin and haunting dark eyes. And her lips—

John flicked the reins in disgust and said in a low voice, "The soldiers can't hear us. We're alone. What did Lady Elizabeth say when you told her about me?"

Anne wore a cloak against the rain, and the hood hid almost all of her face from him but the tip of her nose and chin. He almost demanded that she take it off, so that he could read her face. But he would have to judge by her voice.

"Anne?" he repeated.

"I heard you. Lady Elizabeth was quite distraught over your method to win access to her."

John was tired of apologizing, so he remained silent.

"She refused to believe your insistence that the disaster that has befallen Rame Castle was the late Lord Russell's fault."

"It wasn't a suggestion, it was the truth."

"You may think so, but surely there is another reason."

John didn't press the point; Lady Elizabeth had obviously been enamored of William. He had never considered that he might not be able to win his bride's affection from the ghost of his dead brother. And that angered him.

"She doesn't know whether she can trust you," Anne said softly. "She is very confused."

"But surely she wants to be rescued. Doesn't that matter more than what she thinks of me?"

"Aren't they intertwined?" Anne asked, finally turning to look at him.

He saw sadness and resignation in her eyes.

"It is not just a matter of Lady Elizabeth herself," she continued. "She worries about the fate of Alderley, but mostly she worries about her people."

"I think her people would be relieved to know that she's safe."

"They won't feel that way if Lord Bannaster takes out his wrath on them. He strikes me as a man who feels his connection to the king gives him powers above common men. My lady is worried that he is capable of . . . anything."

"Very well," John said, looking forward again as they crested a hill and Hillesley came into view. "Then I need to convince her of my sincerity. If I write to her, will you take the missive? Only if it is not dangerous to yourself, of course."

"Aye, she would wish to hear your words."

He inhaled. "Was she angry when you told her about the kiss?"

"I didn't tell her yet."

He gave her a reproachful look. "You must. I don't

want you to keep secrets from your mistress on my behalf."

"You want her to know that you desired her maid?"

He glanced over to find her watching him intently. It would have been better if he could have said he'd only pretended to desire her. Anne would think badly of him, but then it would be over.

"She should know the truth," he finally said. "And she needs to know that it is a product of the situation."

She winced, and then nodded. "Very well. She would like to know if you have a plan to help her."

"For the moment, I am biding my time. I have a plan, but I am not ready to share it."

"And why not?" she asked, obviously affronted.

"Because it is not in place."

"But—"

"An alternate plan would involve removing the two guards from the tower, which would be easy enough. Getting Lady Elizabeth out of the castle will be the problem."

"And she won't go."

"What?" he demanded, staring at her.

"As I already said, she fears for her people. She will not leave them. She did try to send a missive to the king, but as you know, Milburn intercepted it. Why don't *you* go to the king?"

There was true excitement in her voice for the first time, and John knew he would drive it away. The dampness soaked down into his shirt, the uneven road jarred his bruised leg—and Anne's idea was about to be crushed. But how could he tell Lady Elizabeth about his plan to win the army's support, if she was so worried about her people that she wouldn't want force used? That was what an army was for!

"I considered going to the king before I even arrived at Alderley. But I am a poor baron, without an army behind me." *For the moment.*

"You have the ring, or so you say."

"I have it. But who is to say he'll believe me, especially if he's heard the rumors?"

He had Anne's full attention. "What rumors?"

"I was going to tell Lady Elizabeth when I met her, but I see it is too important to wait. While I was in Europe, rumors were spread among my people that I was the one demanding money from the estate, and the reason the land and castle were neglected. It was used as a more convenient excuse for why the money was taken. I imagine he thought I would never return, so that it wouldn't matter," he mused.

"He?"

John glanced at her. "My brother."

She gasped in affront, as he knew she would. Lady Elizabeth had delusions about the kind of man William was, and she'd passed them on to Anne.

"How can you make an accusation against such a kind man, God rest his soul?"

The "kind man" had tried to beat and humiliate John in the attempt to make him into a man.

"The steward told me it was done under William's orders," he said, "and who else would have ordered it? William took the money for his personal use, and he didn't want to look guilty of it."

She opened her mouth as if to argue with him, but then she said, "I will tell my mistress what you have said."

"And you will take my missive, as long as there is no danger to you?"

"You worry about me?" she said hesitantly.

"Aye." He kept his eyes focused on the road. "You do not deserve to be caught between Lady Elizabeth and me."

"Very well, I will take it for you."

In Hillesley, a trestle table underneath a pavilion had been set up on the village green for the rent collection, so as not to disturb the recovering bailiff at the manor. Elizabeth sat at John's side, an account book spread out before her, ink and a quill nearby. John had pointed out the column with last month's totals, and told her to write in the next column.

Hugh, the reeve, made casual conversation about the last manor that John had worked at, and she listened in awe and anger as John wove what she knew was a totally fictional account.

She kept reminding herself that he was doing it for her benefit, to rescue her.

And to win her dowry and the title of earl.

Oh, she hated how her mind was going back and forth. And to think he blamed his poor dead brother for another lie! Didn't he understand that someone, probably the steward, stole the money, and wanted to set the brothers against each other?

In John's defense, she was relieved that he'd insisted that she tell her mistress about the kiss. A lesser man would have been glad to keep it hidden.

A sinful part of her almost wished he wanted to keep their intimacy to himself, as a precious thing.

She was so confused, and losing herself playing two very different roles.

Throughout the afternoon, roughly thirty villagers came to pay their respects to the temporary bailiff—and pay their rent. Last year's harvest had been good, and this year's was promising. Several people disputed what they owed, and Elizabeth listened with grudging respect as John asked careful questions, consulted the accounts paid in previous years, and made decisions. On at least one, he was going to have to explain to Milburn why he'd allow the rent to be delayed, but John seemed not to be worried. He was a confident man, one used to being in charge.

And she was destined to marry him.

To look at the man she was supposed to give herself to had a strange reality to it. She had spent the last eleven years of her life imagining herself married to another man, one so perfect in form and face and comportment.

But John Russell had far too many flaws, too many deceptions. After all, might he really have taken his family's money? And if he had, how could she marry him?

They were invited to the local tavern for supper, and this time John accepted without even glancing at her. Apparently he didn't want to eat alone with her again. As if she could ever go back to the dappled glade by the stream without remembering—

The pleasure of his kiss?

Or the eventual feelings of betrayal it had resulted in?

The tavern was hot and crowded, with so many farmers in the village for the day. Elizabeth, who'd been to the king's court in London, had never been allowed inside such a place before, and she found herself curious. She took in the beamed ceiling hung with hams and strings of onions, and she watched John good-naturedly dodge around them. She wished she knew how much of his behavior was for the part he was playing.

Hugh brought them to a table near the wall. There were few women here except the serving maids, so Elizabeth found herself standing uncertainly as the men began sliding onto benches. John would have to remain on the end, due to his "broken" leg, so she slid in next to Hugh, and John pushed in against her. She was shocked how easily people seemed to forget that she was the earl's daughter. Perhaps she looked so different in her plain garments and wimple that they had already forgotten the truth. Since she was used to being deferred to, more than once she almost gave an order, especially where the seating arrangements were concerned.

She tried not to touch Hugh too familiarly, so that put her against John, whose hip was pressed to hers. Their shoulders overlapped, or rubbed against each other as they moved. Serving maids handed out tankards of beer, and the men raised them in salute to their own bailiff's improving health. Elizabeth tried to take small sips, but the beer was potent, and she was soon feeling rather pleased with the world.

"Sir John," Hugh said, wiping the foam from his lip, "what part of the country do ye come from?"

"Cornwall," John answered.

As John leaned forward to see around her, his arm briefly brushed the side of her breast. She froze, but he didn't seem to notice. He was watching Hugh with interest.

"Is it so different than our rolling hills?" Hugh asked.

As long as John wasn't touching her intimately, she was able to pay attention. And she was interested. It had been a long time since her year at Rame Castle. She found it sad to imagine it neglected.

"My village is on a cliff above the sea," John said. "We spend much of our lives in boats riding waves to catch fish to feed our families."

That didn't sound like the truth for him personally.

"There is always wind, and storms are frequent, but 'tis a beautiful place. Yet the sea makes one think of wandering, and in my youth, I traveled much in my quest to become a knight."

"And ye still travel as a bailiff," Hugh said, smiling.

John leaned toward Hugh as if to impart a confidence, and she held her breath as his arm pressed and stayed against her breast.

"Wandering has always called to my soul," John said.

She could barely concentrate on his words, so warm was she becoming, so much did her flesh tingle at his touch. But she sensed that he was telling the truth.

"Each day is different," John continued. "Each place is new and exotic and a thing to be explored and mastered. And the women are never the same."

All the men at the table laughed. John openly elbowed her, everyone laughed harder, but at least his arm was no longer riding her intimately. Maybe he hadn't even noticed or cared.

She remembered that he had left home at sixteen. Could such a man be content at Castle Alderley? Or did he want the money to finance his travels?

She told herself she had always wanted a husband who would go off to court regularly, leaving the running of the estate to her. William would have been such a man.

But strangely, the thought of John doing so made her uneasy and sad now.

Surely she was only missing the life she'd planned with William.

On the journey home, the cart contained a small coffer of coins, so the guards rode one in front, one behind, as they watched the hills, the hedgerows, and occasional woodland for thieves. The rain had let up, and the setting sun peaked through the low clouds directly ahead of them. Elizabeth shielded her eyes and saw John squinting, but he drove without complaint.

She again felt uncomfortable sitting so close

beside him. Her nerves were still frayed from the endless touching they'd shared in the tavern, and she found herself sullen that he hadn't seemed to be bothered. After all, didn't that prove that he hadn't really desired her, had been flirting with her only out of necessity?

But then she realized he was sitting at the absolute edge of the cart, as if he didn't want to touch her either. She tried not to feel too pleased. Surely it was only the beer she'd drunk, giving her fanciful notions.

"What is Lady Elizabeth like?" John suddenly asked.

Taken by surprise, she saw the ghost of her deception rise between them. She reminded herself he deserved it.

"You spent a year living in the same castle with her," she said primly.

"And she turned eleven in that time. I barely knew her."

"And why not?"

"Because she did not have time for me. William was the shining beacon of the family."

There was irony in his tone that reminded her of the lies he thought his brother capable of. Was John jealous that she had paid no attention to him? Or did he only want her because his brother had her?

"You wanted to spend time with an eleven-year-old girl?" she asked slowly.

"I thought she was . . . amusing." He sighed. "And lovely. I am quite certain she grew into a beautiful woman."

Elizabeth looked down for a moment. "And is beauty so important to you?"

"Nay, although, forgive me if I offend you, but is it to her?"

She stiffened. "I do not understand."

"She knew nothing about William. He was eight years older than she, and had no time for little girls. But all he had to do was smile at her . . ." His voice faded away, and then he smiled. "Ah, but I am not perfect. I fear I was the same with her."

Anyone could say such a thing to win a woman's favor, she thought. He probably expected her to run and tell her mistress, easing the way for him. But still she felt . . . flustered.

"With me, Lady Elizabeth will not have to worry about other women swooning over the beauty of my face." He laughed quietly.

Did he want a compliment from her? She didn't understand his motives, so she didn't respond to that.

"Lady Elizabeth is an adult," she said. "She knows a person's worth is in deeds and speech, not beauty." Although she felt a little guilty saying that, because William's beauty had often swayed her. But it was his sensitive, romantic soul she enjoyed the most. "She will not care about the scar on your face."

" 'Tis good. I don't want her to think I'd frighten our children."

Children. Elizabeth shivered. She was a woman raised in the countryside, where plenty of animals roamed, and knew some of what was involved in begetting children. She couldn't even look at him, imagining such intimacies, imagining his nude body.

To distract herself, she asked, "How was your face scarred?"

"During a tournament, a melee. Swarms of men in armor chasing each other with swords across a field, all for the enjoyment of spectators."

"I always thought those particularly barbaric, especially when so many good men were hurt."

"My helm was knocked off, and three men who I regularly defeated in individual competition decided to have their revenge."

She winced.

He grinned. "I'm grateful they missed my eye."

"Does it bother you being . . . disfigured?"

"Does it bother *you* that I am?"

She reared back. "Why should my opinion matter?"

"I learned that it did not affect how most women saw me—commoners anyway. And you are one."

"And are the titled more ill-behaved?" she asked, offended.

"Sometimes, aye."

"Which is why you asked about Lady Elizabeth."

He shrugged.

"You make too many assumptions about her," she said coldly. "She owes you nothing, especially after the way you treated me."

"I will write to her. I vow I will change her mind about me."

" 'Twill be more difficult than you think," Elizabeth said.

Suddenly, she heard a strange sound behind her, and both she and John turned in time to see the stunned expression on the second soldier's face as he stared at the arrow imbedded in his chest.

Before the soldier had even toppled off his horse, John was already pushing Elizabeth face first onto the floor of the cart as he shouted, "Attack!" to the lead guard.

She spat out straw, her heart pounding as she peered over the edge. The soldier in front wheeled his horse about just as an arrow shot past him and was buried in a tree.

"Anne, stay here!" John commanded in a voice she knew she could only obey. He took the dagger from his waist and put it into her hand.

"But will you not need this?" she cried.

He ignored her. There were shouts in the forest now, but she only had eyes for John, who vaulted over the bench, ran across the back of the cart and flung himself at the riderless horse. She gasped as his torso hit the saddle. But instead of falling, all in one motion he pulled himself upright and un-sheathed a sword from the scabbard attached to the saddle. Though the horse was crazed and fought his mastery as it flung itself in a circle, John dominated and controlled it, then lay low over its neck as he rode to join the other soldier. Several arrows missed their mark as the two men galloped into the sparse trees toward the source of the attack.

Elizabeth clutched the edge of the cart and the dagger, squinting into the trees to see what was going on. She could hear both men and horses screaming, and she said a quick prayer for John's safety. He emerged, galloping across the road as he chased a thief who ran for his life. With the hilt of his sword, he hit him across the head, and the thief dropped face-first onto the ground and lay unmoving.

In the fading light, she watched in awe as John wheeled his horse about on its hind legs to return to the woodland. In his face there was no fear, just determination, exultation, and a fierce triumph that made him look like a stranger to her. In that moment, she saw him as a knight, a conqueror of tournaments and battlefields, a man confident in his skill.

She felt shaken and disturbed, and didn't know what to believe about him—or how he, one man with only three soldiers, thought he could rescue her from Bannaster's imprisonment. But at least she understood where his confidence came from.

The cart suddenly shook beneath her, and she turned in time to see a thief climbing onto the back. He was small and wiry, dirty hair wild about his scruffy face. She crouched on her knees, showing him her dagger as if she knew how to use it. He only gave a gap-toothed grin and continued to advance.

She couldn't seem to get enough air as she gasped openmouthed. Her mind flew with questions— should she go for the thief's chest or legs or even his hands as he reached for her? Where was John?

But before she needed to make a decision, two men rose up from each side of the cart, as if they'd been crouched beneath it. She screamed, knowing there was no way she could battle three of them. But to her shock, the newcomers gripped the first thief and flung him out of the cart. As he landed headfirst on the ground, his neck gave a sickening twist, and he lay still.

Elizabeth gaped at the two men and threatened them with her dagger. They grinned at each other, and to her surprise she realized one of them was chewing on the end of his mustache.

"Mistress, I be Ogden," said the man with the mustache, "and this be Parker. We're Sir John's men."

Parker glanced into the woods, where the sound of battle grew fainter. "Just give it to 'er. We 'ave to go."

She tensed, but all Ogden did was show her a rolled piece of parchment. "We've been tryin' to find the right moment to see Sir John today. Might ye give this to him?"

"Come no nearer," she commanded. "Set it down in the cart."

Ogden did as she bid, nodding his encouragement. "Ye done good, mistress. We'll watch ye from the trees to make sure none harm ye before Sir John returns."

She didn't allow herself to relax even though they did melt into the woodland and seem to disappear. Hearing horses galloping behind her, she whirled about and held her dagger with increasing menace.

John and Bannaster's soldier both pulled up in surprise.

"Are there any more?" she demanded, hating that her voice shook.

"Nay, Anne," John said. One corner of his mouth lifted. "Milburn owes you much for your valiant defense of the rent money."

She blinked down at the coffer, having totally forgotten that it was money the thieves wanted more than her. Sinking back onto the bench, she hung her head to her chest and just tried to breathe.

She and John were both safe. Her stomach felt light and queasy, and she put a hand there as if to hold all her emotions inside. She saw Bannaster's soldier eyeing John with grudging respect.

"Me thanks, Sir John," the man said. " 'Tis a shame ye ever left behind the life of a knight."

John swung off the horse, staggered on his "broken" leg, and caught himself on the saddle. Elizabeth arched a brow at his playacting. The soldier dropped to the ground to help prop him up. John, his face streaming with perspiration and dirt, looked at her over the soldier's shoulder and grinned.

"Rest yerself, Sir John," said the soldier. "I'll put poor Baldwin in the cart. We'll leave the rest for the wolves."

"The one on the road is only unconscious," John said. "Tie him up and bring him along for your captain. Perhaps he can tell you more about the thieves' operation."

At last they were on their way back to Alderley. Elizabeth had earlier managed to tuck the rolled parchment into her sleeve. She only offered it to John when they were within sight of the castle, and the soldier had gone ahead.

He frowned down at it as he wiped the perspiration from his forehead with the back of his arm. "What is that?"

"Two men named Ogden and Parker saved my life and left it for you."

He ignored the missive to stare into her eyes with concern. "You are unharmed?"

She nodded. "Although I was about to stab a thief before they arrived."

"I'm certain you would have," he said, a smile returning to his face. "You are a fierce woman."

They were almost to the castle walls. He slid the missive into his tunic unread, and she silently cursed, her curiosity unsatisfied.

Chapter 13

⌒⌒◯◯⌒⌒

The next morning, while John was meeting with Milburn, Elizabeth walked down to the tiltyard. She did not see John's man-at-arms training, so she went to the armory and found Philip inside alone, cataloguing the equipment. With no windows, the room was dark, but for the candle on a shelf.

"Excuse me . . . Philip?" Elizabeth said.

He looked up from his books, and then smiled at her. "Mistress Anne." He glanced behind her. "Sir John is not keeping you at his side?"

She stiffened. "Your master is meeting with the steward about collecting the rent at Hillesley."

His smile was mysterious. "He tells me it went well—but for the attack, of course."

She shrugged. "Is there someplace we can talk and not worry about being disturbed?"

He arched a brow, but nodded and set down his account book. "We have privacy for the moment, but anyone could walk in. Come walk with me, and we can watch the knights train."

The walked to the far end of the tiltyard, where a bench rested near the curtain wall. Elizabeth had resolved to find out more about John than he could tell her, but now sitting here beside his fellow knight—his friend—she almost didn't know where to begin.

"I know you call yourself Philip," Elizabeth began slowly, "but is that your real name?"

He smiled at her, his expression amused. "I am Sir Philip Clifford."

"And you didn't mind pretending to be someone else for John's sake?"

His smile faded a bit, and he watched her seriously. "All he had to do was ask. I owe him my loyalty." He grinned. "I owe him my life many times over."

"And now so do I," she murmured. Taking a deep breath, she continued, "You have been traveling with him?"

"For four years." He cocked his head at her. "Are you conducting an interview on your lady's behalf?"

She lowered her eyes. "Not exactly an interview . . ."

"Research, then?"

"It is difficult for her, locked in a tower, to discover that the man she is to marry is here."

"And that he's lied about his identity," Philip said shrewdly.

She shrugged. "She understands the necessity, but . . ."

Elizabeth trailed off, and to her surprise, Philip was watching her with compassion and sympathy.

"But perhaps *you* don't understand the necessity of all John did," he said.

She felt herself blush. This was not a conversation she wanted to have with a stranger, even a kind one. "Philip, Sir John tells me that he traveled Europe working as a mercenary, or competing in tournaments for prize money. That is how he made his living?"

Philip gave a knowing smile. "Ah, the rumor about Rame Castle's money flowing to him. I can honestly say, never once did he even receive a package from Rame, let alone money. And there were many evenings when the two of us were limited enough in funds to have to stay in questionable inns—or even in a room above taverns. Those are the worst." He shook his head. "But Lady Elizabeth only has my word—and his. She will have to decide whether to believe us."

At least she knew that John inspired loyalty in this man. "Sir John tells me he enjoys the adventure of travel."

"I never saw a man who loved it more. *I* cared about the sleepless nights spent above a raucous tavern—not him. He was even content sleeping under the stars."

"But did he not miss his home, his family?"

Philip hesitated. "He was the youngest son, Anne. Not much was expected of him, and I think he felt the need to prove himself. He had to support himself as well, for everything went to his brother when their parents died."

"I hear the disapproval in your voice, Philip, but you only know what Sir John has told you about his brother."

"That is true. And it's not that Sir John expected the estate. He was just incredibly disappointed to see in how little esteem his brother held it."

Elizabeth gritted her teeth. "You don't know—"

"Your mistress must have been quite in love to defend William so passionately to you."

She didn't like the kindness in his voice. She felt pitied. "My lady's first betrothed is not what I'm here to discuss."

"Nay, you want to discuss my friend. And you cannot believe anything I say," he answered, the amusement fading from his voice. "I can only tell you that I was at his side when he saw the condition of his estate, and the unjust hatred in his people's eyes when they looked at him."

"And that might only be proof that he did not realize how his actions affected Rame Castle."

"Or that *William* didn't care about the results of his actions. John—Sir John gave all he had to begin the restoration."

"Guilt?"

"Duty and honor," Philip said coolly.

"I am sorry if I have offended you."

"You are only doing your lady's bidding," he answered, visibly relaxing.

"Did you ever meet Sir John's brother?"

"Nay, and there again, I only know what I've been told. I am not of much use to your mistress."

"Your loyalty says much."

"Hmm, a diplomatic answer. Are you certain you are only a lady's maid?"

She nodded, trying not to feel guilty for protecting herself.

"Has Sir John told you that we might have more help on the way?" he asked.

She straightened with interest. "What do you mean?"

He lowered his voice. "Have you ever heard of the League of the Blade?"

"I have heard the name, but nothing specific. Maybe my father once mentioned it."

His excitement was palpable. "Was he helped by them?"

She frowned, remembering that her father was supposed to be a farmer. "Not that I know of. They . . . help people?"

"They're a secret organization dedicated to justice. I have heard about them my whole life, and finally Sir John and I met a member in person."

"Philip," said a deep voice.

Startled, Elizabeth turned around to see John only several paces away from them, leaning on his crutch. She'd been so busy studying Philip's every expression, that she hadn't been paying attention.

Anyone could have overheard them. She felt queasy at the thought.

And then she wondered if John was bothered that she was alone with his friend, even though it was in front of the entire inner ward. When he looked at her, she felt the force of his gaze like a physical touch. She reminded herself of her suspicions and his desperation. Logically, she knew these things, but her body did not want to obey, and still craved his embrace.

Philip folded his arms across his chest. "A good morning to you, Sir John."

Softly, John said, "You should not have filled her head with fairy tales."

"The League is not real?" she said, looking between them.

"Of course it's real," Philip answered. "We met a member only days ago, on our way here. You could have told her," he said to his friend.

John rolled his eyes. "And allowed Lady Elizabeth to hope for a miraculous rescue?"

"They said they were going to help her," Philip said angrily. " 'Tis you—"

When Philip stopped himself, John sighed. "Aye, it's me whose worth the stranger questioned." He glanced at Elizabeth. "You can see why I worry about presenting myself to the king, when even strangers who claim to be part of a legend believe the rumors about me."

She was surprised at this disagreement between them, yet she was a practical woman, and hoping for help from a mysterious League seemed foolish.

But Philip turned back to her with interest.

"They'll learn how trustworthy Sir John is; never fear. After all, the League helped the king gain his throne from King Richard."

"Or perhaps his own army did?" John said pleasantly, as if this was a longstanding disagreement between them.

Philip smiled and shook his head. "Someday I'll have proof. Until then, the fact that I've met a Bladesman convinces me they're real."

John turned to Elizabeth. "A stranger told us he was going to offer you aid. Has he?"

She looked between John's skepticism and Philip's anticipation. "I have met no one who—but wait, Sir John, you told me you had not lowered the basket of food to my lady's tower."

Philip stood up and spoke to John. "You didn't tell me about this. Of course it is the League!"

John groaned. "This is the reason I didn't tell you. One of Lady Elizabeth's servants probably wanted to help her, and you're making it out to be more than it is."

"But only a Bladesman would risk his life to do such a thing!"

"You're risking your life for Sir John and for my lady," Elizabeth pointed out.

"You are just as skeptical as he is," Philip said, although he didn't seem offended. "I will leave you two to laugh behind my back."

John shook his head as he watched his friend leave. "And how is Lady Elizabeth this morn?"

She lowered her gaze. "As well as can be expected."

"I have a missive for her."

He looked around, keeping his body between her and the knights at the tiltyard. He pulled a folded, sealed piece of parchment from within his tunic—not the same one that his men had delivered yesterday—and handed it to her.

It bothered her that she noticed it was warm from his body.

"I will take it to her," she murmured, sliding it into the purse hung from the belt at her waist. She was almost disappointed to have to wait for the midday meal to read it aloud. She would be patient and hope that he explained within the letter what his men had contacted him about.

John remained still, standing above her. "You are well?"

She frowned at him. "You saw me but yesterday eve." But she knew what he meant—he was wondering if she'd forgiven him. She would never be his "friend," so there was no point beginning.

"I—" Then a strange expression came over his face, and he limped back a step. "That is good. We do not need to go to Hillesley today. I look forward to your mistress's response. Good day."

John began to walk away, berating his foolishness. He had seen Anne and Philip alone together, talking earnestly, and something inside him had twisted painfully. Logically, he knew she was only discovering the truth about him for Lady Elizabeth.

He told himself that Anne was not his, that she and Philip could very well become—

That was as far as his imagination wanted to take

him. She was his conduit to Lady Elizabeth, and that was all.

Although Ogden and Parker had also used her to deliver their message. And it had been a good one—they had located Alderley's army. Though dispirited, the soldiers were performing their task, ridding outlying areas of thieves. Ogden and Parker should tell them that the road to Hillesley needed their protection, John thought wryly. But Alderley's captain of the guard was not inclined to believe the word of two men-at-arms about John and his purpose. The man wanted proof that their mistress approved of John, that they should do his bidding.

And proof meant that John would have to persuade Lady Elizabeth to give it. But not in his first letter. It would take time for her to forgive him for his conduct with Anne.

Anne. Even thinking of her name made him feel guilty. It would be better for everyone if she found her own life, her own home, because it would be too awkward if she remained here when he married.

But a life with Philip?

He heard footsteps before he could limp too far.

"Sir John?" Anne called.

He turned to find her near.

She linked her hands together, and though she seemed peaceful, he sensed she kept nervousness at bay.

"Sir John, you did not ask me if I told my mistress of our kiss. I did."

Though no one was near, he looked about and then stepped closer. Perhaps he should be the nervous one, but he felt only wary. "I appreciate that you were honest with her. What was her response?"

To his surprise, she stepped even closer, laying a hand on his chest. He could feel the weight of her regard, soft and hesitant, the warmth of her palm even through his garments.

And though he fought to control himself, a shudder moved through him that she must surely have felt. Her eyes narrowed as she studied him.

"She wants to know if she should ever be able to trust that you will be loyal to her, that you can control yourself in all situations."

Though he breathed deeply, he forced himself to pretend her hand was not on his body. "Just yesterday morn, Anne, you attempted to conduct your own test—and punishment as well. I did not react then, and I won't react now. One apology should suffice for you, and if your mistress wants further explanation, all she has to do is ask me when we meet. Is she still willing to consider my help?"

"She will consider it. Reading your words will help."

"Then I await her response."

He stepped back from her hand and walked away. Feeling the first trickle of perspiration down his temples, he was glad that Anne had not seen it. He didn't blame her for her repeated tests of his resolve; for all he knew, her mistress had encouraged it. But when he returned to his bedchamber, he poured water into a basin and splashed his face.

* * *

Elizabeth brought the midday meal to the tower and found Anne staring morosely out the solar window. She hadn't even seemed to realize that Elizabeth was there.

"Anne?" Elizabeth said, setting down the tray.

The maid gave a start, and then put on a smile that was patently false, but so honest with its need to cheer Elizabeth, that she felt her throat tighten.

"Ah, another meal," Anne said. "I am famished."

"No more baskets?"

"Nay, probably because I stick my head out and look up so often that my benefactor can't risk it."

"I imagine you also look out the window often, wishing you were free," Elizabeth said in a low voice.

Anne sighed and took her hand. "I regret nothing. And it is amazing what one sees from the window. I saw you this morn, near the tiltyard."

"How could you tell it was me, from so high up?"

"You are wearing one of my gowns, are you not?" Anne said dryly. "And that terrible wimple—how could Lord Russell even want to kiss you?"

Elizabeth laughed halfheartedly. "I was questioning John's friend. His name is Sir Philip Clifford. John caught us together, but he seemed to understand."

"Ah, if only I could see their faces," Anne said, her hand clutching the windowsill. "I sit here, watching the people move about below, and imagine each person's life—dinner in the great hall, an argument with a parent, even mass. It helps keep me amused."

"You know that if this is too much for you, I will—"

"Nay!" Anne said heatedly. "This is the most important thing I've yet done with my life. Together we will make this work."

Elizabeth drew forth John's missive.

"But will we have help?" Anne asked thoughtfully. "Is that a message from Lord Russell to you?"

Elizabeth nodded.

"Are you going to read it?"

"I have to." She looked down at the missive and sighed.

Anne walked toward her. "You are getting tired of the lie. Why do you not tell him the truth?"

"Because . . ." She stiffened and forced herself to speak firmly. "Because I don't know him well enough." In her mind she saw him defending her against thieves. He had risked his life, but perhaps it was only to persuade her? "Talking to his friend proved no help at all. How do I know he is not lying, too? Although Philip was glad to hear of your mysterious basket. Apparently he's been looking for validation about this League of the Blade, and he feels they're helping us. John—Lord Russell disagrees. It seems he is a skeptic."

"Then read his words and decide," Anne said eagerly. "I'll eat my meal and leave you to read in private."

"There can be nothing here that you can't see. I'll read it aloud." Elizabeth broke the seal and opened the parchment. John wrote in a legible, bold hand. " 'To the Lady Elizabeth: By now you have heard of the lengths I have gone to be of help to you. I would have preferred to come to you with a great army to convince Lord Bannaster that challenging me would be a grave error. Yet I understand from your maid that you wish no violence, no chance for injury to your people. Your need for peace is commendable, although shortsighted. It reveals a soft, womanly attribute that I admire.'"

Elizabeth stopped to roll her eyes.

"He's trying to praise you," Anne offered cheerfully.

"He does not have the way with words his brother did," Elizabeth said.

Anne opened her mouth. Before she could speak, Elizabeth continued, "Aye, I know they were not raised in the same way."

"Imagine leaving home at sixteen to go off to another country."

"I left home at ten to escape the persecution of men who wanted my inheritance," Elizabeth reminded her.

"But you were beloved and adored. And you were only gone a year, fostered as girls usually are. It sounds as if Lord Russell was left to fend for himself."

"He was," she agreed reluctantly.

"And he has honor, to risk his life to complete an oath made by his father to yours."

"And the result will be my money, my castle, my father's title, and me in his bed," Elizabeth said sourly.

Anne smiled. "Not such a terrible prospect for

you. You enjoyed his kiss, even when you knew you should not. Is that not the same for him?"

"I cannot stand when you make sense." Elizabeth sighed. "Let me finish reading. 'Although my estate has come to harm, I vow that I will rebuild it anew to be a shining jewel on the edge of the ocean that I bring to you in marriage. Please forgive my brother's role in this neglect. He was always a man at home in the king's court, and I am certain he thought he would have the chance to make things right before your marriage.'" Elizabeth looked up. "I don't agree that poor William committed this sin!"

"But at least he's defending his brother, and vowing to repair everything. Read on."

"'In closing, my lady, please believe that I am here with the best intentions. Forgive me that I could not arrive sooner and save you from Lord Bannaster's machinations. I promise that with the aid of my men, I will do my best to free you and bring about our fathers' wishes. Yours in peace, John Russell.'" She glanced at Anne. "He has a plan, but he doesn't wish me to know it yet, not until he can say with certainty. And he didn't tell me what was in the message sent by his friends!"

"He is protective of you."

Elizabeth carefully put the letter on a table and looked at it with indecision. He expected a reply, but she didn't know what to give. There was no poetry, no praise, no attempt to woo her, and no declarations of affection. She didn't know what to make of it.

Yet the words sounded like the man she was growing to know, single-minded in his determination to make things right, a man who would have himself beaten as an adequate reason to remain at Castle Alderley.

"How are you going to respond?" Anne asked. "He seems to be trying to win your approval."

"I know he is," Elizabeth replied sadly. "He is trying by deed and now written word. But I have not grown to trust him, Anne. I have known him only a few days. How will I know when I can believe him?"

"My mother always said to watch a man's behavior when he doesn't know you're watching. He'll reveal all."

"But he knows when I'm watching—we're with each other all the time. Milburn is keeping us together. Surely I would begin to trust him if I knew absolutely he was who he says he is."

"You still do not believe?"

"Perhaps I do, but I cannot trust my own intuition anymore. He made me doubt myself, and now I cannot resurrect trust in my impressions. But if I saw the ring, if I knew without doubt that he is my betrothed, perhaps I could begin to accept a future with him."

"Then ask him to show it to you. If you're worried about being a mere maid, say that I asked you to do this."

Though the ring might help her believe, she could not ask him to show it to her. He might become suspicious, and she was not yet ready to reveal her identity.

"So are you going to write back?" Anne asked.

"Should I? What if he is caught with it? It will implicate him as a man against Lord Bannaster."

Anne smiled knowingly. "I think you know not what to say."

"But I have to explain to him my conversation with you. Believe me, that is far more difficult."

But she was already thinking ahead to how best to look for the ring, as if that would magically solve all their problems.

Chapter 14

❧❧❧

John waited for Anne to reappear after her visit with Lady Elizabeth, but when an hour passed, he went to find her. He started in the kitchens with her friend Adalia, who told him she'd asked Anne to weed in the kitchen garden when her work with Lady Elizabeth was finished.

Anne had deliberately avoided him, John realized, and it didn't bode well.

The cook herself seemed very hesitant with him, even suspicious, which seemed strange. How could she be upset with his role pursuing Anne? Would Adalia not want a maidservant to have the chance to marry a bailiff?

Outside, he entered the kitchen gardens, which were laid out with the vegetables needed for the consumption of the castle residents. Though he saw several maidservants bent over the rows, it didn't take him long to find Anne. She was the only one wearing a wimple.

Considering she was an unmarried young lady, why did she wear it?

But he could hardly ask her such a personal question, not when he was trying to keep his distance.

The neat rows of greenery posed a challenge for his crutch—he was heartily sick of it after only a few days. He ended up straddling a row of beans and limping very carefully toward her. She looked up as he neared, shading her eyes from the sun, her face impassive. Nodding to him, she went back to weeding.

"Is this what a lady's maid does now?" he asked, standing above her.

"A lady's maid who has been deprived of her usual duties."

He waited, looking down at the back of her head and her slim back, but she remained silent. All around them, he saw several servants giving them wide-eyed looks and trying to hide their giggles. At least the shocked stares of the past few days were finally being replaced by amusement.

When she continued to ignore him, he said, "Anne? Did you speak with your mistress?"

"I did."

"And does she have something for me in return?" he asked in a low voice.

She sat back on her heels and wiped her perspiring face with the back of her hand. It left a streak of dirt that he found endearing—and then he was angry with himself for noticing.

"She feared its discovery would compromise you or her," Anne said, "so she directed me to say that she read it, and would consider your words."

He frowned. "That is all?"

"What would you have her say?" she asked, a puzzled expression on her face.

Although John felt angry, he was mostly frustrated with the whole situation: his inability to immediately help his betrothed; her refusal to leave should he infiltrate the tower; and mostly his overwhelming attraction to Anne and his increasing fears that she would not be easy to forget. Never had a woman occupied his mind as much as she did. Even watching her work in the dirt only reminded him of how supple and strong she was, how much he wanted her in his bed.

He gave a weary sigh. "Thank you for delivering the item for me. You are a loyal servant to her."

She gave him a nod and went back to weeding as if it challenged her both physically and mentally.

Or gave her a good reason to ignore him.

Early that evening, just after supper, Elizabeth watched John's movements carefully. When he was beginning a game of Tables with Philip and several knights, she snuck out of the great hall and hurried to his bedchamber. Once inside, she closed the door in relief and looked about, wondering where to begin. After throwing open the shutters to catch the last of the sunlight, she started with a satchel on

John's bed. Though she deserved to know the truth, she felt guilty for spying, for continuing her deception after John had told the truth.

She rummaged through the satchel, finding only garments. There was another satchel on Philip's pallet, but she would not touch that unless she absolutely had to. A coffer against one wall was only filled with bedding. She ran her fingers along the mantel of the hearth, even searched for loose stones that a treasure might be hidden behind. Her breathing quickened, her heart raced, as more and more time went by and she felt the need to escape. She was just sliding her hands beneath the mattress when the door opened and closed. Her eyes went wide, and she held her breath.

Just as she was trying to quietly slide beneath the bed again, John said, "I know you're here. By now the whole castle does."

His voice was full of anger, which she wasn't used to from him. Before she could even get to her knees, he was beside her, pulling her up by the arms until she was standing, then leaning over her, his face dark with fury.

"What did you think you would accomplish with this?" he demanded, flinging his arm wide to encompass the whole chamber.

"I—"

"A soldier saw you. He told another. Who proceeded to tell me, in front of the rest of the knights, what a lucky man I was to have you waiting in my bed."

She gasped. "I never meant—"

"Your mistress will hear about it someday and assume that I—that we—" With a groan he let her go and stalked away from her, running his hand through his dark hair. "And now the rest of the household will someday think that their lord took his wife's maid to bed."

She lifted her chin. "I will tell them the truth. They'll believe me."

"They barely speak to you. Why should I assume they'd believe you? And what were you doing in here?"

She bit her lip and said nothing.

He looked around the chamber and saw his open satchel.

"Now she has you searching my things?" he said in a low voice.

"She needs to know for certain that you are who you say you are."

"The ring," he said, advancing on her.

"Aye, the ring." Her back hit the wall.

"My word is not enough."

"Plenty of men give their word," she replied with heat, looking up at him. "And sometimes it means nothing."

He reached beneath the neckline of his shirt and lifted up a chain, from which dangled a massive ring, set with a carved emerald. She stared at it, transfixed, as it glimmered in the last rays of sunset through the window.

With sarcasm, he said, "Do you need to feel the ring to make certain 'tis real?"

She would have declined, but he took her hand

and fisted it around the ring, holding it in place. The ring was warm from his body; his hand around hers was full of a strength she couldn't match. His arm brushed her breast. She should have been angry or uneasy, with her back to the wall, alone in his bed-chamber.

But a terrible arousal swept over her, tingling her skin from her toes to her nape. Her eyelids felt heavy, her mouth dry, and she found herself staring at his lips, remembering the magic he had wrought within her with just his kiss.

He was staring at her with intensity, and he leaned closer, as if he would complete the kiss. She didn't care about the deception between them, the mistrust. Her body only wanted him to make her feel complete, to finish what his pretend seduction had started.

In that frozen moment, a thousand thoughts raced through John's mind. Lady Elizabeth didn't trust him, probably preferred almost any husband to him. But Anne . . . Anne desired him as much as he desired her, though both knew how wrong it was. If King Henry broke the betrothal contract, John could have Anne, and then—

He inhaled suddenly and backed away, letting her hand go. The ring on its chain swung away from her, and he tucked it back beneath his tunic.

What was he thinking? How could he dishonor himself and his family in such a way? All because of his lust for a maid. He was the only one left to resurrect his family pride, to prove to his parents that he could fulfill their wishes.

Harshly, he said, "Go back to your mistress and tell her she has her proof."

She licked her lips, and although John noticed her trembling, she spoke with a cool detachment he reluctantly admired.

"And how will she know you haven't stolen it?"

He needed no more proof for how little he was trusted, after all he'd risked helping Lady Elizabeth. Before he could answer, there was a soft knock on the door.

Anne's eyes widened, and he saw her worry.

"It is too late," he said. "They already know you're here."

But he went to answer the door, picking up his crutch and tucking it beneath his arm. In the corridor, Adalia stared up at him.

"I—I heard the maidservant Anne is . . . with ye?" she said tentatively. "I need to speak with her."

He opened the door wide and gestured her in. Without hesitation, she moved past him. Her stiff shoulders seemed to ease when she saw the undisturbed bed, and Anne fully dressed.

Instead of freely speaking, Adalia walked right up to Anne and whispered something in her ear. John watched with curiosity, and though Anne obviously tried to compose her face, her eyes widened in dismay.

"Thank you, Adalia," she said. She looked to John, not quite meeting his eyes. "I must leave. A good evening to you, Sir John."

She swept by him as Adalia gave a quick curtsy

and followed. John watched them walk swiftly down the corridor.

Did Anne think he would just remain here, after such a curious encounter? He followed at a discreet distance.

When Elizabeth felt they were far enough away from John's bedchamber, she whispered to Adalia, "How could my sisters have come unannounced?"

"Apparently, the rumors of your captivity had finally reached them. I know not what they intended; mayhap to surprise Lord Bannaster?"

"Where is their foster father?" Elizabeth asked in exasperation.

Adalia shrugged helplessly.

"What did Milburn do when they arrived?"

"Told them they could not see you, and said he'd return them to their foster father with an even larger escort tomorrow. I think they would have caused trouble right there, but I signaled for them to be quiet. They behaved like meek young ladies and let themselves be escorted to their bedchamber."

"Your presence worked wonders, then," Elizabeth said dryly. "Meek young ladies? I may not have seen them since our parents' funeral six months ago, but they can't have changed *that* much."

After climbing a circular staircase in a corner of the castle to the second floor, they arrived at the girls' shared bedchamber.

Elizabeth knocked, and when one of the girls called for her identity, she said, "'Tis Anne, lady's maid to your sister."

The door was thrown wide by a shocked Sarah, the eldest of the two at sixteen. "I thought I recognized your voice!"

"Be quiet!" Elizabeth hissed, pushing her way inside.

Adalia retreated. "I must see to me son," she said with a grin. "Good night, ladies."

When the door was safely closed, both girls, redheads without Elizabeth's height, hugged her and started talking at once.

"That man said you were secluded!"

"Did you call yourself Anne?"

Elizabeth, her arms full, patted their backs and finally disengaged herself. "I am all right. Aye, they think they've held me captive, but Anne and I exchanged places."

"Then why haven't you escaped?" Sarah demanded. She was the practical one of the two.

"Because Lord Bannaster would punish our friends and servants. I couldn't permit that to happen. I'll find a way to make everything right."

"So you're acting as a maid?" Katherine said, looking appalled. "But you're the eldest daughter of an earl!"

"I am doing what is necessary. And it's not as if I have much to do, since the steward only allows me in the tower at mealtimes."

"Anne is imprisoned there?" Sarah asked. "How long has it been?"

"This is the fifth day."

"Oh, Liz," Katherine whispered, using Elizabeth's childhood name. "I am so afraid for you."

Elizabeth put her arm around her youngest sister. Katherine may be old enough to marry, but the girl had been sheltered within this loving family—as Elizabeth had once been, before her parents' deaths.

"It may seem frightening," Elizabeth said, pressing a kiss to Katherine's head, "but Lord Bannaster does not want to harm me. He only wants guardianship—and perhaps marriage. That is illegal, since I'm betrothed."

Sarah put her arms around them both. "You must promise me that if you can't free yourself, you'll get word to us. Our foster family will gladly come to your aid."

"I promise," Elizabeth said, although she could not imagine bringing another family, especially one with so little wealth and power, into what might become a violent situation.

The door suddenly slammed wide, and all three women jumped in fear. Elizabeth had a momentary terror of discovery—and then when she turned around, she realized that the next worst thing had happened.

John was standing there, looking angrier than she'd ever seen him. He must have been listening at the door. He closed it hard and came into the room, the crutch useless in his hand.

"Ladies, have no fear for your *sister*," he said.

His low voice was so pleasant as to be frightening.

"She has not told you all of the truth. I am Lord Russell, her betrothed, and I will take care of her."

But the look in his eyes was anything but pleasant. He stared at her as if she were Eve caught talking to a serpent in the Garden of Eden.

As if she'd betrayed him.

She lifted her chin and gave him a cool stare in return, though her stomach was churning with nausea. He had lied to her, too, she reminded herself. He'd used her.

But she found herself wishing she'd chosen to tell him the truth before now.

She waited for John to blame her for misleading him, but he only turned to her sisters, who were looking at him with relief, as if he'd already managed to save them all.

She could have saved herself without his help, Elizabeth found herself thinking with anger.

"Ladies," he said to her sisters, "I came here in disguise to rescue your sister. Though some delicacy will be required to extricate her from this situation, I promise that she and I will make this work."

Elizabeth found herself even angrier, because he included her in his plans, as if she were his partner. She couldn't trust that—to her, it sounded like he was placating them all. And trying to take over. And he hadn't even told her his plan!

But Sarah and Katherine were looking at him as if he were a rescuing knight at the head of an army. How could she tell them that he couldn't even afford armor?

"But it will be more difficult if we have to worry about the two of you," John continued. "I ask that you return home and await word from us."

"We will," Sarah promised, her smile bright and full of hope. "We're so glad to finally meet you."

"And we're so sorry about the death of your brothers," compassionate Katherine added.

John nodded. "My thanks, ladies. Now if you don't mind, I need to speak to Lady Elizabeth."

Elizabeth heard the slight emphasis on her name, and she winced.

"If you see me in the morning before you depart," John added, "I will not speak to you, and you must not seem to know me at all. And you cannot speak to your sister, except as to a maidservant."

"As we would speak to Anne," Katherine said cheerfully.

"It is not worth the risk," Elizabeth said. "Perhaps we should not even see each other in the morning." She hugged each of them in turn. "Take care of yourselves. Thank you for coming to see after me. Do your foster parents know where you are?"

Sheepishly, Sarah said, "We told them we were visiting Lady Louisa."

"Then you need to return immediately, before they discover the danger you almost got yourselves into."

Katherine looked between John and Elizabeth with interest. "Do you want to talk here? We could leave . . ."

"Nay, that will not be necessary," John said. "Good evening, ladies."

In the corridor, he once again slid the crutch beneath his shoulder and walked with a limp. He took

Elizabeth's upper arm in a firm grip. A valet who usually served in the great hall stared as he walked by them.

When the boy was far enough away, she whispered, "You do not have to hold on to me."

He just gave her a look.

"Where are you taking me?"

"To my chamber," he answered in a cold voice. "You cannot possibly mind—the entire castle thinks you're mine anyway. God's Blood," he added with a harsh laugh, "when they discover my identity, they'll be grateful I took you in hand and kept you safe."

She gritted her teeth and said nothing, knowing she would have to weather the storm of his anger. They went down one flight of stairs rather quickly for a man who supposedly had a broken leg, but John didn't seem his usual cautious self.

When they reached his bedchamber, they found a candle lit, as if Philip had been there and gone. Elizabeth waited for the door to close, then turned to face John, prepared to hear his arguments.

But he threw the crutch on his bed, grabbed her by both arms, turned to put her back against the door, and then kissed her.

This was not the delicate, romantic kiss that their first one had been. Nay, this was a full-scale assault, hot and invasive and powerful. Her head was tipped back, her body was pressed hard into the door by the sheer strength of his. His tongue swept her mouth, announcing his possession of her right here, right now.

One of his large hands held her face, as if he thought she'd revolt. The other swept down her neck and then lower, cupping her breast, an intimacy that shocked and angered her. This desperate need to touch her made her realize how much he'd been holding back since he'd told her the truth of his identity.

And how angry that seemed to make him.

In the heat of the moment, every emotion from passion to fury swept through her, and she kissed him back, hard, putting her tongue in his mouth, battling with his for supremacy. Their mouths opened wider and slanted, their heads twisted as they sought to merge deeper.

She could not press herself into the heat and power of him any more than she already was. She put her arms around his neck, pulling him into herself, a wild desperation making her reckless.

Her anger and her passion merged and she became something she didn't recognize anymore, more animal than human.

Chapter 15

As he kissed Elizabeth, John's anger dissolved into the passion he'd felt for her since the moment they'd met. He couldn't get enough of the taste of her mouth, of the soft fullness of her breast in his hand. And she wasn't fighting him—nay, she was as aggressive as he was, holding fistfuls of his tunic to keep his body against hers.

It took both his hands to remove her wimple even as he continued to kiss her, but finally he was pulling the pins from her hair and letting down the reddish-blond curls. He buried his face in them, knowing the ultimate satisfaction: she was his.

But she'd let him go on feeling guilty for desiring "Anne," when he was really desiring the woman he was to marry.

He stumbled back from her and wiped his forearm across his mouth as his fury returned.

Bathed in candlelight, she stood against his door, curls tumbling down her body, her breasts rising and falling with each quick breath. Her eyes glittered as she stared at him.

She had matured into a beautiful woman, although it was easy to see why he had not recognized her with her hair hidden.

"You haven't changed all that much since childhood," he said in a low voice. "You still want everything your way."

Her eyes narrowed. "You cannot blame me for trying to protect myself and Castle Alderley."

"*I* am here to protect you and your castle! I should take you out of here right now—"

"And prove yourself no better than Bannaster."

"And that's what you believe of me, isn't it," he answered coldly.

"That you want me for my property and title? Aye, why should I think differently? 'Tis true, isn't it?"

He paced away from her. "I want you to fulfill a contract between our parents, a vow they made to unite our families. 'Twas what my parents wished me to do."

"Nay, they wished your brother William to marry me. Instead you've done nothing but slur him since you arrived, although he is but months into his grave."

He closed his eyes, trying to control his temper, knowing and regretting that she still loved William.

"I am not lying to you about what happened to Rame Castle."

"And I say that mayhap you don't know the full truth yourself. And that fact that you lied about your identity—"

"As did you!" he countered.

"Aye, we both misled because we felt it necessary."

"You continued to lie even after I told the truth and asked for your help."

She ignored that. "And your attempted seduction of me—"

"I attempted no such thing!" he said, stalking up to her and putting his hand on the side of her face so she'd be forced to look at him. "If I would have wanted to seduce you, I would have done it."

She slapped his hand away and ducked away from him into the center of the room. "It is not my fault that I know not if I can trust you."

They glared at each other in silence, both breathing heavily, both full of mistrust.

"Say what you will," John said, "but you will be my wife. You may think that you preferred my brother, but your body and your lips say otherwise."

"You are crude."

"And someday you'll admit that you enjoy it. Do you still want to escape what Lord Bannaster has planned, although it is to me that you must submit yourself?"

He saw her flinch at his words, but her chin came up. "Our betrothal is binding. I will not dishonor my parents by trying to escape it."

It almost sounded like she wanted to, and he suddenly felt very tired.

"Then I need a missive written in your hand," he said.

She narrowed her eyes. "Explain this to me. Please."

"My men—the two who handed you the parchment yesterday—have found your army."

She inhaled, and he saw the relief in her eyes.

"But your captain of the guard is loyal to you, and will not take the word of two common soldiers that I am your betrothed. He wants proof from you that he can trust me."

She looked away, and he knew that she still debated that herself. Certainly she didn't trust him—she had withheld the truth from him for too long.

"You need to be rescued," he said coldly.

"But not with an attack by an army."

"I am a knight. I give you my word that I will attack only as a last resort. But I need soldiers, Elizabeth."

"What will you do with them?"

"Train them. My men are experts in warfare, techniques from Europe that are only just making their way into England."

"Warfare!" she cried.

In one stride he was against her, hand on her mouth. "Silence," he murmured against her ear. "Do you want someone to hear of this conversation?"

She struggled, and he gladly let her go. Touching her only confused him, made him forget everything except that she would be waiting in his marriage bed.

For a moment, he considered suggesting that he take her right now, sealing their union, denying Bannaster. But they were both still so angry, and he didn't want to begin their relationship like that. And besides, if Bannaster were only concerned about the title, he wouldn't care if his bride came to him impure.

Anne strummed her lute in the tower bedchamber, trying to find a cheerful melody, but only haunting, sad ballads came to her fingers. For some reason, the loneliness tonight seemed like a heavy weight that pressed against her. Each night she battled it, hated putting out the candle and surrendering to the darkness, when her fears seemed to expand. She found herself staying awake later and later each night, leaving her more tired when the rising sun woke her.

Suddenly she heard a sound outside her window. Her fingers froze on the strings, her head cocked. Surely it was a bird taking rest, as had happened often in these last days. She would try to coax them into the room as if she could make a pet of a wild creature.

The sound came again, like a giant brush against the shutters.

Could someone be lowering another basket?

She vaulted to her feet, setting the lute onto a table, and threw the shutters wide. At first she saw nothing in the darkness. Suddenly, something swung in at her, and she stumbled back. But it was only the end of a rope, knotted at intervals, and it was vibrating.

A moment later, a booted foot lowered to the windowsill, followed by another. A man bent and peered in.

"Lady Elizabeth?"

She knew she should be frightened—who knew what Lord Bannaster would do to win Elizabeth to wife?—but his face looked so friendly that she could only nod.

"Forgive the intrusion," he said, still gripping the sill, perched precariously on the outside of the tower. "Might I come in?"

She covered her mouth to hide her shocked giggle. He could mean her harm, she reminded herself.

But she was desperate for company. "You may, sir," she said, "but I have a dagger, and I am familiar with its use."

He lowered himself until he sat on the sill, then ducked his head and rose to his feet. He was a tall man, slim and wiry with muscle rather than excessively broad. He had dark hair tinged with red, and the greenest, most open eyes she had ever seen.

He bowed low with a flourish. "Lady Elizabeth, I am Sir Philip Clifford."

The name was familiar, but she couldn't remember why. "Are you a member of the League of the Blade, Sir Philip? I was just told of that secret organization. Did you send me down the basket of food?"

"Nay, to all of your questions, my lady," he said

with true regret. "But I have heard about the legendary Bladesmen, and also about your basket of food. I had to test my theory on how they got it to you, and before I knew it, I decided to try the descent myself."

"You heard about the basket?" she said thoughtfully. "I only told my maidservant."

"And Anne told my lord."

"Lord Russell," she breathed, finally understanding. "You are the man who serves him."

"And you are the woman he is betrothed to," Sir Philip said, his gaze admiring. "I will tell John that he is the most fortunate man in the kingdom. Your beauty is unequaled."

She found herself blushing, for no man had ever praised her in such a romantic way. During her few trips home, her father's neighbors had only commented that her hips were broad enough to make more babies to add to the motherless ones they already had.

If Anne weren't careful, she would find herself swooning at the admiration in Sir Philip's beautiful green eyes. She tried to collect herself. "Sir Philip, do you believe it is truly the League who are trying to help me? I understand that Lord Russell does not believe it so."

"Lord Russell is a man used to being in command, where he must weigh decisions on the facts available." Sir Philip gave an exaggerated wink. "He's still waiting for all the facts."

"And you don't need 'facts'?" she asked with a smile.

"I have done extensive research. I already have the facts. And we were approached by a member of the League, who *told* us he would help you. There are enough facts for me."

He looked back to the window. "It is good to know that I can come down to you this way."

She moved past him to stare out the window to the darkness below. Torches were pinpricks of light along the battlements and in the ward. "It seems very dangerous."

He grinned. " 'Twas exciting. And with the moon out, I could see surprisingly well. If we ever needed to remove you from the tower by this method, I think we could."

She backed away and shook her head. "Nay, I will not leave and risk—"

"That your people will be punished," he interrupted, sighing heavily. "I know." He brightened. "I'll have to tell John about this. He could come to meet you."

"Nay, please do not. What if he is killed in a fall? I could not live with myself."

"And then you would be available for Lord Bannaster's taking," Sir Philip said shrewdly.

Anne shrugged.

He looked around and saw the lute. "I heard you playing. You are quite good. In fact, I think I've heard you playing before, but I wasn't certain where the sound was coming from."

"I have to do something to occupy my mind."

"And you read," he said with admiration, looking at the few books on her table. "I'm thinking of recording the chronicles of the League for future generations."

"You are quite an admirer of theirs," she said. "But if they're so secretive, perhaps they don't want their exploits known."

He frowned. "We'll see."

She regretted putting a damper on his grand ideas, because he decided to leave soon after that.

"Would you consider returning to visit me?" she asked too quickly.

He gave her a curious look. "You want me to visit, but not your betrothed?"

She felt a blush heat her face. She'd made a dreadful mistake.

He smiled with sympathy. "Ah, you're lonely, of course."

"Forgive my impulsive request," she murmured. "I am not in any immediate danger. You would think I would be able to handle a few days alone. But 'tis surprisingly . . . stressful."

"I understand. You enjoy talking to people."

"That's it," she murmured, trying not to watch him in fascination.

"You must miss the evenings down below."

Tears stung her eyes, and she felt ridiculous to be so choked up that she could only nod. Luckily, Sir Philip didn't seem to notice.

"It will be over soon," he said, reaching outside and yanking on the rope as if he felt the need to test it. "Continue to be brave, Lady Elizabeth. I promise that John will make everything all right. Fare well."

"Do be careful," she called, as he stood on the windowsill, his upper body now outside the tower.

With a jump, he braced both feet on a knot in the rope, and then pulled himself up out of sight.

John was glaring at Elizabeth when the door opened and Philip walked in. He came up short when he saw them and glanced at the wimple on the floor.

"Should I leave?" he asked uncertainly.

"Stay and close the door."

John knew his voice was abrupt, but Philip, arching a brow, did as he asked.

"Philip, meet Lady Elizabeth."

Philip's mouth fell open, and he didn't bother to hide his shock.

Elizabeth folded her arms over her chest and gave a brief nod.

"My lady, I—" A strange look came over his face. "So you switched places. Clever."

John glared at him.

"And deceitful," Philip amended, smiling.

Elizabeth took a deep breath. "I had to—"

"Do not go into it all again," John interrupted. "Suffice it to say that she doesn't trust me, and wishes my brother were alive."

She frowned and looked away, remaining silent.

"Well, your maidservant is doing a good job impersonating you," Philip said. "I just left your bedchamber."

John and Elizabeth both gaped at him, but he held up a hand.

"I decided to see how easy it was to come down from the top of the tower, as a Bladesman might."

"And since your neck isn't broken," John said with sarcasm, "I can see you managed the feat."

"It was quite exhilarating. And the poor girl was starved for company, but she never once led me to believe she was anyone other than Lady Elizabeth." He rubbed his chin. "A maidservant, eh? Seems she and I have things in common: we do much for our friends. I allowed myself to be severely beaten, and she allowed herself to be imprisoned."

"And you'll both receive our gratitude when we straighten out this mess," John said.

"This *mess* is my life," Elizabeth responded with anger. She grabbed up her wimple, and with practiced ease she secured her hair, wrapped the cloth about her head, and walked toward the door. "Now, if you'll excuse me, I need to find my pallet."

John stepped in her way. "Remember the missive. I'll need it by tomorrow."

He saw her hesitation, knew her worry. He tried to soften his tone, but it still came out harsh. "Your army wants to defend you, to fulfill the oaths they swore to your father. Do not be cruel enough to deny them."

She drew in a breath and closed her eyes, whispering, "I don't want anyone hurt."

"And I will do my best to ensure that."

She finally nodded. "You will have the missive—and the imprint of my ring in the wax. Now let me go."

He let relief surge in and replace his anger. "And where do you sleep again?"

"In the kitchens."

"That is not a safe place for an earl's daughter. You should remain here. Everyone already thinks you're in my bed."

"Not my own people," she said in a low voice. "They trust me."

"No wonder they barely talked to you these last few days. They were afraid to reveal your identity. They are very loyal to you."

"And I cannot betray their loyalty. Let me go."

When he didn't move right away, she raised her eyes and implored him. "Please."

He stared down at her, and saw a woman in circumstances not of her making, whose parents and betrothed had just died. She was responsible for a castle full of people, while two grown men fought over her.

And he felt the first bit of sympathy for her.

He stepped aside, and she swept out of the chamber as majestically as any countess.

Philip closed the door behind her, and then put his back to it as he gave John a grin. "I must say, this works out for you. No more worries about who you desire."

"Aye, that is the one bright spot in this whole mess. But 'tis easily overshadowed by thoughts of a long marriage full of mistrust, and a bride's wish that she was marrying a different man."

Philip put a hand on his shoulder. "It has only been a few days. Give her a chance to let passion become more. You're a good man, John. She'll realize that soon enough."

Though John nodded, he had his doubts. He felt like a fool, like he was that little boy again that no one expected much of, least of all himself. He'd grown into a confident, talented man—why was it so easy for Elizabeth to make him feel otherwise?

He would win her trust and respect, make her realize that he cared more for the honor of his family than a title. He would become a man of her people, rather than one who craved adventure. Surely he had had enough travel for one lifetime, he insisted to himself.

Yet none of that mattered when he needed her money. Wishing it weren't so didn't make the guilt go away.

Chapter 16

❧

The next morning, as Sarah and Katherine were mounting their horses to leave for their foster home, Elizabeth secretly watched them, hidden behind a bush in the lady's garden. They were so young, with their lives yet before them. They were learning all that was involved in being a lady of the castle, basking in the attention of another family. Neither one of them was betrothed, although she knew that that duty would fall to her husband.

To John. And he would probably take great pride in performing his duty as the head of the household. Elizabeth wished that she could be the one to help shape such an important decision.

Strangely, she could barely stop from crying as her sisters and their party of soldiers departed through the gatehouse. She wished to be them, young enough to be confident that everything would work out. Elizabeth didn't even know *how* she wanted everything to work out.

She took a breakfast tray up to Anne, and let her talk excitedly about the man who'd come through her window.

Finally Anne noticed how quiet Elizabeth was. "So what has happened?" she demanded, hands on her hips. "You let me chatter on like—"

"You deserve to chatter on. You never have anyone to talk to."

"Aye, but it makes me the worst sort of friend not to see that you're troubled. What is it?"

Elizabeth heaved a sigh and tried to smile, although it came out as a grimace. "John discovered who I am."

Anne gasped. "How?"

"He overheard me persuading my sisters to leave."

"They're here?" she cried.

Elizabeth explained what had happened, how John had behaved with her sisters. She grudgingly respected that he had not shouted accusations at her in front of them.

"Did he want to speak to you alone?"

"Of course. He was angry."

"But he must be relieved."

"Relieved?" Elizabeth echoed in confusion.

"He was . . . enamored of you, was he not?"

She tried not to blush. "He was playing a part."

But she remembered his passionate kiss, and wondered if part of his response to her had been relief.

Perhaps he was only glad that his standing among the castle residents would not be in jeopardy when they discovered his identity.

There was something . . . bothersome about being the object of his physical attention, when she still loved the memory of his brother.

Surely if she'd had a chance to be intimate with William, she would have felt more desire for him, her first betrothed. When William smiled, the sun had shone brighter, and she had basked in its warmth.

When John's smoldering gaze caught her, a darkness seemed to sweep through her mind, taking all her rational thought away. She lost control; she lost herself.

John had slept little during the night. His thoughts had run in circles as he analyzed what he was supposed to do about Elizabeth.

After mass, when he broke his fast, he sat alone with his thoughts while he ate. He still couldn't believe the woman he knew as Anne was his betrothed. And though she mistrusted him severely, at least she wasn't demanding an annulment of the contract. That only meant he was a better prospect than Bannaster, or that she was determined to honor her parents' wishes, regardless.

Although he could not forget all the things he was angry with her about, dwelling on it would not make the transition to marriage easier. It was time to convince her that marriage to him would not be a terrible thing. He had to put aside his anger, in hopes that she would, too.

Wooing her physically did not seem to be what she wanted—not right now. Though she desired him, it somehow seemed to make everything worse in her mind, as if she didn't want to feel the way she did.

She wanted the courtly tradition of romance: a man at a distance, professing his admiration and love with politeness and poetry rather than passion.

He could do this, although the necessity of it grated on him. But in the long run, he preferred a grateful bride to an angry one. He would learn to live with his own doubts and disappointments. And if the marriage did not turn out as he'd hoped, he would remember all the lives he was helping.

Even if his own seemed incomplete.

When Elizabeth entered the great hall after returning Anne's tray to the kitchens, she saw John talking to Milburn. Both men glanced at her, Milburn nodded, and John limped toward her, leaning on his crutch.

"Anne," he said politely, "Master Milburn wishes us to return to Hillesley. He would like the orchard inspected in anticipation of the autumn harvest, to see if there's enough for Alderley's needs."

"With the combined harvest from all the surrounding villages, we've always done well."

John's smile remained fixed, too polite. "Regardless, he wants us to go."

"Very well."

Elizabeth wondered if John was using this as an excuse to get her alone. But once they were driving in the cart outside the castle, a soldier in front, and Philip behind, he did nothing but drive. Even when she handed him the letter she'd written to her captain of the guard, he only tucked it away as he thanked her.

"You don't want to know what it says?" she asked.

He glanced at her. "I trust you."

She barely restrained from rolling her eyes. She didn't even sense residual anger from him, as if he was keeping everything locked away.

Yet she couldn't. Side by side with him, she found herself dwelling on how he'd felt in her arms, the mortifying way she'd clung to him, pulling him against her.

Though the day had a chill, she felt overly warm. She could not forget the way his hand had felt on her breast, the ache of pleasure he'd evoked, and the way her nipples had hardened against him.

They passed the stream where they'd first kissed, and he didn't even suggest stopping.

She hated that she felt disappointed.

Now that he had her beneath his thumb, did he feel no more need to seduce her? Was she just a thing he'd already acquired?

"Tell me about William," he suddenly said.

She gave him a surprised stare. "Why would you want to hear about a man I was betrothed to for so many years, and whom you are accusing of so many sins?"

"Because I had not seen him in eight years."

"I only saw him once or twice a year myself. But I did receive letters from him." She almost wished she hadn't brought that up. It was uncomfortable to discuss one's first betrothed with one's second.

"Maybe he had changed," John said musingly.

"Changed from what? Even when we were first betrothed, and I was but eleven, he was always attentive to me. That never changed through the years."

"How attentive could he have been if you are twenty-two and never married?"

"That was my father's doing," she said crisply.

"Really? He did not want to see you safely wed?"

She sighed. "With my sisters fostered, my parents decided they would miss me too much. I was learning so much about running Alderley. And William was busy in London. We thought there was so much time," she added sadly.

"What was William doing?"

She frowned. "He was at Parliament for part of the year, in the House of Lords."

"But when King Henry came back to England and won his crown, how did William switch allegiance?"

"I know not. He did not talk of such things in his letters."

John wasn't surprised. He was positive William took whatever seemed to be the easiest course. Yet in this instance, he'd somehow saved Rame Castle from retaliation from the new king, for supporting the old king. That was a positive accomplishment, and John was grateful to be able to find something good to remember about his brother.

"What did he discuss?" he asked. "This might seem too personal, but he was my brother."

"Our letters were filled with our plans for Alderley. It was the future that mattered, our marriage, not the present."

"He didn't tell you about himself? What he was doing at court?"

"Nay, he often talked about . . . me." She looked away, as if she was embarrassed.

"Ah, the poetry," he said, feeling grim, but trying not to show it.

"He could make one feel special," she murmured.

"And when he was with you?" Though he hated hearing the details, he wanted everything in the open between them, so that he knew the memories he was up against. How else to change her opinion of him?

"He was often with my father, of course, but he never forgot about me, even if it was a smile as I crossed the room, or a song he sang dedicated to me."

John didn't like the dreamy sadness on her face—and he couldn't sing. But he told himself that it was good that his brother paid attention to Elizabeth.

"You did not know these things about your brother?" she suddenly asked.

"We did not have a close bond."

"I've already gathered that," she said dryly.

"I was younger enough than he that I proved something of an embarrassment because I was small and—"

"Plump?"

He shot her a startled look. "I was going to say awkward, but aye, I was that, too."

"And William didn't try to help you? He seemed so considerate of others."

"He thought I should already be better than I was. He decided when I was fifteen that training me would be his mission in life."

"Then he *was* trying to help," she said brightly.

For just a moment, John saw true happiness on her face, instead of endless worry or the mask of her disguise. He wondered if she would ever smile like that for him.

Was Elizabeth right? Had William been trying to help in his own stupid way?

"So he worked with you every day?" she asked.

If he told her the truth, would she just think he was trying to make his brother look bad again?

"He did," John said gravely. "And I was bloody and bruised every night."

"He worked you hard."

Too hard, John had always thought. But had he? Had John taken it all personally, because it was his brother? Were not other squires as beaten as he was? It had seemed so humiliating to him, and the fact that his father hadn't stepped in and put a stop to it was the worst part.

"Mayhap . . . though I didn't see it," he began slowly. "They thought they were helping me."

"They?"

"My father and my brother. After the humiliation of failing so often, I was glad to squire at my cousin's home. In fact, maybe I trained hard there just to prove myself to my family."

Something deep and troubling shifted inside him, and he didn't know how to react. Suddenly Elizabeth's knowing gaze was too personal. He was not yet ready to forget William's last betrayals.

And here he was trying to clear William's legacy between them, and this conversation had probably convinced her that she was right.

She faced forward again, saying with resignation, "William was a good man, who didn't deserve to die young."

John remained silent, considering.

For the rest of the journey to Hillesley, Elizabeth considered John. He was obviously a man who had felt the need to leave his family permanently at a young age, and some of the reasons were now clear. She tried to imagine how she would have felt were her father a strict, cold man. Maybe she would have wanted to marry earlier, to escape.

But maybe William wouldn't have wanted to marry earlier. She'd always thought it was her father's doing that she was yet a maiden, but could her father have been protecting her from knowing that William wasn't ready? That he was having too good a time in London?

She'd thought John had abandoned his family to go off on a personal hunt for glory. But when he heard about her parents' death, he'd left that life to come to her, even though he was vulnerable without an army. So much more was at stake for him than her happiness: the resurrection of Rame Castle, his access to power and wealth beyond anything a mercenary knight could know. All of it without having to bow to his family's needs.

When they arrived at the village, she continued to watch him carefully throughout the afternoon. She saw him hand her missive to Philip, who galloped away after giving her a smile. A little girl brought John a sweet, and he got down on one knee to talk to her while he ate it. After they'd examined the early growth of fruit in the orchards, they watched several little boys playing at sword fighting with sticks. John had freely given advice, had even delayed their meeting with Hugh to show the proper technique for holding a sword.

Elizabeth had a sudden memory of William's impatience when dealing with his squire. Had he treated his youngest brother the same way?

She didn't like to think of William's flaws, but he'd been human like everyone else. She'd never been able to see that.

Could he have neglected his own castle?

Nay, surely that was too much.

But he hadn't returned home to see for himself. He'd been too busy in London with his amusements.

From long ago, the betrothal contract had been written that she was to marry the heir, the baron, not William in particular. Had even his parents had their doubts?

And was some of her anger directed at William,

who had died so foolishly and left her in this mess, watching the death of all her childhood dreams of romance and marriage? She'd always had everything planned to perfection, and it was all gone now.

Was she taking some of this out on John?

On the way back to Castle Alderley, she decided she needed to resolve some confusion. "John, last night you were so furious with me. What changed overnight? I was expecting a miserable trip, and instead you talked about your family as if all our disagreements had never happened."

He didn't look at her, but she thought he clenched his jaw. "I simply realized that arguing would serve no purpose."

"So you're still angry."

He glanced at her. "Are you not? Does it not anger you that we have been put into this situation not of our making?"

She braced her elbows on her knees. "Aye, I'm angry," she said in a low voice.

"At whom? Tell me. I know you're angry with me. The method I chose to get close to you hurt; if not you, it would have hurt Anne. My apologizing doesn't make it go away."

She pressed her lips together and shook her head, worried that if she started to talk, the tears would start, too.

"I've spent the day trying to treat you as you want to be treated," he said.

"I never—"

"Every chance you get, you throw into my face the deference William paid to you. You seem to want an abstract man, not a flesh and blood man with needs."

"I thought you treated me in this distant fashion because you now have everything you wanted from me."

"Everything I wanted?" he said in disbelief, letting the reins go slack. "I'm torn between ending this captivity the way I want, or finding a solution that suits you. I'm actually beginning to hope there *is* a League of the Blade, because we could use them. But most of all, if I had everything I wanted, I'd be touching you, instead of doing my damnedest to keep my hands to myself, like this mythical, romantic man you seem to want."

The cart came to a stop in the middle of the road, the horse dropped his head down to nibble grass, and Elizabeth gaped at John. He was trying to behave as he thought she wanted? As if she even knew what she wanted anymore. There had been so many revelations in the past few days that her head was spinning from it all. She felt confused and uncertain, and so formless as to be shifting with any wind that passed.

The soldier who'd accompanied them for protection now glanced at them over his shoulder, shrugged, and kept riding.

"Aye, I'm angry," she said again. "I'm angry that every plan I made is gone. I'm angry that your brother was stupid enough to die, and maybe wasn't the man I thought he was. I'm even angry at my parents, God rest their souls, for not finding some way to have me safely married."

"That is one thing I am glad did not happen."

His voice was low and fierce and husky. His desire was a thing she didn't trust, too raw, too primitive, and too full of sensations that she didn't understand. Just the look in his eyes affected her powerfully. She had to turn away, holding herself, trembling.

She heard him pick up the reins to urge the horse to trot again, leaving her alone with her chaotic thoughts. She had a need of him, in more ways than one, and she wasn't used to needing anyone.

Chapter 17

The next afternoon, Viscount Bannaster returned with an armed troop of guards. Word
spread before he was even in the great hall, and
Elizabeth found herself instinctively looking for
John, but he was not in the castle. She ran to the
double doors in time to look down upon the inner
ward, and the chaos of Bannaster's arrival. Dogs
barked and ran about the horses, people darted
away from the pawing hooves of the ill-controlled
animals, and Lord Bannaster rode in the center of
it all.

Looking too well pleased with himself, Elizabeth
thought. Nausea swirled through her stomach. She
looked about anxiously for John, and finally saw
him limping toward the castle from the tiltyard,

Philip right behind him. Oh heavens, was she already starting to depend on his presence? She looked up at the tower and wondered if Anne was watching, too.

Was it already too late? Elizabeth had come up with no method to free herself that would not hurt other people. So little time had passed since Bannaster had left for London; King Henry must have needed little persuasion. What if the king had skipped guardianship and settled on marriage as an end to the problems of Elizabeth and her dowry?

Bannaster swung his leg over the side of his horse and jumped from the saddle. His fur-lined cloak swirled about him, and he tossed it back over his shoulders. He left his soldiers to deal with the horses, and came up the steps to the great hall two at a time. Elizabeth stumbled back, and to her relief he didn't even notice her as he swept by. She was only a lady's maid he'd met once, after all.

"Bring me an ale!" he called. "Travel parches my throat."

A dozen or more knights followed behind him, laughing too loudly, pushing each other like boys, and looking about as if for prey.

For women.

And Elizabeth felt very vulnerable against the wall. Just then, John came through the door, and his big body was between her and the rest of the hall.

"Are you all right?" he asked in a low voice.

She nodded, absurdly grateful for him, though she knew he could do nothing should Bannaster's men decide to amuse themselves at her expense.

"So this is the man who wants to take what is mine?" he said near her ear.

That annoyed her, and she flashed him an angry look. "It is all still mine," she answered.

He rolled his eyes. "Has he revealed anything?"

"Nay, though does he not seem far too pleased with himself?"

John drew her hand into the warmth of his elbow, and turned to watch the viscount again. She found herself clutching John tightly.

"He is exhilarated," John said, "but he hardly seems like a man who'd show uncertainty. And he could not have stayed in London more than one night, to arrive back here so soon."

"I thought we would have more time," she whispered.

She was startled at her own use of the word "we," and tried to tell herself that she was including Anne. John glanced down at her, but didn't remark on it.

"Patience," he murmured.

She was reminded of that same word written on the note in the basket.

John continued, "I cannot believe that the king could break a betrothal contract so easily."

"Maybe he simply named Bannaster my guardian."

"Then let us find out."

Though everyone had just finished the midday meal, Bannaster and his men were starving. Servants swarmed out of the kitchens with some initial offerings of bread and cheese, while poor Adalia must have been working frantically to reheat what was left of the meal.

Milburn greeted his lord civilly, and then sat at his right hand to relay his own report. John and Elizabeth walked casually around the perimeter of the room, hoping to get close enough to overhear them.

Instead, Milburn looked up, saw them, and called, "Sir John, please attend to us."

When Elizabeth released John, Milburn motioned her toward the kitchens. "Bring more food, Anne."

As she walked away, she looked back over her shoulder as John was introduced to Bannaster. When she returned carrying a tray of salad bowls to the high table, Milburn was explaining about the illness of Hillesley's bailiff, and John's ability to take over quickly.

And Bannaster was looking distracted, as he broke off a piece of bread and slathered it with butter. When she set his salad down, he looked up and paused. The recognition in his eyes chilled her.

"Are you not Lady Elizabeth's maid?" he asked.

"Aye, my lord."

"How is her ladyship?"

"She is well."

"Not crying to be let out?"

"Nay, my lord."

He sighed. "She is a brave woman. Perhaps she will be glad to see me."

Elizabeth wished she could snort her response to that.

"Has she given her situation thought? After all, she was silly enough to think she could run this estate by herself."

Without thinking, she responded, "She did so for six months, my lord."

Milburn broke his usual impassive expression to gape at her.

But Bannaster only laughed. "Aye, mayhap she did. Or mayhap her people helped more than she knew."

Elizabeth curtsied and moved on to the next hungry man before she could get herself in real trouble.

John was not invited to eat with the viscount. Out of the corner of her eye, she watched him retreat to the hearth and prop his leg up as if it pained him.

Her outspokenness had earned her the interest of Bannaster. While he ate, he watched her occasionally, and she did not like the interest in his gaze. He drank too much throughout the meal, and as the day wore on, he continued to drink. Never once did he mention his audience with the king. He was far too jovial at supper, and tried to entertain the occupants of the hall with the great deeds of the noblemen at court.

They all sounded like pompous fools to Elizabeth. She hid her thoughts, even as she was getting better at hiding herself from the viscount's gaze. She was trying not to get her hopes up that he stayed away from the tower because he hadn't been successful in his quest.

But early in the evening, as the torches were being lit and the supper dishes were removed, Bannaster slammed his tankard down and rose to his feet. He swayed precariously, caught his balance, and announced to the hall, "Now I go to see your mistress."

After exchanging glances with John, Elizabeth ran ahead to reach the tower before Bannaster did.

The two soldiers frowned at her. "You do not bring Lady Elizabeth a meal?" said Bannaster's man.

She had forgotten. And it was too late to turn back now, for she could hear Bannaster's loud, off-key whistle as he approached.

"Tonight I thought to ask her preference," she said. "Might I be let up?"

But the soldier, glancing over her head, came to attention, and Alderley's soldier did as well, though with obvious reluctance.

It was too late for Elizabeth to warn Anne. She turned to face Bannaster, but he merely looked over her head at the soldiers.

"Has anyone dared to defy the guards I placed here while I was gone?" Bannaster asked.

"Nay, milord," said his soldier.

" 'Tis good. I shall go up to speak with her."

"My lord," Elizabeth said, drawing his gaze, "I need to come with you."

"Nay, what is between my lady and me is private." He gave her a bleary grin.

"But my lord, you cannot see her alone. How will it look to her people—to your people?" she added for his benefit.

"But I care not who—"

As Bannaster waved an arm to encompass the whole castle, he stopped talking when he saw that half a dozen people were nearby, some passing by in the corridor, or like John, coming from the great hall in curiosity.

Bannaster sighed. "Very well, maidservant. What is your name again?"

"Anne, my lord."

"Then you come with me, Anne, only you."

"Thank you, my lord."

She went through the door ahead of him, but he was right behind. It made her nervous to walk up the stairs that hugged the wall of the tower. She didn't like him behind her, staring at her lower body. She felt like she could hear his breathing.

At the door to the solar, she knocked and called, "My lady? 'Tis I, Anne, and Lord Bannaster."

For a moment she could hear nothing inside.

She gasped when Bannaster put a hand on her hip and said, "Move aside, and I'll knock louder."

But the door suddenly opened, and warm light spilled down the stairs. Anne stood there, looking subdued and regal in a gown of blue silk. "Good evening, Lord Bannaster," she said softly, as she stepped back to allow them entrance.

Elizabeth entered first and although she probably should have taken her place behind Anne, instead she stood at her side, facing the viscount.

As if the drunken walk up the stairs had winded him, he sank down sloppily onto a stool and smiled. "You look the same, Lady Elizabeth, beautiful and untouchable."

"I watched you arrive, my lord," Anne said. "You looked pleased with yourself."

Elizabeth thought confinement had made Anne increasingly brave.

Bannaster grinned. "So you were anxious for my reappearance?"

"Anxious? Nay, my lord. But what else do I have to do but look out the window?"

She smiled as she said it, but she made her point. Yet Bannaster was just drunk enough that all he did was laugh.

"You are so refreshing, Lady Elizabeth. I will never grow bored with you."

Anne inhaled. "Let us be direct, my lord. Has the king granted you guardianship over me?"

Elizabeth held her breath.

Bannaster leaned his head back against the wall, and suddenly his eyes looked hooded. "He is contemplating his decision and will advise me of it."

Elizabeth stared at the floor, because she was afraid her expression would betray her relief.

"You don't have to look so happy," he said sourly.

She looked up in time to see Anne's smile fade.

"Can you blame me?" Anne asked softly. "My betrothed will come for me soon, and I don't wish your interference."

"Yet the king thought my wish to protect you was a good one. I feel it is only a matter of time before I win the ability to guide your future."

He looked down Anne's body in a way that made Elizabeth step closer to her. Even the two of them together could not stop a man of his size from doing as he wished.

"In fact," Bannaster continued, rising unsteadily

to his feet, "if I take you now, the king would not refuse my right to wed you."

His true intentions were finally in the open, but Elizabeth never thought he'd be fool enough to resort to rape to get what he wanted.

Anne backed up a step. "Nay, sir, you cannot force yourself upon me."

"It will not be force, my girl. I am quite persuasive."

Elizabeth put herself between her dearest friend and Bannaster. She would allow no harm to come to Anne, even if it meant confessing her identity. Bannaster impatiently grabbed Elizabeth's arm, but before he could push her aside, Anne started screaming. She was impressively loud, and full of enough terror to bring anyone within hearing distance running.

"Shh!" Bannaster said, thrusting Elizabeth aside. "I wasn't going to hurt you, girl!"

Elizabeth tripped and fell to the floor.

"A kiss is all I ask!" he shouted.

Anne continued screaming.

"One kiss and you'll see that I can make the best husband!"

Even as Elizabeth stood up, she could hear the sound of pounding feet coming up the stairs. The door burst open and the two soldiers spilled inside. Anne started sobbing, Elizabeth threw her arms around her, and Bannaster swayed and put a hand on his soldier's chest.

"A misunderstanding," Bannaster said. "I was just leaving."

Anne calmed down until her sobs were hiccups. Elizabeth continued to pat her back as Bannaster backed down from whatever he'd planned. She could not be satisfied, though, because he could try again another time. And who could stop him from what he truly wanted to do?

When Bannaster and the soldiers had gone, Elizabeth and Anne hugged each other.

Elizabeth gave her a handkerchief to dry her tears. "You know I would never have let him touch you. This is growing too dangerous. Let me take back my life."

"Nay! I knew you were going to say that. That's why I was crying, trying to make him leave before you did something foolish!"

Elizabeth sighed. "You did a fine job scaring him off."

Anne shook her head, her expression worried. "For now, Elizabeth, only for now. His meeting with the king did not go at all as he'd planned. He seems a bit desperate."

"Mayhap it was only the drink in him talking. If he'd have wanted to take you, he could have tried it a sennight ago. I promise I will have more of our people keep watch on him and the tower. We'll make sure he never has a chance to sneak up here."

Anne nodded, but she looked unconvinced. How vulnerable she must feel! Elizabeth felt terribly guilty, but she knew Anne would reject the offer to switch places.

"Let me bring you up a supper tray," Elizabeth said. "Food always makes you feel better."

Anne gave a shaky smile. "You make me sound like a glutton."

"Nonsense. But surely you're hungry. I'll be right back."

Elizabeth left the solar, closed the door behind her, and began to hurry down the stairs. She'd only taken a few when something rose out of the shadows in front of her. She gasped and fell back against the wall, catching herself.

Lord Bannaster smiled at her, the torchlight gleaming across his teeth.

Oh God, what had he heard? If he'd listened at the door, he knew who she was.

"Anne, you're a beautiful girl," he said.

She told herself to relax, that he didn't know the truth, but something in his gaze made her fear rise instead.

"And I want company tonight," he continued pleasantly.

He sounded like they were going to spend the evening playing Tables in the great hall, but she knew that wasn't what he meant. Without a word, she turned and tried to run back up the stairs, but he caught her arm, and she fell onto her knees on the cold stone.

"There, there, you'll hurt yourself," he said. "You must be careful. It's a nasty fall down."

There was no railing. The tower stairs were made for hand-to-hand combat, where one knight could pitch the other over the edge.

Bannaster helped her up. "Come, let me show you the bedchamber I use here. It was the earl's, and 'tis magnificent."

The thought of him dragging her to her parents' bed made her nauseous. But they were in too precarious a position to struggle. He turned her about, put his arm around her and started walking her down the stairs.

"This is far too slow," he said, laughing quietly to himself.

She cried out as he picked her up by the waist like a sack of grain. She dangled against his side as he began to take the stairs faster and faster. She hung out over the edge, with the darkness and the torches whirling around her. She couldn't scream or cry, couldn't breathe from fear until they were closer to the ground.

He stumbled when they reached level ground, and Elizabeth fell and rolled away from him. Her breath came in gasps; she realized her face was wet with tears she didn't remember shedding. She stared up at him, not concealing her fury and her fear.

Bannaster frowned as he looked down at her. "I was very careful not to drop you. Why are you on the ground? Come, let's get up, girl, so we don't frighten the soldiers."

He reached for her, and she had no choice but to take his hand and allow herself to be pulled up. When he opened the door at the base of the tower, she ducked past him, between the soldiers, and started to run.

"What fun!" he called. "A chase!"

He might have been drunk, but he was fast. She couldn't quite get away from him. Though she led him through mazelike corridors, she never lost him. The occasional servant pressed himself against the wall as she flew past, but she didn't stop. But why didn't he pass out?

Whenever he got close, he laughed like it was a childhood game; to her it was a childhood nightmare come back to life. When she was a girl, before her betrothal, there had always been men visiting Alderley, pushing themselves or their young sons on her, making her feel hunted. She had stopped sleeping from the nightmares; her appetite had faded, until finally her parents had taken her away—

To John's family castle, the first place she remembered feeling at peace. The betrothal had protected her, made her feel safe again, but all of that was gone. Would she ever in her life be able to stop running?

The need for John was like a sudden, vivid ache in her chest, but she did not lead the viscount to him. John would protect her even if it got him imprisoned or killed.

And she didn't want him dead.

At last her lungs could no longer bear the strain. She couldn't stop alone in a corridor, knowing what would happen. She could only go to the great hall in hopes that Bannaster could be distracted.

She ran beneath an arched doorway and to the hearth in the great hall. Soldiers were dancing with maidservants to the music of a pipe and lute. Milburn was playing Tables, moving his pieces on the board; he looked up and frowned at her. She could only imagine what she looked like. Her face was hot with perspiration, and she wished she could pull the wimple from her hair and toss it into the fire.

Though her breathing was unsteady, she tried to walk instead of run across the room, but the muscles in her legs were shaky. John was there; he had been seated beside Philip on a bench, but he had risen to his feet at the sight of her. His brows drew together ominously, and his hand went to the dagger at his waist.

Nay, she had not meant to involve him—what had she been thinking? She shook her head frantically at him, and was grateful when Philip grabbed his arm from behind.

"Anne!" Bannaster shouted her name. "You've had your fun."

He was right behind her. He whirled her about, pulled her to him, and kissed her. Though the soldiers cheered, even Elizabeth heard the unnatural silence that descended on the rest of the great hall.

The viscount lifted his head and looked about, his drunken smile uncertain. "Who stopped the music? I wanted to dance with Anne."

"Fire!" a voice shrieked.

Bannaster let go of her immediately, turning about, and Elizabeth did the same. She saw no evidence of fire—but Adalia, the one who had shouted, was motioning frantically to the kitchens.

Everywhere people started running—many of the soldiers fled for the great double doors to the outside, but her own people, bless them, went running for buckets. Bannaster, probably fearful that his hoped-for home would not be ruined, followed everyone toward the kitchens.

Elizabeth would have also, but someone caught her from behind. She cried out instinctively.

" 'Tis me!" John said.

With a shudder, she threw her arms around him. He picked her right up off the floor and held her.

"Did he hurt you?" John said against her ear.

"Nay, I am just frightened, and so weary from leading him about the castle. Even drunk, he can run!"

John put her down, and she awkwardly stepped away from him. "Is there truly a fire?" she asked, suddenly shy about the way she'd reacted to him. Surely she was so frightened that anyone but Bannaster would have served the same purpose.

"I doubt it," he said. "But we'll go see."

There were shouts coming from the kitchen, and only the smallest wisp of smoke. Bannaster stood in the doorway, looking at the confusion within, and just before Elizabeth and John got there, a bucket of water drenched him.

He stumbled backward looking down at his wilted silks and brocades.

John pulled Elizabeth back against him, his arm about her waist, and she didn't protest. All around them her people gathered in a close group, maidservants, valets, and grooms, leaving the center of the gathering to Bannaster, who sputtered as water dripped down his face.

"My garments are ruined," he said, wringing out the skirt of his doublet. "Anne, I'll need you to—"

He broke off as he saw the people around him. No one smiled or offered to help. Bannaster's gaze focused on her, and he couldn't miss John's arm about her waist, and the protective way he held her.

"My lord," said a young man, who had pushed his way through the group and now stared about with uncertainty. "I unpacked your coffers in the master suite. Shall I help you change?"

Surely this was his squire.

Bannaster peered about him, his smile growing as if in amusement, and he finally nodded. "Aye, Henry. I'll go with you. Strangely enough, I'm feeling rather tired. I think I drank too much."

Elizabeth blinked in surprise as Bannaster turned about and followed his squire from the hall. She received several friendly good-nights as people dispersed for the night. She could only smile her thanks and try to hold back tears. They had all helped rescue her.

She tried to step away from John, but his arm tightened, and he spoke in a low voice against her ear. "He will try that again."

"I think not. He saw the way everyone had gathered around him." But she knew she could not count on that.

"Anne—"

"Shh." She turned about in his arms, patted his chest and stepped away from him. "I have to take a meal up to Lady Elizabeth."

"I will come with you."

"Nay. I will speak to Adalia and thank her for what she did. I'm sure she'll accompany me."

"But if you run into Bannaster—"

"And if you were at my side, you would try to solve the problem with *force*."

"I am a knight!" he said in a low, harsh voice.

"And you would have gotten yourself killed or banished. Do you think I want that?"

He opened his mouth, but no words came as he blinked down at her in surprise.

"Now let me go. I promise I will be escorted."

"For as long as he's here."

"Aye, I promise. And then I need to speak with you. I'll come to your bedchamber."

Elizabeth tried not to think about the speculative look in John's eyes as he nodded. She would tell him of the desperate plan that had begun forming in her mind when Bannaster had tried to force himself on her. It was the only way she could think of to solve her dilemma without involving an attack by her army.

Chapter 18

John paced his bedchamber, avoiding the bathing tub with its steaming water. He'd forgotten to cancel his request; the water would just have to grow cold.

Philip packed a satchel.

"I regret having to send you away," John said.

Philip grinned and shrugged. "Lady Elizabeth needs you."

"Only because she has something urgent she needs to tell me," he insisted.

"Of course," Philip said lightly. "And what will be the excuse tomorrow night?"

John couldn't protest. He wanted Elizabeth safe, and that meant staying with him, if he could convince her. But to Philip, he said, "I cannot see farther than tonight. Where will you go?"

"I'll sleep in the great hall. I've slept in worse places, as you know."

"You have my gratitude."

Philip laughed and shook his head. "Maybe I'll request my own chamber from the captain of the guard. I *am* his assistant and clerk."

Not for the first time, John found himself wishing that he were the one without the "broken" leg. He missed the excitement of training, of pitting his skills against a worthy opponent. Sometimes he just wished he could challenge Bannaster and be done with it. But of course the king might have a problem with that. . . .

And Elizabeth as well. She wanted Alderley to be the most important thing in their lives. And it was, for now. What would happen when everything was peaceful and placid and . . . the same, day in and day out?

Focusing on Philip again, John said, "And has your position among the soldiers helped us in any way?"

"Someday, perhaps. But right now, all it has told me is that as in any troop of soldiers, there are mostly good men just doing their duty, and there are a few bad men who enjoy making trouble."

"Did you see Alderley's army?"

Philip shook his head. "Parker told me that they are roughly one hundred strong. If you have them on your side, you should be able to retake the castle."

"*If* I have them on my side. And as for taking the

castle, I might have to do it without the lady's permission. I'm not sure my wedding night will be a happy one. But I am grateful for your help."

Philip walked to the door. "And what else would I be doing were I not here? Selling my sword arm to the highest bidder?"

"Instead you lent it to me for free," John said.

Philip rolled his eyes, saluted a good-night, and left the chamber. And John continued pacing. He knew that Elizabeth would probably linger with her lady's maid, telling her what had transpired. But it seemed an abnormally long time before he heard a soft knock on the door. He threw it open and found her standing there alone.

"You promised me you would be escorted," he said, pulling her inside and closing the door behind her.

"I was, but I sent Adalia away just now. John, Bannaster cannot even be awake, so inebriated was he."

He closed his eyes to control his temper. "Elizabeth, the soldiers are all his. He could have you summoned before him with just a word. I am bothered by how little you care for yourself. From now on, you are sleeping here, where I can protect you."

He was ready for her protest, but instead she squared her shoulders. "That works well with my plan."

"Plan?" he echoed suspiciously.

"I told you that I would think of one, and I have." She swallowed and met his gaze gravely.

To his surprise, she unwrapped her wimple and

tossed it onto a table. Her unbound hair spilled down around her shoulders and breasts. Pulling it over one shoulder, she reached behind her neck and began loosening the laces of her gown.

The dark place deep inside him, where he forced his desire into check, now began to unfurl and spread its heat through him.

"What are you doing?" he asked hoarsely, unable to stop himself from watching the bodice of her gown begin to sag.

"I can no longer risk remaining a virgin," she said impassively. "You must take me to bed, so Bannaster won't be a threat."

He had thought she would need comfort this night from the fright of Bannaster's attack, but she was too strong for that. And with her offer, she was going to prove him the weakest of men, for he could not imagine refusing her.

He felt like a statue, so unable to move was he. With not a trace of emotion on her face, she stepped out of her gown, to reveal her long-sleeved linen smock, gathered high about her neck. She sat down on a stool to remove her shoes and stockings. He swallowed as he glimpsed the smooth slopes of her legs when she removed her garters. Then she walked to his bed and climbed in, pulling the coverlet to her waist, but leaving an edge turned down invitingly.

For him.

A part of him wanted to tear off all his clothing and join her, showing her just how much passion he would bring to their marriage. He could never imagine tiring of her, of her spirit and courage, and even her need to lead him. He would do whatever she told him to do—in bed. And she would finally have proof of how much she really wanted him. No more of her foolish wish for a distant, romantic courtship.

His gaze traveled from the hint of her breasts within the delicate smock, up her throat—to her pale face. Suddenly her brown eyes seemed frightened, vulnerable, but only for a moment, and then determination filled them once again.

How could he begin the intimacy of their marriage with the future bride feeling forced, capitulating only as a last resort?

John sighed heavily, knowing he would have to ignore the painful ache of his erection. His nightly bath would be a cold one.

He sat down on the edge of the bed and tried not to wince at how she stiffened. "Nay, Elizabeth, sweetling, not like this."

She frowned at him. "What do you mean? Are you so bothered by the fact that it is my idea?"

He smiled. "Nay, your suggestion was a valid one—deeply appreciated, you may be certain. But we'll find another way."

She looked shocked. "But . . . every man has always wanted me, and what marriage to me brings to him."

"Trust me, Elizabeth, this man wants you badly, and I don't give a damn about what property you bring me. But I want to find an honorable solution, one you're not forced into."

She looked away, her shoulders slumped. "It has not always been a good thing, to be so wanted."

He said nothing, hoping she'd continue to talk.

"When I was ten years old," she began in a low voice, "just before I came to Rame Castle, an old friend of my father visited, and brought his young son with him. I was used to meeting eligible boys; I didn't mind knowing that my father would pick someone for me. I trusted his choices. But . . . for the previous year, the fathers had become more insistent, the sons kept trying to get me alone to play, and although that was all we did, it was as if . . . they were being told to do it. The earldom was a powerful lure, even though the king had not settled on how it would pass beyond my father. But we thought we could trust this old family friend. It was a relief to be with him and his son."

John wanted to hold her, sensing that the story would not have a happy ending, but Elizabeth seemed lost in her memories.

"He was going to take his son and me on an outing to a nearby pond and back. I was thrilled to be showing off my riding skills, as well as getting away from the tension of the castle. We always had guests trying to convince my father to give me in marriage to them. But before I mounted my horse, something seemed . . . wrong. I was only ten, but even I could see that the horses' saddle bags seemed rather full for a simple ride."

John nodded. "He was going to take you away?"

"He never admitted it to my father," she said softly, "even when his bags were searched. He kept insisting that he and his son were leaving afterward, and he'd just prepared in advance, but no one believed him."

"What did your father think he meant to do?"

"Blackmail?" She shuddered. "Or something even more sinister that had nothing to do with his son. His wife had recently died."

"Elizabeth, that was a terrible ordeal for a child to go through."

She tried to smile. "But it was the direct reason my parents decided to send me to your family."

"And I wager there are days you're not so happy that that happened," he said dryly.

"Nay, the immediate result was wonderful. I came home, and for a long time Alderley seemed peaceful. I enjoyed myself for many years."

"Until your parents died?"

Nodding, she said, "And once again, everyone wants to own me."

Elizabeth felt an ache deep in her heart that never quite went away, no matter how hard she forced it down. They had tried to protect her from the world, and now there was no one between her and the men who fought over her. She was so sick of feeling helpless, and had hoped tonight to take matters into her own hands.

But John was being honorable and noble, though she could see in the tight lines of his face what it cost him. He was a man who'd returned home to do his duty by his family and found himself alone, with few resources. The respect for his family name was gone, regardless of who had caused it. He had spent years building a reputation in Europe, to no avail. Though he was a man who hid his own pain, there was a haunting, answering look in his eyes that called to her, made her want to make things better for him.

She found herself reaching up to touch his face. He went utterly still, his eyes closed, his expression for a moment twisting with tension, then smoothing out with understanding. When she leaned in and kissed him, his lips parted, and he shuddered.

"Elizabeth." His spoke against her mouth, his voice full of subtle warnings.

"Just a kiss," she murmured, kissing his top lip, his bottom lip, and then sucking on it gently. "How will I learn not to fear what happens between a husband and wife?"

She knew that he let her lead, and she felt a quiet thrill. She tilted her head, deepening the kiss, her tongue circling his lips before darting inside and retreating. She put her hands on his, felt the way his were fisted in the bedclothes. Stroking them gently, she hoped to ease his spirit, but he was a man, and already she was learning that they were unalike. She only seemed to fire his passion, for with a groan, he caught her hand and pressed it flat against his chest, where she could feel the pounding of his heart. She had a flash of memory, from when he had touched her body in the same place, and it made her shiver.

His hand slid over her hip, though it was covered in blankets. Up higher, indenting on her waist, over her ribs, skimming up the side of her breast.

She broke the kiss and gazed questioningly into his eyes, unable to control her breathing.

"Let me show you some of what you came for tonight, sweetling," he murmured, kissing her cheek, nibbling her earlobe. "I promise that I still believe we should wait for everything that marriage entails, but ah . . . the taste of you makes me ache to show you more."

She nodded silently, knowing that he would keep his word. But as the power of their attraction rose higher inside her, she began to wonder if even her own vows mattered next to the flame of desire. She couldn't resist it, and it frightened her; but he was kissing her mouth ever deeper, mating with her tongue, tugging at the lace that held the gathering of her smock.

And she wanted him to; she wanted to be overwhelmed, to forget.

The smock loosened and began a slow slide down her shoulders; still he kissed her, pressed his hand against her back, urging her ever closer. His mouth took a torturous path down her neck, as he licked and nipped, then circled the hollow at the base of her throat with his tongue. With both hands he lifted her up until she was kneeling on the bed, though he yet sat. In this position he didn't need to bend over her. He was eye level as her smock clung for a moment to her nipples, and then fell to her waist.

He inhaled deeply, staring at her. "You are perfection," he murmured.

She didn't know how to feel, what to do, only knew that it was heavenly to be worshiped by what she saw in his eyes.

He pressed his mouth between her breasts; the brush of his hair and the roughness of his whiskers teased her with pleasure and pain. He held her like that, and she finally allowed herself to thread her fingers through his soft hair, as she'd longed to do. With a roll of his shoulders, he growled his pleasure.

And then he began to move, tasting her skin, pressing light kisses along the rising slope of her breast. Her need rose just as high, only to subside in frustration, when his teasing kisses slid another way instead of finding the peak.

He tormented her like this for several minutes, until finally a moan escaped her. Only then did he seem to have what he wanted, for he cupped one breast gently, then gave it a long lick of his tongue.

It made her convulse in an overpowering shudder; yet he held her still and continued inexorably, licking her as if she were marzipan candy. When his mouth moved to the other breast, he used his fingers on the first, and the twin sensations were like nothing she'd ever felt before. There was a fire deep in her belly that was stoked by everything he did. Her smock was caught on her lower arms, and she longed to free herself of the last of the garments, to give him what he desired.

But would it be *her* choice? Or his will?

He finally suckled her, taking her deep into his mouth, so that she barely felt him lift her smock from behind until a draft caressed her buttocks a moment before his fingers did. His other hand slid down her front, cupping the most intimate part of her through the garment.

When she stiffened, he murmured her name as if she were a wild cat he needed to soothe. He was petting her, stroking her, reaching to tease her from behind. She would have fallen bonelessly onto the bed if he had not held her up, so unable was she to understand the way he controlled her, the sensations that coursed through her body.

And then his bare hand slid up her thigh, beneath her smock and he touched her without the barrier of clothing between them. His fingers played her effortlessly, as if he knew all the secrets. She was lost, unknowing, feeling a rising panic beneath the layers of heat and passion. His fingers moved deeper, and she realized her body moistened his passage. His mouth teased her breasts, while his fingers circled and teased and plucked below. She found herself stiffening, waiting, almost begging for him to give her what she needed.

And it came over her so suddenly, that she arched back with it, lost in the overwhelming convulsion. Her only awareness was him, with his hands and his mouth claiming her, possessing her, giving her this release so steeped in pleasure.

He lowered her back on the bed, and she lay still and stared up at him in wonder and growing unease. This was a powerful connection between them. She wondered if she would do something desperate to feel this again. Her mind was no longer her own; had she been seduced by his will?

He watched her face, and she saw the quiet understanding in his eyes. Without speaking, he gently pulled her smock up to cover her nakedness, then brought the coverlet up to her waist. Somehow this was worse, because she knew he sacrificed his own pleasure to show her just the beginnings of intimacy.

"Sleep," he whispered.

And suddenly she wanted to be tired, to close her eyes and not see his face anymore. She had no control when she looked upon him, and it frightened her. She lowered her lids.

But she wasn't sleepy, not really. She felt . . . invigorated, different, and her mind whirled trying to understand all the new sensations that her body experienced. She heard John moving about, and she realized that she didn't know where he would sleep—on Philip's pallet on the floor? With her?

That thought sent another quiver through her. She had to know. She opened her eyes the tiniest bit, looking at the chamber through her lashes. She saw John immediately, for he stood near the bathing tub.

To her shock, he was removing his clothing.

Of course he would, she told herself. He could not sleep in all of his garments. But then she realized that he might be planning to bathe.

She slammed her eyes shut again, mortified to intrude on such a private thing.

But hadn't he just *touched* the most private parts of her? All she was going to do was look.

Once again, she peered through her lashes. John was just removing his shirt. She had seen parts of him before, when Rachel the healer had worked on his wounds. But the full breadth of his chest set off another quiver deep inside her. It was pleasurable and embarrassing, yet . . . she still continued to watch.

His muscles bulged where hers gently sloped. Hair was scattered across his chest and narrowed down his abdomen, which was ridged with more muscle. Scattered scars of combat were white lines of honor across his skin.

And then she remembered that he had not been able to wear hose, due to the splint on his lower leg. He only wore his braies, the barest scrap of linen about his loins. With his back to her, he removed them, and was naked.

His buttocks looked so firm and perfect that she wanted to touch them; she was scandalized by her own indecent thoughts. But since she'd had the pleasure of his intimate caresses, she discovered a yearning to explore him the same way. For now she used her eyes, and what they saw next could have blinded them.

He leaned over to feel the water in the tub, which must surely be cold by now. When he turned in profile, she saw his penis sticking straight outward from his body.

The inside of her suddenly throbbed, as if it needed him to be whole. She knew that male and female came together that way; her mother had not wanted her ignorant when her wedding night came. She hadn't been able to imagine it then—but now it was fully evident.

He still desired her. He had given her the ultimate pleasure, and not received it himself.

Would another man have been so selfless, especially when she had allowed him to continue pleasuring her?

He climbed into the tub and sank down with a sigh, even though the water must only come to his waist. He was a big man who needed a big tub, but the only one large enough was in the family wing, which her father had had built to order. She would have it sent to John and—

She was behaving like a wife already, she thought in wonder, considering his comfort, his needs.

Had she finally accepted that he was to be her husband?

She continued to watch him bathe, lulled into sleepiness by his slow movements as he used a cloth on his skin.

She told herself that he was her last hope, even as deep inside, a part of her warned that she was losing herself to him.

Chapter 19

⟨⟩

I n the morning, Elizabeth left Anne inspecting another basket that had been lowered to her during the night, more sweets and books, even a flute. Had Anne's music been heard by this mysterious man?

At the bottom of the tower, John was waiting for Elizabeth. She felt surprised that she was so relieved and glad to see him. She knew he could only have been dragged from the castle by force, but still . . . He turned to walk at her side, limping, and she remembered how considerate he'd been, sleeping on Philip's pallet instead of sharing the bed with her.

She'd almost been disappointed to awaken alone.

In the great hall, Milburn stepped in front of them, and they both came to a stop. She had a sick feeling of panic, so unusual for her. Had John's identity been discovered? Had the fact that she slept safe in his room caused too much notice?

Milburn took the tray from her hands and gave it to John. "Lord Bannaster would like to see you, Anne."

In that moment, her years of training resurfaced, and she found herself becoming calm. There were people all around them; it was the start of a new day, and Bannaster was no longer drunk.

But John stepped forward with his hand on his dagger, and Milburn arched a brow.

She put a hand on John's arm. "Nay, 'tis all right," she said quietly. "I will not leave the hall."

She saw the way his jaw clenched, but he only nodded once. The relief inside her gave way to gratitude—he trusted her to make her own decisions. How many women could say that of the man they would marry?

She felt warm inside just looking at John. Milburn, usually so impassive, seemed almost . . . amused. Elizabeth schooled her features into stern lines and walked to the dais, where Bannaster sat at the head table, breaking his fast.

The viscount looked up at her, and there was no embarrassment in his expression.

Of course not—he was the kind of man who believed he could have any lowly maiden he wished.

"Anne," he said, after chewing and swallowing a piece of bread, "you can tell Lady Elizabeth that I heard of her betrothed in London."

She stiffened in surprise, but only nodded, hoping he would continue.

"Quite to my surprise, the king has received regular reports on him for many years. It seems he's quite famous in Europe."

"Lady Elizabeth had heard of his talent as a swordsman," she said cautiously.

"He's won many of the major tournaments, and apparently he's quite in demand as a mercenary. A gifted fellow."

She didn't understand what Bannaster's purpose was in telling her all this.

"But sadly, although he may be gifted, it is obvious he cares as little for family obligations as his brother did, for he's not come back for your lady."

She lowered her eyes, for she couldn't show triumph. And then her good feelings faded away, as she realized that yet another person believed the worst of William.

Bannaster sighed. "William was a pleasant companion, though, and I must admit to missing him. No one could sway a roomful of wenches with his handsome looks as much as William could. He knew just what to say. When he died, I was worried what would happen to this estate. It is only fair that as his friend, I make sure it is taken care of."

He sounded like he believed everything he was saying, too, as if marriage and an impressive dowry were a great hardship no one wanted to bear.

Bannaster scrutinized her again. "You make sure to tell Lady Elizabeth what I said."

"Of course, my lord." She curtsied and turned away from him.

John was waiting for her before the hearth, propped on his crutch. He'd been right about his brother all along, and she'd doubted him.

She walked toward him, and he smiled, and even the pull of his scar made her all soft inside for him.

When she stopped before him, he said, "Milburn has asked me to record the amount of sheep grazing Hillesley's pastureland."

"I can be ready to leave."

He arched a brow.

"For Hillesley, anyway," she amended.

In a lower voice, he said, "Are you well? What did he want?"

Elizabeth looked about, but the hall was emptying except for a few valets who cleaned the trestle tables. "I'm fine. He wanted to slur your name."

Surprised, he glanced at Bannaster, but the man was already talking to Milburn as he walked toward the double doors leading outside.

"My name?" he echoed, amused.

"It seems the king has been following your famous exploits. I would have thought the king's interest in you would bother Bannaster, but he seems far too sure of himself."

"How is that a slur?"

She took a deep breath. "He compared you to your brother, and said that you obviously cared as little for your obligations as he did."

Silently, John watched her. His eyes were so warm with understanding that she could have cried. Oh, how she was sick of these emotions she could so little control.

She sighed. "So it seems the king is an admirer of yours. That might help us someday. I don't want to be caught unaware, so tell me of the condition of Rame Castle."

"You know, I've come to believe that William might not truly have known what was going on there. The steward could have been the one deceiving him."

"John, you don't have to protect me. Regardless of whether he knew or not, William should have visited his family seat, evaluated its condition with his own eyes. And he didn't."

"I'll tell you anything you want to know, sweetling," he murmured. "Rame will be yours as well, and I know how you take care of everything that's yours."

She wasn't just giving her property away, she realized. He was offering to share his own. "Come, you can tell me all about it on the journey to Hillesley."

As they walked outside, she felt as if she finally put the ghost of William to rest. Though he had tried to please her in ways that mattered to a little girl, he'd had his flaws. And he might have ruined Castle Alderley and all its property, if he'd have taken control from her.

But not John. She trusted that he would know that she had the best interests at heart of all of her people. He seemed to value her help and her opinion. If all he had wanted was her property, he wouldn't care what she thought.

Could this be love? she suddenly wondered. Was she finally growing up, realizing what was important in her life?

She went on with her day, feeling better than she had in a long time. She was going to make this work. The king would want to hear John's side of the story. Patience might be all she needed to cultivate.

After supper that evening, Adalia hesitantly approached Elizabeth when she came into the kitchen for a tray for Anne.

"Might I speak with ye a moment?" Adalia asked.

"Of course," Elizabeth said with concern. The cook did not seem her usual sunny self. Was something else about to go wrong?

As Elizabeth had promised, she turned to see if John saw them. He nodded to her, and she told herself she wasn't asking permission, only granting him a courtesy so that he would not have to worry about her.

Elizabeth followed her into the cook's chamber, across the corridor behind the kitchens.

Adalia shut the door, then came to Elizabeth and took her hand. "You did not sleep in the kitchens last night."

"Forgive me for not telling you. I did not know myself what would happen."

"Bannaster did not . . . come back for ye, did he?"

"Nay!" she quickly said, patting Adalia's hand. "I was safe."

"You were with Sir John?"

Warily, Elizabeth nodded. "But not in the way you might be thinking. He has not— He is only protecting me."

Adalia closed her eyes in relief. "Oh, thank God above for that. I know he's been sniffin' around ye. Poor man, he thinks ye're but a maid."

She wanted to tell Adalia the truth, but how could she give the woman information she would have to keep hidden? It would make everything so much more complicated.

"He understands . . . how things are between us," Elizabeth finally said.

"Yet he still wants to protect ye. He's a good man. Maybe *I* should be flirtin' with him next!"

Adalia laughed, but Elizabeth realized she had to force an answering smile.

Was she already *jealous* of any attention John might give someone else? She didn't like the kind of woman that made her, one doubting of her own abilities.

Before these last few months, she'd never doubted any of her skills! Or perhaps she'd never been truly tried in a time of adversity.

John spent a tense evening, constantly watching Bannaster. Though Elizabeth had remained near his side as he'd asked her to, John kept expecting Bannaster to notice her again.

But the viscount did not seem to be imbibing like he had the previous evening. In fact, he seemed almost . . . melancholy, as if he'd been so confident in his plan to approach the king, but now had had proven to him that being a cousin did not necessarily sway a monarch.

And a man who'd lost confidence in one way to deal with a matter, often found a more dangerous method. John had warned the four Alderley guards to be extra cautious when on duty at the base of the tower. Philip was supposed to be suggesting the same thing to Bannaster's own soldiers, to see who among them would be inclined to protect a lady, regardless of what she was to his master.

Finally, John had confirmation that Bannaster had retired to his bed. Philip, who was playing dice with the soldiers, casually met John's gaze across the hall, and slightly inclined his head toward the corridor. Philip needed to meet with him? John wondered, feeling his tension begin to rise again.

But first, John escorted Elizabeth to his bedchamber. When he did not enter behind her, she gave him a questioning glance.

"I have to speak with Philip," he said. "I won't be long, and I'll be nearby in the corridor."

She frowned. "You do not have to worry about me constantly. Bannaster did not confront me today."

"You should not assume he is finished with you. Desperate men do desperate things. And a man long without a woman is a danger as well."

"Is that a hint?" she asked sweetly. "Or a threat?"

He had an urge to laugh, and it felt good. Why was he letting himself get nervous about his life with her? She was even amusing, and he liked that about her.

"I don't need to threaten," he whispered, backing away.

"Oh, I'll just succumb?" she answered.

He grinned. "You were the one who wanted to."

He left her looking nonplussed.

He walked down the corridor, took a turn, and found Philip waiting for him, leaning negligently against the wall.

"Well?" John said softly.

"As I said before, there are several good men in Bannaster's army that I would trust with my life—were I fighting on their side," Philip added.

"But do they at least agree that Bannaster should not be allowed up into the tower alone?"

"They did, but he is their lord. How would they stop him?"

"They would have the help of Alderley's soldier on guard, but what would stop Bannaster from having his own man killed for disobeying him?"

"And then again, in his anger at being denied, he might turn to the real heiress."

Though Philip spoke in a low voice, John winced. "You should not speak such things aloud."

"I was not followed."

"Are you so confident in your abilities?" John asked, telling himself to relax.

"You taught me to be that."

Suddenly Philip's head jerked forward, and he pitched into John's arms, unconscious. John only had the briefest glimpse of a club aimed at his own head. He let go of Philip's body to bring the crutch up, but he was too late. The blow caught him across the temple, a sharp, searing pain. The dark corridor turned to deep black as he passed out.

As John woke up, he couldn't decide whether his eyes were open or closed. There was nothing but blackness, and a dank, unused odor, and the faint sound of dripping water echoing in the distance.

And pain; he winced with the way his head pounded. It took him several moments before his thoughts became clear. He remembered Philip falling into him, then a club aimed at his head. It had all happened too fast for him to see the man wielding it.

He was lying on something hard and uneven, damp in spots. He reached above him as he sat up, not wanting to hit his head again.

A pounding ache made him hold still until the nausea subsided. He reached up and felt his face; he wasn't wearing a blindfold. He touched something wet at his temple, and knew he was bleeding. He followed the trace down his face, to his clothing, and detected no terrible wetness, so hopefully it was not too serious a wound.

He ran his hand over what he was sitting on, and it had the deep coldness of stone, rough where it had been carved.

Someone nearby groaned.

John went still. "Philip?" Was he actually lucky enough to be imprisoned with his man-at-arms?

For a moment, all he heard was deep, sporadic breathing.

"John?" Philip's voice was husky, ragged.

"I'm here. I just woke up."

"Can you see?"

"Nay, I cannot. At least we've not been blinded."

"Unless we've been blinded together."

John grunted. "I'm lying on a rock ledge."

"And I as well. You've explored no farther?"

"I was about to, until I heard you."

"Do you know what happened? I remember speaking with you and then—nothing."

"You were hit from behind, fell into me, and then I was clubbed across the head. From the way my voice sounds, I don't believe we're in a big room. I am going to follow the wall behind me and see where it leads. Can you stand?"

"I think so."

"Then you go to your left, I'll go to my right, and hopefully we'll meet."

It didn't take long. They shuffled their feet over the uneven floor, stepping in shallow puddles. The wall was rough, obviously carved, wet with moisture and moss. They met in minutes, then worked their way back. Several other "benches" were carved out of the rock.

Before they met again, John touched something made of wood. Splinters pierced his fingers as he explored. "I've found a door."

Philip was beside him a moment later. "It is as I feared then."

"We're in a dungeon."

"Alderley has a dungeon?" Philip wondered.

"I hadn't heard of one, but then I'm a bailiff. No soldiers mentioned it?"

"They're as much strangers here as we are."

For several minutes, they tried to break down the door, but it wouldn't budge.

"Then we have nothing to do but wait," John finally said, rubbing his aching shoulder.

"And wonder," Philip added darkly. "Think you we should yell?"

"A dungeon is usually deep enough for sound to be trapped, but you can give it a try."

Philip did, until his voice grew hoarse. Conversation was pointless, since they didn't want to discuss anything private for fear someone was listening. They both tried to sleep. John wasn't successful. His eyes were wide open when the first light registered.

"Do you see that, Philip?"

"Light in the cracks of the door?"

"Aye."

They remained silent, waiting. The light grew brighter, outlining the solid door. They stationed themselves on either side of it, hoping someone was fool enough to come in alone.

"Sir John," boomed a voice that echoed from the corridor outside.

"Who are you?" John demanded. "Let us see who falsely attacked us."

The man laughed. "No falsehood applies. I have been suspicious of your clerk for several days now. Our captain relies on him too much."

"You wanted my position?" Philip asked dryly.

Do you know him? mouthed John.

Philip grimaced and shook his head.

"You are too talented on the tiltyard for a clerk,

Sutterly," the man said. "I began to follow you yesterday, and tonight my patience was rewarded."

"With what?" Philip asked. "You found me talking to my first master."

"I heard your words. You said Lord Bannaster might turn to the real heiress if he was denied access to the tower."

Philip winced, and in the soft glow of faint light, John could see him mouth *I'm sorry.* John shrugged. It was too late for recriminations.

"I have been waiting for a chance to prove my loyalty," the soldier said. "When I bring you to Lord Bannaster, he'll recognize my ingenuity."

"No one knows we're here?" John asked dubiously.

"You're my captives. When Lord Bannaster awakens in the morning, I'll bring you both forth as my prize. Tell me who the real heiress is, and I'll see that you live."

As if a common soldier had control over that. John said, "I know not what you're talking about. I was referring to my fears for the heiress in the tower, should Lord Bannaster decide to harm her."

"Nay, that's not what was said," the soldier replied.

There was enough frustration in his voice that John hoped he'd open the door. But it didn't even rattle.

"You implied that Lord Bannaster is being duped," the soldier continued. "And if you know that, you're not who you seem, either. It will be a pleasure to get the truth from you both."

"I'd like to see you try," Philip said. "Come in here and test my skills yourself."

"Nay, I am no fool. Your confession can wait until morning. Sleep well."

"Who are you?" John yelled. "Your cleverness impresses me."

But the light faded away.

Philip said, "His prize tomorrow is obviously worth the wait."

"If it's just the two of us against him, we can overpower him," John said. "Let's try to sleep."

But John's thoughts moved crazily through his head. He was used to this feeling of expectation, of his muscles preparing for battle. God's Blood, hadn't he been desperate for action, to rid himself of his crutch and fight as he was able? But much as he told himself that he and Philip could triumph in the morning, he felt uneasy, worried.

And it was all because of Elizabeth.

For the first time in his life, someone else truly depended on him. As the youngest son, he'd had no responsibilities except to himself. Each day had been an adventure—but had he used that to replace his family? Now the weight of a title, two vast estates, many smaller properties—and one lone, vulnerable, but strong, woman—rested on him.

What would happen to Elizabeth should he not survive? Bannaster would probably have her. Or perhaps she'd fight so hard for her own choices, that the king would give her a stronger man to control her.

He was helpless, and now understood how Elizabeth had been feeling for a long time with so little to say in her life. Though he had thought her mistrust of him was about his family's neglect or the false rumors about himself, he was making everything too personal. She just had to learn to trust someone again. Maybe by not accepting her offer to share his bed, he'd taken a step toward proving he could be the one she should trust.

Chapter 20

Elizabeth came wide-awake in the middle of the night, and she didn't know why. Finding herself in bed alone, she was disappointed. Had she expected John to crawl into bed beside her, when he'd already refused the offer of her body?

But ah, she could not fault him for that. And he had given her a gift of pleasure she had never expected. She came up on her elbow. The fire had burned down, and she could see little in the shadows.

But the pallet was empty, and looked as if it had not been slept in.

She threw the coverlet to the side, and then lowered herself to the cold floor. How many hours had passed? She cautiously opened the door and peered into the corridor, but she saw nothing. She whispered his name, but heard no response.

John had said he'd be nearby. She could not imagine he would leave her unguarded.

She dressed in a hurry, then cautiously followed the torchlit corridors to the great hall, but remained out of sight behind the arch of the entrance. She peered in to see several dozen people sleeping on the floor, wrapped in blankets. But none of them looked like John—or Philip.

She could not search every chamber, so she headed back to John's. He would not abandon her. Even if she ascribed the worst motives to him, he would not abandon Alderley, and its power and wealth.

But nay, he was not like that. He might have come to fulfill a bargain between their families, but he had feelings for her now. He was a good, honorable man.

Whom she'd proven over and over again she didn't trust. Had she driven him away?

She had to stop thinking such things. When dawn arrived, she would not rest until she discovered what had happened to John.

But before she reached John's bedchamber, she spotted what she had not noticed earlier—his crutch laying against the corridor wall. She picked it up and stared all around her, as if suddenly there was menace in the darkness. She ran into his room, slammed the door behind her and leaned against it, her every sense alert to the possibility of someone out there trying to get in.

Minutes passed, and nothing happened. She

clutched the crutch to her as if it were the last remnant she had of John. For a moment, her future stretched out endlessly, and without him it seemed bleak and lonely and frightening.

Where was he?

When John next awoke, it was still black as pitch in the dungeon, but he had an instinctive feeling that dawn was approaching—and his confrontation with Bannaster.

Before he could speak, Philip suddenly said, "I remember!"

"You remember what?"

"Oh, 'tis good you're awake. I spent half the night wrestling with the identity of our captor."

"Hardly half the night. You were snoring almost immediately."

"Then I must have awakened hours ago. But I've finally put a face to that voice. I can't tell you his name, but he's a common soldier in Bannaster's army. I'll recognize him when I see him. He challenged me one day, and I might have made the mistake of defeating him rather too easily."

"How intelligent."

"I know. I humbly beg your forgiveness."

"I'll grant it when we're free."

"At least you're confident."

They settled into a tense silence that seemed to last a long time.

"Do you think he's forgotten about us?" Philip asked.

"I cannot believe so."

John found himself picturing Elizabeth in his bed, sleeping there without him. That made him a little too uncomfortable. He adjusted himself, and then sat up. Though he still had a lingering ache in his head, he felt good. He was restless with the need to move, but he couldn't pace and risk falling.

Perhaps he could hear something. He went to press his ear to the door—and found it ajar.

"Philip, the door is open, and you didn't hear it happen." He felt Philip at his back as he opened the door wide and moved out. "I knew you weren't awake hours."

Philip only snorted.

John's hands encountered the wall soon enough, proving that they were indeed in a corridor. They went left first, hit a dead end, and then walked back the other way. They found another door ajar, and stairs leading up.

"What do you make of this?" John asked, hesitating at the bottom. "Could it be a trap?"

"He had us well held. What would be the point?"

"I wish I had a sword," John said in frustration. "But let's go."

He led the way, climbing up slowly, regretting the annoyance of the splint still bound to his lower leg. He held one hand in front of him, and one trailing against the wall. After awhile, he wished he would have counted the steps, because it seemed to go on a long time.

Until he slammed his head on something above him.

"Ow!"

"What happened?"

John reached above and ran his hands over wood. "I think it's a trap door." It budged, although not much. "Come up beside me and help push."

Between the two of them, they lifted it up enough to see the shadows of a storage room, lit by a single torch in a wall bracket.

"'Tis the undercroft beneath the castle," John said, upon spotting the curved arches supporting the ceiling. "If there's someone in here, he's not paying attention to us."

"But someone left a torch to light our way," Philip said.

"I'll hold the door up, and you climb out and lift it farther."

The trap door was more unwieldy than heavy, and John was able to brace it with his legs spread and elbows locked. Philip climbed out, remaining low to the ground as he looked about.

He nodded down at John. "All set."

When John was beside him, and the trap door lowered, they discovered another set of steps, leading to the first floor above them.

"Someone deliberately let us go," Philip said, as he squinted up at the next trap door.

John eyed him. "Or 'tis a way to make sport out of our capture."

"Or 'tis the League of the Blade," Philip said solemnly.

"They said they wouldn't help me."

"Aha! So you believe!"

"I did not say that. But our fireside visitor told me I wasn't worthy."

"He had his doubts then. Apparently the League has decided in your favor."

"So somehow strangers got into the castle, found the dungeon, silently left all the doors open—when they could have just told us what they were doing."

"They don't like to work hand-in-hand with people. You have to be intelligent enough to work on your own, within their plans."

"You mean we were supposed to wake up at the right time?" he asked darkly.

"We did, did we not?"

"Hmph. Regardless of who let us out, we still have to tread carefully until we find this soldier who imprisoned us. He might have told Bannaster everything by now."

Philip shook his head. "I think not. He was all about the surprise and consequent adulation."

"So we need to find him before he sees us."

Philip looked him up and down. "You're filthy. We have to wash before anyone sees us."

"You, too."

After they climbed up through the next trap door, they found themselves in a corridor behind the kitchens. It was just dark enough that they only received an occasional curious stare from the servants they passed.

John opened the door to his chamber, Philip trailed in behind him—and then he saw Elizabeth. Her expression was shocked and relieved, and he thought there might be an extra sheen to her eyes.

But she simply drew herself up and calmly said, "I was worried when you didn't return." Her eyes widened as she took in their appearance. "What happened to you?"

John found himself wishing she would have thrown her arms around him, but she had herself well in control. He explained what had happened, and though she remained calm, he could sense her rising panic.

"Philip recognized the soldier's voice," John said. "We will find him."

"And do what?" she demanded. "You can't mean to kill him."

John shook his head. "We'll have to imprison him as he did to us, and hope that no one finds him until we've resolved this situation."

" 'Tis getting more and more complicated," she whispered. "I feel like a failure. You both will be in even more danger. When will it end?"

John tried to touch her arm, but she stiffened, and he let her turn away from him. "Elizabeth—"

"Do you think the League really helped you?" she asked with sudden hope.

John glanced at Philip, who put up both hands and remained silent.

"I know not," John said. "If we have unseen help, I don't know what they're doing, but I'll attempt to communicate with them, to join forces. Elizabeth, once again, I have to ask: let me take you away from here. We'll leave Bannaster a message, so he knows that Anne is not the true heiress."

She was already shaking her head. "He won't

believe that. He'll think it a trick to make him leave the castle in pursuit. He's already shown that he would take Anne to bed. I cannot risk it."

"You are a stubborn woman," he said angrily, gritting his teeth. "You care so little about your own life."

"There are others who need my care," she insisted.

He reluctantly admitted to himself that her loyalty and bravery were part of what drew him to her. "Very well. First we have to make sure that this soldier who suspects us is taken care of."

She looked between them with concern. "Be careful."

He gave her a smile. "Always. Now turn your back while we wash and change."

She glanced at the door.

"You're not going out of my sight," he added.

With a roll of her eyes, she found a stool and sat on it with her back to the chamber. "Hurry!"

Twenty minutes later, when they were ready to leave, Philip said, "The soldiers will be on the tiltyard. Let me go alone to find our captor."

"Nay, I will not have it," John said, feeling the need to accomplish *something*. "I have sat on my ass for days now and watched you have the fun of training."

"Fun?" Elizabeth said.

John glanced at her. "There is nothing in the world like pitting yourself against an opponent, using only your skill and brains to vanquish him."

"And a sword," Philip added.

"And then the next day being able to do it all

again," John continued, feeling pride in his accomplishments.

None of which would have happened if his father hadn't allowed him to leave home at sixteen. Had his father been helping him?

"But John, there's no point in all three of us going," Philip said. "The risk of capture will be greater."

"And if *you're* captured, Philip?" Elizabeth said.

John frowned. "Let us worry about that if it happens."

"And it won't," Philip said jauntily. "I can be very stealthy. You two wait here. I'll leave the castle by the lady's garden, avoiding the great hall, and return as quickly as I can."

When Philip had gone, John and Elizabeth looked at each other, and a tension rose between them.

Elizabeth was still feeling flustered by how overpowering her relief had been when she'd discovered that he was all right. She'd almost flung herself on him, dirt and all, when he'd walked into the room. She could have easily wept, which had made her feel weak.

But it wasn't weak to care for someone, and John was soon to be her husband. He pleased her in many ways, but there was so much she didn't know about how he would treat a marriage. And she desperately wanted to think about something else rather than Philip's vulnerability.

"John, when we're married—"

His head came up, and he grinned.

"Aye, I'm optimistic," she said.

"You just assume you'll always get your way."

"And will you mind if I'm the same when we marry?"

He made a great show of crossing his arms over his chest and frowning as if in contemplation. "Will you make my life miserable if I disagree with you?"

"Not as long as you have a good reason." She tried not to smile.

He leaned back to sit on his bed, and she found that incredibly distracting, as she remembered what had happened in that bed. And the scene afterward, where she'd seen him naked.

"Are you going to lose your thoughts when we marry?" he asked.

"You're very distracting," she said primly.

"I can be more distracting."

His gaze wandered down her leisurely, and she found herself wishing she were wearing her own clothing, which showed off her figure.

As if he hadn't touched everything already.

"So what about our marriage?" he asked, a half-smile on his lips.

For a moment, with John looking at her, her mind went totally and completely blank. "I cannot believe you've done this to me," she murmured. "I should be thinking about the danger Philip is walking into. I should be wondering how to handle a man so desperate for approval that he imprisoned you—"

He walked toward her slowly, and put his hands on her waist. "Nay, I will take care of that."

"Is that how it will be when we're married? You'll want to protect me from everything?"

"If I was the kind to keep secrets, you wouldn't know the condition Rame Castle is in."

"If I remember correctly, you didn't immediately tell me that."

He grinned. "That's because I thought I was talking to Anne."

She frowned, knowing that she could not protest. "And when we are married, you promise to tell me everything."

"Everything."

"Even if something happens while you're at Parliament?"

"You'll know everything I know. I'll send so many missives, my courier will be sick of us."

"You think I'm too controlling, don't you." She almost pouted, and was annoyed with herself.

"You can control me all you want," he said softly. "Just tell me where you want my hand."

She felt a little thrill go through her, and then was embarrassed at the same time. No man wanted to be overruled by a woman. He would be off in London, she would remain here, at Alderley, in charge of everything that mattered to her. That was how she'd always dreamed it would be. And he had his dreams too, of bringing his skills and fame to England. But as an earl, surely he would not have the time he'd once had for such adventures.

She would miss him, she realized suddenly. She had been separated from him for mere hours, and it had taught her the ache of the absence of him.

He was still waiting for an order, and the mischievous look in his eyes teased her.

"Put your hand . . . on my cheek," she said, lifting her chin in a challenge.

He grabbed her backside and squeezed.

She gasped, and in trying to get away from his hand, only pushed herself even closer to the rest of his body.

His very aroused body.

He leaned over her as if to bestow a kiss.

She quickly said, "Nay, I have not permitted such a thing. You may kiss me"—she thought about a safe spot, then pointed to her forehead—"here."

He pressed his lips very gently between her brows. He was warm all around her, and she felt very safe.

A male voice said, "You can kiss me if you'd like."

Elizabeth tried to break away, but John continued to hold her as he said, "And why would I kiss you, Philip?"

"Because I've solved today's problem."

John allowed her to turn about in his embrace, but kept an arm about her waist from behind. Philip seemed to think nothing of this, so gradually she relaxed.

"You found the soldier?" she asked.

"Nay, but I discovered that he's simply gone."

"What?" John said.

"It seems our captor has not been seen since last night. When he didn't appear for guard duty this morning, the others went searching for him. His possessions are gone, as is a horse."

"He just . . . left?" she asked in surprise.

"That makes no sense," John said.

"Unless he was forcibly removed," Philip offered, smiling. "I told you that the League has decided to help you now."

"If that's true, then they could help more."

"Maybe they are," Philip said.

Elizabeth said, "But how do we know this soldier didn't tell someone about who he had in the dungeon?"

"He didn't want to share the glory," Philip answered. "And also, I walked about in plain sight through the great hall, where Milburn was, and no one said a word."

In a low voice, John said, "That could have been dangerous."

"But don't we live for the thrill of it?"

The two men grinned at each other, and Elizabeth felt . . . left out, even uneasy.

"Well I'm hungry," she said, and they both looked at her. "I'm certain Adalia saved us some food. And I have yet to go to Anne this morn."

John sighed, and his arm fell away from her waist. "By all means, you must have food. Allow us to escort you."

She handed him his crutch, and he sighed as he put it under his arm. "I'm sore from this thing."

In the kitchens, instead of smiling, Adalia greeted them with a worried frown. She opened her mouth to speak, then glanced at the two men.

"We'll wait near the great hall," John said.

When he and Philip were far enough away, Adalia said, "Bannaster just received a messenger, and immediately he doubled the guards on the tower."

"And you don't know why?" Elizabeth asked, as all the worry that had eased with John's playing came rushing back.

"Nay. He said not to prepare a tray for her ladyship. And worst of all, he wants to see ye."

"Where is he?"

"In the great hall. His scowl is terrible to behold. He was out on the tiltyard training with his men when he received the mysterious news. So he's still in there in training armor, his sword in its scabbard."

"At least he's not waving it around."

"Promise me ye'll be careful," Adalia said, touching her arm.

"I'll be in front of the whole hall. I'll be fine."

"Ye weren't last time. I had to set fire to me own kitchen to stop the brute."

"You were the heroine that day."

"And don't ye forget it." Adalia glanced at the two men. "What about them?"

"I'm going to ask them to remain here," she said. "Will you mind?"

"I might put them to work."

"I wouldn't blame you." Elizabeth walked over to John and Philip and relayed the news. "I need you both to remain here."

"I'm not leaving you unguarded," John said predictably.

"But what if this has something to do with your captor? What if he was too frightened to go through with the plan, and sent word to Bannaster instead?"

"You didn't hear his gloating," Philip said. "He's gone—and he had help disappearing."

"Still, I need you to wait here. You can watch, hidden, but please, trust me. Something feels very wrong."

Once again, she stared at John, waiting for him to overrule her. But he only nodded, and she felt profound relief.

"Thank you," she murmured. "I won't worry so much."

"But I will," he said softly. "You are a woman who takes on too much."

She gave him a fleeting smile, then walked into the great hall. Bannaster stood near the hearth, speaking to Milburn.

They both turned to look at her, and then Bannaster gestured for her to come forward. Wearing a chest and back plate, he looked more impressive than in his fine court garments. The scabbard belted to his waist looked as if it housed an intimidating weapon.

To her surprise, Bannaster sat in one of the cushioned chairs before the fire, and motioned her to the other one. She had a flash of memory, her parents sitting there, smiling at each other, smiling at her.

She sat down and waited.

"I just received a missive," he said, wasting no time.

She nodded politely, trying to look baffled.

"Someone at Rodmarton Castle overheard news that interested me."

A cold sweat suddenly broke out over Elizabeth's

body, and she prayed it was not visible. Rodmarton Castle was where her sisters were being fostered.

Bannaster smiled grimly. "He wants me to pay him well for it, and I shall."

"My lord, I don't understand why you're telling me this."

"I am told that somewhere in Alderley, Lord Russell is in disguise, trying to aid his betrothed."

She whispered a silent prayer to God. *Let John remain hidden.* Had her foolish sisters discussed her plight where someone could overhear? Though it was the hardest thing she ever did, she gave him a puzzled frown. "Surely this courier misheard, my lord."

He ignored her protest. "Milburn and I have been discussing who Russell could be. Milburn believes he could not be a regular servant—after all, the man is a knight, hard to disguise."

She was dying to glance at the kitchens, wishing she could somehow signal John and Philip to flee.

"There is only one knight who is not a member of the household," Bannaster continued.

She could not pretend ignorance without looking like she deliberately lied. "Who—you mean Sir John Gravesend?"

He was watching her carefully as he nodded.

"But my lord, I have been working with him every day. Never once did he portray anything but a bailiff. Aye, he was once a knight, but he could not afford to remain one."

"He's been waiting for the right moment, using you to get to Lady Elizabeth."

And that's what he'd first been doing when he arrived at Castle Alderley, Elizabeth thought, feeling the threat of hysterical laughter.

"That cannot be true," she said firmly.

"We've simply found him out before he had the chance. Now why don't you tell us where he is. I understand you have spent the last several nights in his company." Bannaster's eyelids were half closed in sensual mockery.

"My lord, I do not—"

"We have found him, my lord!" a man cried.

Chapter 21

E lizabeth spun in her chair in time to see John and Philip dragged forward by two soldiers. Before she had more than a moment's feeling of terror, John sent one to the floor and came up with his sword. The other soldier pulled Philip away and forced him to his knees.

There were shouts and screams as people backed away from the armed man. With a flick of his wrist, John cut the bindings of his splint, and it fell in pieces.

Bannaster had already surged to his feet. But instead of looking dismayed at John's freedom, he wore a grin of triumph as he drew his own sword.

"Get back!" he shouted at his soldiers.

Why had she not noticed how many soldiers there

were in the great hall at midmorning? she thought desperately. Bannaster must have been lying in wait to surprise John.

"Russell," Bannaster called, striding into the center of the great hall, "How good to finally meet you."

There were gasps all around, and several people looked at Elizabeth, wide-eyed, betraying their knowledge of her identity. Luckily, Bannaster and Milburn were focused on John.

John circled slowly, his sword raised, keeping an eye all around him, even as he watched Bannaster warily.

"Nay, no one shall challenge you except myself," Bannaster said. "It is only fitting, as we fight over a woman."

"We fight not over a woman," John shouted. "We fight over your unchivalrous treatment of my betrothed."

Bannaster closed the gap between them, but still circled. "I am only righting your wrong. You left Lady Elizabeth alone for months."

"I came the moment I heard," John said, feinting forward with his sword.

Bannaster hopped nimbly to the side. "Ah, yes, how did it feel to discover that you were third choice?"

John smiled. "I am the youngest son. Being third comes naturally to me."

"You will lose, you know," Bannaster said, then slashed suddenly at John's legs. "Why not just take the maidservant you already seem fond of?"

"I simply used the girl."

Elizabeth gasped and tried to look outraged. Adalia walked to her side and put a comforting arm around her.

The two men finally crossed swords in a great blow that echoed through the hall. Both sprang away unharmed.

During the shouts and cheers, Adalia whispered, "Did ye know who he was?"

Elizabeth gave the slightest nod of her head.

"And he you?"

Another brief nod.

"Ah, what a man," Adalia said in appreciation.

Elizabeth glanced at her in surprise. But at another clash of swords, she gave her full attention to the sword fight—and watched in awe at the demonstration John gave. He moved with a speed difficult to see, thrusting, cutting, parrying away his opponent's sword before it came anywhere near him. Bannaster's glee gradually faded as a look of concentration came over him.

Wringing her hands together, Elizabeth glanced at Philip, who was still on his knees, held at each elbow by a soldier. All three of them seemed engrossed in the combat.

John stepped away again. Bannaster was breathing heavily, but John looked barely winded. He only smiled with confidence as Bannaster tried to hide his anger.

"You have been at Alderley for many days now," Bannaster said. "You have yet to even see Lady Elizabeth."

"I don't need to see her to know she needs my help," John parried Bannaster's sword away as if a child swung it. "Can you not find a woman without having to imprison her?"

"She's being kept safe, not imprisoned."

John laughed without humor. "I don't think she'd agree with you."

Once more Elizabeth looked at Philip—but he was gone, the two soldiers who'd been holding him left groaning in a heap. No one else seemed to notice, so she quickly looked back at the sword fight.

But . . . how could this possibly end? John couldn't very well kill Bannaster—he was a viscount, and the king's cousin, who'd just appealed quite legally to the king in a matter both men were involved in. They could not fight to the death, as if hundreds of years of civilization had not passed.

If Bannaster put John back in the dungeon, this time there would be guards. The League could not so easily provide aid.

Yet John was obviously the stronger, more skilled swordsman. She found herself wishing she could have seen him win those tournaments in Europe.

Perhaps Alderley could host a tournament. John could—

What was she thinking? John could die right now—or he could marry her and go off on his adventures like before. And she'd convinced herself that that's what she'd always wanted.

But she found she couldn't imagine being separated from him, even if it meant she had to share the management of Alderley with him.

But would he want to remain with her? Once they'd slept together, perhaps he'd tire of her. She couldn't imagine tiring of his kisses and caresses, but he was a man of the world—he had had lovers before her.

She had to stop distracting herself. Two men might be battling to the death over possession of her. Each wanted the biggest share for himself. She knew she was just the newest toy for Bannaster, but what was she to John?

A great cry went up from the spectators, and all fell back as Bannaster began to chase John. John jumped up on a table and went running down it, vaulting to the floor at the far end, closest to the doors. Suddenly, she saw Philip there, and he looked dramatically shocked to find himself in the midst of soldiers. He dove back into the center of the great hall, and a great mass of men followed him as he led them on a chase to the far end, and through the corridor.

Leaving the entrance to the great hall free of men.

John suddenly swept into a bow, though a table separated Bannaster and him. Then he turned and left the castle.

He'd made a fool of Bannaster with his skill, but no one had gotten hurt, not even a scratch.

"Seize him!" shouted Bannaster, as he went running to the doors.

But many of the soldiers had followed Philip, who was probably leading them on a merry chase through the castle. The others had been caught off guard by

John's unexpected retreat. By the time they followed their lord to the inner ward, Elizabeth had no doubt that John would be gone. She went to the doors and leaned against the frame, watching the commotion in the ward below, as soldiers picked their way between carts and horses, dogs, and chickens.

She stared at the gatehouse, feeling almost lost.

John was gone.

How could he possibly return? Bannaster knew who he was—everyone would recognize his face. The danger to John would be too great.

Elizabeth hugged herself, feeling the strangest urge to cry.

And Adalia was there again, standing beside her. "Will ye be all right?"

Elizabeth nodded. "Of course. John won't give up. I only hope he's not killed."

"He seems rather good at takin' care of himself. But he hasn't been too good at takin' care of you."

Elizabeth looked about, and then said in a low voice, "He wanted to take me away, but I wouldn't let him."

"Why ever not?"

"I could not leave you all here to suffer for what I'd done. I said I would find a way to fix things, and I will."

But things were looking more and more bleak. She had never even asked John where to find him should he have to leave the castle.

Adalia tsked and shook her head. "Ye're tryin' so hard to be brave. I wish ye'd see that ye're not in this alone."

"I feel very alone," she whispered.

Bannaster charged back up the stairs to the great hall, and Elizabeth fell back. But he came right at her.

"You tell your mistress that I've driven Russell away. Like a coward, he obviously does not want her enough to fight to the end for her."

She bowed her head.

"Tell her that she will soon understand that I am doing what is in her best interest. I have sisters—I know how silly women can be." He swept by her, calling, "Milburn! We need to strengthen our defenses. More soldiers up on the battlements and in the gatehouse. That man is not getting back in here."

Elizabeth heaved a sigh when the men were far enough away. "Adalia, I need a tray for her ladyship."

"You go on up to her, Anne. She'll be able to comfort ye."

Adalia was right. Up in the tower, Anne put her arms around Elizabeth after hearing the news.

"You betrothed is a man who can take care of himself," Anne insisted.

"And you know this even though you haven't met him?" Elizabeth asked, trying to keep her words light.

"Everything you have said about him convinces me of it. Be confident, he will return for you."

"I keep trying to tell myself that I don't need him," Elizabeth whispered. "But 'tis a lie. I think I might be in love with him."

Anne drew her to a bench and sat beside her. "Then that is a good thing."

"How can it be good?" she cried. "I had my whole life planned out, and loving someone so desperately was never a part of it. I never meant to give my husband such power over me. I wanted my heart free, so that I could have my own life while he had his. Now I might not even be permitted to marry him, when I want so much to—" She broke off, finding herself dangerously close to tears.

"He will return for you," Anne said firmly. "We both know it."

"And possibly be killed," she whispered, hugging herself.

"Nay, Bannaster seems to be a man who takes his king's word seriously. He will not jeopardize his future by harming a fellow nobleman. He thinks the king will rule in his favor, so he won't have to. But the king will honor your betrothal. Surely he will not risk alienating two such impressive houses as Alderley and Russell. And then you and Lord Russell will discuss your marriage, and make it work to the satisfaction of you both."

"John is a man of adventure, Anne. He'll leave me much of the year as I've always wanted a husband to do."

"Stop this foolish worrying and trust yourself."

Elizabeth had always done that—and now she didn't know if it was enough.

John and Philip met up at a clearing in the woods, a place decided on from the moment they'd gone into Alderley in disguise. Philip was leading two horses.

"You're none the worse for battle," Philip said, smiling. "Did it feel good?"

"It would have felt better to separate his ribs with my sword, but I am patient."

"Surely the soldiers will give you another try, since they're probably looking for us."

"Let them look. They won't find us."

"Will Lady Elizabeth be all right with us gone?"

"She'd be the first to tell us that she can take care of herself. But I'll return to her side tonight. For now show me the way to the army."

After a journey of several miles, they passed the inspection of several guards before entering the encampment spread out across a meadow in the heart of a woodland. Pavilions for the higher-ranking knights were scattered between many campfires. Though several soldiers worked over cauldrons preparing the midday meal, the rest were gathered in an open area of the meadow, where the grass had been stamped into dirt as a hundred soldiers trained.

Still mounted, John and Philip watched the training exercises for several minutes from the cover of the trees. Ogden and Parker rode up to join them in the woods.

Parker, short and broad, squinted up at John. "Good to see ye again, milord."

John smiled briefly. "My thanks for your help when we were attacked by thieves. My lady and I will not forget it."

Ogden grinned. "She's a fine woman, milord. Had a dagger out ready to defend herself."

John nodded and looked back at the training. "I would have thought that learning new skills would make Alderley's men eager. Why is it not so?"

Ogden spit out the end of his long mustache. "The missive from Lady Elizabeth settled 'em down a bit, but they don't trust us—nor you. Just another suitor fightin' over their lady, accordin' to them. Maybe ye're her last hope, and not the right man."

John arched a brow at him.

"Just repeatin' their words," Ogden said, reddening.

John debated simply riding up to the soldiers and introducing himself, but how could he just demand their allegiance, when they were already doubtful of him?

And then an idea came to him. He glanced at Ogden. "Have you had an informal tournament to test their skills against each other?"

Ogden frowned. "Nay, milord, though it be a good idea."

"I'll be joining."

"Won't they hesitate to—"

"But they won't know who I am. Find me a helm and training armor and bring them to me here. Parker can distract them all by organizing the tournament. Group the men informally to fight each other, with a winner being declared before any blood loss. The winners continue to play each other, until there is only one man left standing."

Philip smiled. "And you assume you'll be one of the winners?"

"I don't assume it will be easy," John said, "not if they've learned Parker's skill with the sword."

Parker cleared his throat. "Go on with ye, milord."

John waited in the forest while his three men-at-arms gathered together Alderley's soldiers. The idea of a tournament was at first greeted without spirit, but gradually the men began to become enthused, especially when everyone was ordered to keep their helm on. The knights recognized each other of course, but not all of the simple soldiers. Ogden mixed everyone up, and John was able to slip into a group as it spread out near the trees.

His first opponent was a common soldier by the look of his garments, but he fought with an eager skill that was impressive. Where John wanted to circle, getting an impression of his foe, the soldier was too eager and tired himself trying to chase. Ogden was judging their group of fighting men, and called a winner when John had the man on his knees, his sword knocked from his hand.

By John's fourth bout, there were only a dozen men left, most of them knights. More than one man had angrily demanded to know his identity, but John spoke only with the skill of his sword. Everyone was exhausted, and the sun's heat rose in waves off their armor. The losers became the spectators, falling and propping their heads on their helms to watch the tournament.

When it came down to the final two men, one of them John, he sensed the crowd's curiosity, knew they were still trying to guess his identity. Though tired, he was ready to battle, especially against an opponent who was trying to pretend he could keep his sword arm up. But John could see the trembling in his hand. This was no time for a cautious approach. John came out swinging his sword with purpose, forcing his opponent to jump over his blade and stagger. But the knight raised his sword enough to parry another hard blow. John felt the concussion right up through his shoulder. His breathing was a harsh gasp; the heat inside his helm made perspiration flow freely down his face, stinging his eyes. But he couldn't lift his visor to wipe it away. Distantly, he heard men cheering. With his sword he battered the shield until it crashed against the knight's body.

The knight groaned and tried to stumble away, but John didn't allow him to retreat. Only when he'd fallen and was unable to lift his sword did Ogden and Parker call the match and declare John the winner.

His opponent managed to stand, swaying. He pulled off his helm. "I am the captain of the guard. Who has defeated me?"

John sheathed his sword and removed his helm. The cheering was suddenly replaced by a tense silence.

"I know you not," the captain said. "I am Sir Jasper. Who are you?"

John reached down inside his shirt and pulled forth the chain about his neck. He donned the ring slowly, letting the emerald catch fire in the sun. "I am John, Baron Russell, and by contract with your late liege lord, I am betrothed to Lady Elizabeth."

The captain's eyes widened. "My lord, why did you not show yourself to us?"

"Doubts about my abilities and my claims have been spoken here among Alderley's soldiers." John turned slowly in a circle, meeting as many eyes as he could. "I wanted it understood that I am capable of standing at your side, defending Alderley, defending your lady. We cannot allow Bannaster, who banished you from your own home, to succeed. When I need you, will you be at my call?"

One by one, the soldiers and knights rose to their feet, their expressions ranging from determination to exultation.

Sir Jasper nodded to him. "We gladly offer you our support, my lord. We will march with you now, if you need us."

John finally smiled, looking at all the exhausted men who puffed out their chests and reached for their swords. "Now is not the time, Sir Jasper, but you have my gratitude."

A low murmur of voices began behind John, and he could see the wary expressions of the soldiers in front of him. He turned around to see four strangers emerging from the trees.

Philip came to his side, his expression intent. "More guests?"

John recognized the stranger who had not denied his connection to the League of the Blade. Though the three other men with him were not dressed alike in livery, they all moved with a unison and professionalism that marked them as trained by the same master.

Sir Jasper said, "Lord Russell, shall we disarm them?"

John shook his head. "I recognize one man. Wait until you have my orders."

Together, John and Philip walked across the meadow to meet the four strangers. The man they'd met before they arrived at Alderley now bowed courteously to John. In his face glowed the wisdom and experience that made his age so hard to determine. The other three men with him wore expressions of interest, but it was plain who led them.

"Lord Russell, it is good that we meet," the stranger said.

John nodded. "I think you and I have been in close proximity recently."

Philip grinned. "You do enjoy making an entrance. You'll have to tell me how you snuck into the castle, released us from the dungeon, and removed that pesky soldier all in a night."

The man merely smiled and shrugged.

"You *did* release us from the dungeon," Philip said.

"Since you deserved to be released, I am glad that it was done," the stranger said.

"Not exactly an answer," John said. "But since I 'deserved' to be released, have I earned your approval?"

"You have been a source of strength for Lady Elizabeth Hutton. So far you have been able to aid

her without allowing her people to be harmed."
He glanced at Alderley's soldiers behind John.
"Your next move is of interest to me."

"Then perhaps you would help train Lady Elizabeth's soldiers? Philip tells me that the legends claim
your knowledge of stealth is impressive. They will
need everything you can teach them, if we are to invade the castle with little death and destruction."

The stranger glanced at his three men. Though
no one spoke, it was as if they could read each other's expressions.

"Very well," the stranger said at last. "Our aid
will be a tool to use as you deem fit. It will be up to
you to choose your course wisely. You may have the
use of my men for a sennight, no more."

"Then that will have to be enough," John said. "I
think matters will come to a head before that. You
have my gratitude. Allow me to introduce you to Sir
Jasper, the captain of the guard. You will be working
with him, for I am needed urgently elsewhere."

The day passed with excruciating slowness as
Elizabeth tried to pretend that everything would
work out. She avoided the great hall, because Bannaster was too happy with himself, as if the king's
decision was a foregone conclusion.

And she was avoiding her own people, who
looked on her with pity. Maybe they were disappointed to think that her betrothed had been there,
but had proven unable to overcome Bannaster.

She found herself hoping for a clandestine message from John, but received none.

That night, she retired alone to his bedchamber. It had been stripped bare of his few belongings by soldiers searching on Bannaster's orders. Yet it gave her comfort to be in John's bed, to imagine his scent lingering on the cushions.

She fell asleep pretending that he was with her, and awoke hours later to find him hovering over her, his hand covering her mouth.

Her body went stiff with shock, and then when he released her, she threw her arms about his neck and just held on.

He was warm, and he was safe, and he smelled like—

Straw.

She lifted her head off his shoulder and looked up into his face. "John, how did you get back into the castle?" she whispered frantically. "What if someone saw you? What if—"

"No one saw me," he said, caressing the side of her face, and then her hair.

"You came back," she murmured, looking up into his strong face.

As she traced the scar down his left cheek, she felt her emotions overwhelm her. He had risked everything for her, and she wanted to risk everything for him. She pressed her lips to his scar, and felt him go rigid in her arms. Her mouth worshiped the hurts he'd sustained in his hard life, when he'd thought himself unwanted by his family, when he'd thought himself alone.

She didn't want him to be alone anymore.

He was breathing heavily when her light kisses traveled across the stubble covering his jaw.

"Elizabeth—"

She silenced him with a kiss on the mouth. His lips, so firm and smooth, finally shaped themselves to the pressure of hers. She held his face in her hands and pressed her mouth to his over and over, memorizing the texture and the touch.

And then the taste. She angled her head and deepened the kiss. He groaned, but did not take control, just allowed her to do as she wished.

And she was so grateful, so appreciative. He understood her as no man had ever attempted to. She tasted him with her tongue, darted into his mouth and retreated over and over again, until she could feel him trembling. She ran her hands through his hair, fisting them in it to hold him to her, although it was unnecessary. He was grasping her by the waist, sitting by her side on the bed.

It wasn't enough. She was desperate to be closer to him. Dressed only in her smock, she climbed to her knees, letting the coverlet fall around her.

She finally broke the endless kiss, her lips tender and trembling, to stare into his eyes.

Then she pulled the smock up her body and over her head, leaving her naked.

He inhaled sharply, and his hot gaze traveled down, lingering on her breasts, and especially at the curls that hid her womanhood from him. She pulled the leather tie that held her hair plaited behind her, and it slid across her back and over her shoulders.

He would have reached for her, but she spread his arms wide, so that she could touch his chest. She'd seen the wonders he could perform with a sword, and now she wanted to see even more. She pulled the belt loose at his waist, and it came free, along with his scabbard, which she let fall gently to the floor. She pulled him to his feet beside the bed and rose to stand with him. He was wearing a black doublet and hose, which must hide him in the shadows. But it made him look different than he had as a simple bailiff with a splint covering his bare leg beneath his tunic. Now he looked like a knight, like a baron.

And it thrilled her to know he wanted her as much as she wanted him. Naked, she moved around him, loosening the laces of his doublet, helping to push it up his body as he pulled it over his head. Next came his shirt, and she slipped her hands beneath it to touch the bare skin of his chest while he fumbled trying to pull it over his head.

"I watched you bathe the other night," she whispered, when the handsome expanse of his chest was before her, the ring hanging over his heart.

While his hands slid down her arms, he gave her an arched brow of surprise.

"I wasn't asleep," she continued. "I watched you disrobe, and I studied your body with a curiosity that rather shocked me."

"I hope I measured up," he murmured against her ear.

She sighed as he spread kisses down her neck and pulled her against him. Her breasts were pressed to the hard heat of his skin, and they ached with an insistence that drove her farther in this wicked display of her need for him.

She slid her hands down the slope of muscles that played across his chest, through the feathering of hair scattered there, down to the belt to which his hose was tied. She undid each point with a tug, and the fact that he shuddered each time sent an answering wave of desire through her. She felt alive with the need to join with him, to be one with him. Her skin itched with it; her mind was consumed by it. When she was able to push the last of his garments off, she stared down at his engorged penis, which brushed against her body, making her shudder.

He lifted her chin and searched her eyes. "Do not be afraid, sweetling."

She gave him a wicked smile. "Oh, fear is the last thing I'm thinking about."

When he returned her smile in relief, she kissed him again, pressing herself to him, feeling the promise of his erection caught between them. His big arms crushed her to him, as if he needed to be closer. His kisses were wild and passionate, and the brush of his chest hair across her sensitive nipples helped fan the rising flame that her need had become. She reached to touch his penis, but he only allowed it for a moment.

"Ah, sweetling, I want this night to last, and your touch is sure to hasten my pleasure."

"But I don't understand. I need to touch you."

"First, I need to touch you. I want you prepared for me."

Though she frowned her bemusement at him, she

did not argue. Though she had led the encounter to this point, he now took over.

And she loved it. She didn't know what he would do, and that only increased her pleasure. They swayed in the center of the chamber, their hands seeking, caressing. He bent her back over his arm, so that his lips and tongue could arouse her breasts. Even the ring dangling against her was an erotic sensation. She let herself lean back in his embrace, knowing he would never drop her. His lips tugged at her breasts, and when his teeth nipped her, she shuddered and sagged in his arms. One hand slid down her back and over the rounded curve of her buttocks. Her flesh tingled with the pleasure of it, especially as the tips of his fingers gently teased the cleft between them.

His hand continued its decent, tugging at her knee, lifting her leg from the floor to press himself deeper between her thighs. The length of his erection rode the depths of her as she hung in his embrace. His hardness was the most intimate caress, and he used it against her with precision, knowing where to rub himself.

His mouth moved between her nipples, suckling and licking, his big hands held her body to him, while his penis rubbed and probed. As the rising pleasure became a madness that seemed to have no end, she groaned and tried to press his entrance into her body, but he would have none of it. She lost touch with the floor, lost herself in the sensations, and then lost her last touch on reality when pleasure exploded inside her. Her body shuddered helplessly, as waves kept rising through her.

With a groan, John turned and braced her against the edge of the high bed, pulling her thighs about his waist, at last beginning his entrance into her body. She couldn't stop moving, couldn't stop pulling him tighter against her and the pleasure continued to throb inside her.

"Easy, sweetling," he murmured, bending over her on the bed. "I don't wish to hurt you. A woman's first time—"

"I don't care," she said, using her feet against his backside to push him into her.

His brow was wet with perspiration, his face a grimace as he held back from her, as if he knew her body better than she did.

Maybe it was so, but right now she needed to be joined with him. She ran her hands over every part of his body she could reach, arched her hips off the bed to press him deeper. He gasped when she touched his nipples, so she concentrated her efforts there, knowing how wondrous such ministrations on her body felt. His skin, at first so smooth and soft there, pebbled beneath her fingers.

At last, with a shudder, he pulled on her hips and buried himself inside her.

The pain was a momentary burn that swiftly faded beneath the thrill of knowing that, at last, she was one with the man meant to be her husband, her mate. He began to move inside her.

And pleasure, so new and wondrous, began to

unfurl again, beginning at the fullness of him stretching her flesh, rubbing even more intimately against her. His skin, smooth on his chest, rough with hair on his legs where he pressed her thighs wide, made her own flesh come alive with sensation.

His feet on the floor, his body pinning her to the bed, he held himself up with his arms. His eyes were closed, his expression intense as he concentrated on their joining. She was glad to give him the pleasure he'd given her, which was even now working back into feverish intensity. She clutched his hips with her thighs, linked her feet behind his back, and let him ride her. Once again he teased and tormented her with his body, surging deep, or pulling out a second too long until the loss of him made her panic. Her craving of him was a wild thing all on its own, and she lost herself within it, mindless, knowing only the craving of pleasure that he could give her.

Chapter 22

John was lost. Never had he let himself become a part of a woman during lovemaking, almost forgetting where she ended and he began.

But this was Elizabeth—beautiful and bold and so demanding, even though she was a virgin before tonight. The depths of her had a heat that burned him. He felt grasped by the tightness of her body, and it was bliss to pull away, then thrust deeper.

The taste of her breasts, the little cries that passion wrung from her, the slap of their bodies coming together, all conspired to send him hurtling toward his own release, though he tried to delay it.

At last, when she climaxed again, arching her hips up beneath him, with a shudder he gave himself up to the bliss of it and joined her.

They came back to themselves slowly, their skin wet with perspiration. She left one leg draped around his hip, and the casual rub of her heel against his ass was a bold reminder of the uninhibited way she had accepted the pleasures of lovemaking. He was still propped on his elbows, looking down into her face, knowing he wouldn't be able to stay in this position much longer, braced as his feet were against the floor.

But he didn't want to leave the comfort and pleasure of her body.

She grinned up at him, breathing hard, letting her fingers trace down his scar. He turned his head and caught the tip of one finger in his mouth.

She closed her eyes and sighed. "It is so easy to forget that there is another world outside this bedchamber," she murmured.

"When we are married, it will be many days before I allow you to even remember that."

She laughed, and her breasts bounced pleasantly against his chest.

With a groan, he started to lift himself away, but with her arms and legs she caught and held him tight.

"Don't go," she whispered.

"I won't. Let me make us more comfortable in bed."

Pulling from within her body seemed like the hardest thing he'd ever done, but then he swept her up in his arms, deposited her in the middle of the bed, and then climbed in beside her. He pulled her back against him and leaned into the cushions, so grateful for the warm weight of her. Her hair spilled across his chest, and he tipped her head up to kiss her lips, now red and swollen.

His possession of her had done that. And she'd accepted it all.

"Tell me how you came back here," Elizabeth said. "Is that mysterious League finally helping you?"

He smiled. "Aye, we do have the aid of the League, but returning to Alderley was all me—with some help from my men and your healer friend, Rachel."

"Rachel?"

"When Philip and I left here, we met up with Ogden and Parker. They took me to your army, where I was impressed with the skill of your captain of the guard."

"Sir Jasper?" she cried softly. "They are all well?"

"Aye, and they live to serve you. They are training hard, even as we speak, with assistance from the Bladesmen."

Her smile faltered. "Training for what?"

"Training in case they are needed. No attack is planned, but we must be prepared, sweetling." That was the truth—for now. "Bannaster would not be foolish enough to think he had frightened me away. He had to know I'd try to return."

She pressed a kiss to his chest, and cuddled against his shoulder. "There were so many soldiers on guard today. They searched everyone who came in."

"Philip thought the ultimate disguise would be as a woman with child."

She gaped at him, and then bit her lip, probably to keep from laughing.

"Oh, I knew it wouldn't work," he said. "Even pregnancy could not explain my size. So we decided I had to come inside a shipment regularly expected."

"The soldiers inspected everything that came through the gatehouse! I sat there in the inner ward this afternoon, watching, as if—"

She paused, and his heart beat faster inside, knowing that she cared about him.

"As if I would finally see them capture you," she continued in a whisper. "I found myself praying that you would give up trying to help me, that you'd protect yourself rather than come back here."

As she turned her head away, he saw her face in profile, knew that she was still troubled. And who could blame her? They were not free to marry yet— and he sensed some deep part of her still resisted the true dependency of such a relationship.

"As if I would leave you to him," John scoffed, trying to keep her mood light. "So I hid in a shipment of straw for the stables."

"And they didn't search the cart?"

"Of course they did, but this is where we used Rachel's help. She took us to the village blacksmith, who laid boards across me to create a false bottom in the cart."

The admiration in her eyes warmed him. He would be content to make her happy for the rest of his life. Such a notion startled him, and he almost lost his thoughts. Content to stay here in Alderley, one home, seeing the same faces every day?

"A false bottom?" she prodded, twirling his ring about her finger.

Her thigh slid up his.

"Sweetling, the more you move, the less I'm able to remember how to talk."

She rolled away, looking guilty. "Forgive me."

He pulled her back. "So where was I? Ah, yes, the false bottom. It was very narrow under there and hard to breathe. I lay flat on my back, the floor literally resting on my chest. The journey to the castle seemed to be the longest of my life—not to mention the bumpiest. My back must surely be a mass of bruises."

She lifted herself and pushed him. "Roll over and let me see what you suffered in pursuit of my castle and me."

He arched a brow. "I already have a castle. Think not that there's any reason but for you that I suffer such indignities."

She stared at him for a moment too long, her expression suddenly serious. Did she truly still harbor doubts about his motivations? As if she realized what she revealed, she lightened the moment by rolling her eyes. With a push, she had him on his stomach, where he propped his head on his crossed arms. She swept the sheet away and he was naked. He felt the lightest touch of her fingers across his shoulder blades. He shivered.

"Ah, I see the bruises," she murmured.

To his surprise, she placed gentle kisses there. Her hands swept down his back, and she cupped his ass.

"More bruises. You have not enough flesh to pillow you."

He received another kiss there, and the fanning of her breath across his thighs put any thought of discomfort from his mind.

"So go on with your story," she said.

But she was draped across the back of his legs as she spoke. He felt her hair curling about him. He couldn't remember what they'd even been talking about.

"The uncomfortable cart?" she prodded, and then lightly slapped his ass.

He shook his head to clear his thoughts. Pressing his forehead into his arms, he said, "Of course. The cart was inspected at the gatehouse. A farmer brought me through at his own peril."

She stopped touching him. "Another man who risked himself for me."

He looked over his shoulder to see her sad face. "Elizabeth, don't. Think you they all wish to be ruled by Bannaster? They much prefer the master they know."

"They don't know you," she countered.

He heard the edge in her voice. He would have rolled over to face her, but seeing his erection up close might make her think he only had sex on his mind. "Elizabeth, you have been the woman in control of their lives these many months. They trust you and want to help you."

She gave him a smile, but it was solemn.

"Come here," he said, pulling her back up next to him. They lay side by side, and he was careful not to press his hips near her. "I'm here. The farmer is safe. The soldiers inspected the cart, and I could hear them prodding through the straw, as if I hid beneath it."

"But you did," she breathed, staring into his eyes in wonder.

He shrugged and adjusted the cushion beneath their heads so they could continue to face each other. "They didn't find me. The cart was driven to the stables, then left to await unloading. I waited for night. I heard a lot of conversations, even some about myself."

She smiled and leaned in to kiss his chin. "And what did my grooms say?"

"One of them claimed that he knew all along who I was," he said, using his finger to slide a lock of hair behind her ear.

"Oh, he did?"

He loved the way her nose crinkled when she smiled. Freckles lightly scattered there. "The other groom didn't believe him either. To be fair, one groom thought I was a coward for retreating."

"As if you were supposed to defeat Bannaster and his entire army."

She was affronted on his behalf, and he found himself pulling her closer. When their hips met, she eyed him dubiously.

"You are aroused by my defense of you?" she asked.

He leaned in and kissed behind her ear, inhaling

the sweet, womanly scent of her. "I'm aroused by anything you do." He rolled his hips against her. "All you have to do is walk by me in the great hall carrying a tray, or kneel at mass or—"

Shocked, she covered his mouth with her hand. "The priest would say such a thing is a sin!"

"I am betrothed to you, and the priest says that is almost the same as a marriage. A husband is supposed to desire his wife, so that babies will be born. How can you say that is a sin?"

She started to laugh, and he kissed her until she was breathless and looking at him with longing. That was what he wanted to see for the rest of his life. He wanted her to desire him—to love him, to not wonder about his greed when she looked on him. Somehow he would make it happen.

Between kisses, he said, "When all was silent . . . I lifted the false bottom . . . replaced everything . . . and came right to you for my reward."

He rolled on top of her, settling himself between her thighs. But before he could make love to her, she put both hands on his chest and pushed.

"Nay, John, we cannot use the time so selfishly again."

He lifted up on his hands to look down at her. Though her face was flushed, and he felt the heat at the core of her, he would not press such an advantage. He rolled off her and collapsed onto his back with a groan.

Elizabeth came up on her elbow. "You cannot stay here. What if the soldiers return, thinking you might press your advantage with me?"

He gave her a leering grin.

She pushed at his shoulder. "You know what I mean. What will we do now that you're here?"

John's smile faded. "I will allow nothing to happen to you, sweetling. I will be here to protect you. Sometimes I find myself wishing that you and I were simple people, who could marry freely as they will. I would take you without dowry, without a title, without concerns about households and money."

She sat up, pulling the sheet up about her breasts, distancing herself from him. "But we aren't those people, John. I know you are a man of honor. You made something of yourself when your family thought you couldn't. You honored your family's promises to mine, though it took you away from the life of travel that you love."

Something flashed in her eyes so quickly, he almost thought he imagined it.

Softly, she said, "You've risked everything for me—"

"And I would risk it again. I love you, Elizabeth."

But instead of joy, he saw pain in her eyes, and she swiftly looked away. He'd meant to woo her, to seduce her, to show her that they could love one another, and instead he only added to her pressure.

"And I have brought you heartache," she continued in a low voice. "I know not how this will end with Bannaster. Tonight I fear that dawn is approaching, and our time cut short."

"Elizabeth—"

"Nay, you must leave now. I could not live with the guilt should someone discover you here."

He got out of bed and saw that she couldn't meet his eyes as he dressed. He knew that he could not leave with something unstated between them. He left Elizabeth seated in the middle of his bed, the sheet as her defense, though he wanted to drag her to him and coerce the truth from her.

"I will not leave you until you tell me what you're thinking," John said.

Her glance was uncertain, but that regal way she had of seeming untouchable, unattainable, returned. "I am worried that the only plan we have to protect my people might cause even more harm."

" 'Tis not what I'm talking about, and you know it," he said. "I told you I loved you, and you immediately became distant with me. Aye, mayhap I should not have spoken my feelings so quickly. You are frightened and—"

"I am not frightened." Her eyes flashed at him.

"Then tell me what it is. I am not pressuring you to make such a declaration yourself. These are dreadful times for you, watching everything your family has worked for come under the power of an outsider."

"And that is just it!" she whispered furiously, her fists gripping the bedsheet. "I am faced with a situation I cannot resolve, yet it was so easy for me to—" She broke off and looked away from him.

He wanted to touch her, but he knew the dilemma she wrestled with. "Easy for you to what, Elizabeth?"

After a hesitation, she spoke in a low, firm voice.

"I don't like feeling like this, unable to . . . control myself when I am with you."

Though inside he softened in sympathy for her, he knew she didn't want such emotion from him, not right now.

"Passion that brings two people together can feel overwhelming," he said quietly. "Maybe it even feels unsafe to you, unnatural, but only because you have never experienced love before."

"And you have?"

"Nay, I do not claim that. You are the only woman I have ever loved."

"Or thought you loved," she quickly said.

"Because you are confused, you think I don't know my own heart? I may not have loved before, but I have been intimate with women, and I enjoyed it each time."

She flinched, and he hated hurting her.

"But enjoying sex is not the same thing as giving of yourself in every way. What I had here with you tonight I have never experienced before. There is an intimacy between us that humbles me, that makes me realize that I want to share this with you for the rest of my life."

"And you are not . . . afraid of it? Afraid of change? Afraid of . . . losing yourself?"

"Of giving you power over me, you mean?"

She bit her lip.

"I want this, Elizabeth. I want it more than any-thing else I have in my life. I am willing to give up the things that I once thought were all I needed to feel happy. I don't care about the life I had before, the travel, the combat. If you could not be with me, what would such things matter to me?"

"I cannot believe that something so important to you would cease to matter."

"I did not say that. 'Tis just that you matter more. I think I used my love of adventure as a replacement for real love. I never thought I could hope for it, being the third son and with little to offer a bride."

She stared up at him with wide eyes swimming in tears.

"So if I travel again, I would want you with me," he continued. "You mean so much to me."

She closed her eyes, and two tears fell down her cheeks. "I usually know the right things to say," she said. "But now, with you, I don't."

"It is you demanding perfection of yourself, Elizabeth, not I. You have a castle full of people depending on you, and I am one more, I know."

"I do not think of you as I think of my servants and my friends."

He gave her a gentle smile. "That's all I can ask for right now. Be patient with yourself."

"It is you who have all the patience," she said. "You returned and I practically attacked you—"

"It was wondrous, and I enjoyed the display of your feelings for me. I don't need the words, at least not at this moment."

She bowed her head. "You should go. Hide yourself. If he finds you here—"

"He will think you aid the enemy."

She grabbed his hand. "Nay, I care not for myself!

It is you who will suffer in my place, and I could not bear it."

She kissed the back of his hand. He felt her tears, knew her torment, and softly cupped her head.

"Then I will go, sweetling," he murmured, stooping to kiss the top of her head. "I will see you again tomorrow night. Know that you are not alone."

"I know," she whispered.

John left her and returned to the undercroft, where there were so many places to hide. He made himself as comfortable as possible on sacks of grain and tried to sleep, but he kept seeing her sad eyes in his mind.

Chapter 23

The next morning, Elizabeth waited in the kitchen as Adalia prepared food for Anne. Elizabeth felt rather dazed, and she told herself it was lack of sleep. Adalia gave her several worried looks, but did not pry beyond an initial, hesitant good morning.

It wasn't just lack of sleep overwhelming Elizabeth. She did not know what to think about John, his gentleness, his understanding. She felt unworthy of his attentions, when she herself did not know yet what to offer him in return.

It seemed like it would have been a simple thing to offer her own hesitant confession. Hadn't she already wondered if she loved him? Shouldn't lovemaking have convinced her of that?

Instead it made her pull back, and John didn't deserve that, not after everything he had sacrificed for her.

She was a coward, and she was startled and disappointed by that fact.

Yet was it cowardly to want to spare him, should her feelings prove less than his? Plenty of people had good marriages without true love.

But not her parents, she thought with sadness. They'd shared everything together, even death.

How foolish she was to think that she had loved William. There had been none of this whirlwind of emotion—this fear, this ecstasy, this despair.

This terror. How would she bear it if something happened to John?

"Anne?"

Elizabeth shook herself back to awareness to find Adalia watching her with concern.

"I've called yer name twice now," the cook said softly, "but I couldn't hand a full tray to a woman who wasn't payin' attention."

Elizabeth tried to smile. "Forgive me. My thoughts have been scattered. I'm here now."

" 'Tis a good thing." She looked about and whispered, "He will make it all right."

Elizabeth smiled brightly. "Who?"

Adalia only shook her head and handed her the tray.

Elizabeth walked through the great hall, ignoring the looks of sympathy she was still receiving. What was surprising was how many soldiers watched her, too, and that made her uneasy.

At the base of the tower, she found Bannaster waiting for her, and now she understood the soldiers' curiosity.

Still holding the tray, she curtsied. "A good morning, my lord."

"Good morning, Anne."

He looked at her so innocently, as if he hadn't chased her through the corridors of Castle Alderley, trying to bed her.

But why was he waiting for her?

"I will accompany you up to visit Lady Elizabeth," he said.

"My lord, permit me to go up first, and prepare her for you. She likes her hair styled just so—"

"Such vanity is unnecessary with me," he said. "Lady Elizabeth's beauty is readily apparent. I will follow you up."

Neither soldier looked at her as they stepped aside. Bowing her head, Elizabeth stepped past the viscount and preceded him into the tower and up the stairs. She kept expecting him to touch her, and that made her climb so quickly that she was breathless near the top.

What did he want? Did he mean to hurt Anne by telling her that John had been driven from the castle? Did he wonder if "Lady Elizabeth" had somehow been aiding her betrothed?

Elizabeth knocked on the door, calling out, as she had before, that Lord Bannaster was accompanying her this day.

She heard him chuckle, but he said nothing as they waited.

Anne took a long time coming to the door. Had she received another basket that she needed to hide? Finally, she opened it and stepped back.

"Good morning, Lord Bannaster," she said in a soft voice.

"Aye, it is," he said agreeably.

He was too insufferably pleased with himself. Thank goodness Elizabeth had already explained the revelation of John's true identity to Anne. Yet her maid did not know that John had returned, and was even now hiding in the castle. Perhaps her ignorance was for the best.

"Might I break my fast with you?" he asked.

Anne gestured to the table, and they both sat down. Elizabeth silently split the meal onto plates between them.

When they were eating, Elizabeth retreated to a corner chair and picked up an embroidery hoop to pretend to busy herself.

Bannaster handed Anne a chunk of bread. "I am sure your maid told you that John Russell had been spying on us all."

Spying was an interesting way to put it, but Anne only inclined her head to wait.

"He is determined to have you, even though the king knows by now that he is unsuitable to become an earl."

"And how does the king know that?" Anne asked.

"My cousin was sending a man to investigate Russell's castle and finances. It cannot look good for him. Since it is only a matter of time before the contract is invalidated, I have decided that to protect you, it is best if I decline guardianship of you and offer marriage instead."

Elizabeth poked herself with a needle and tried not to wince.

Anne stopped pretending to eat. "You may offer marriage, my lord, but that does not mean—"

He interrupted her, and his smile seemed forced. "*Offer* is the wrong word. I intend to marry you, Lady Elizabeth. Russell is a scoundrel unworthy to serve my royal cousin. I will present the king with our marriage. He will void the betrothal contract negotiated by a dead king. What bishop would stand against him?"

"You cannot force me to wed you," Anne said.

Her voice was shaking now. What would happen if she were pushed too hard? Would she betray herself by looking to her lady's maid for guidance?

Bannaster smiled. "I won't have to force you to marry me."

Anne rose to her feet. "And I will not let you . . . touch my person, as if *that* would convince me to marry you!"

"I won't do that either," Bannaster said calmly. "Russell is in disgrace, and his unworthiness will already be apparent to the king. I have told the parish priest that we wish to be wed on the morrow, and that I have already purchased a special license to be married without the banns being read."

He had planned for this a long time, Elizabeth realized in growing fear.

Bannaster stood up, and Anne just stared at him, her fear apparent.

"I suggest, my lady, that you prepare yourself for a beautiful ceremony. And stop looking as if I mean to harm you!" he added with distaste.

After he'd left the room, Elizabeth closed the door behind him and crossed to Anne, who sat still, looking ashen.

"I won't let it come to this," Elizabeth said fiercely.

"I know you won't. But I fear for what you will do."

"He put it out of my hands," she answered softly. "I think I might have only one option."

"Elizabeth, you're frightening me."

"You don't need to be frightened anymore."

By that night, John had already overheard the news—Bannaster planned to marry Lady Elizabeth on the morrow. A feast had been ordered, and servants moved about too quietly. John had to wait to go to Elizabeth until the sounds of supper overhead faded away.

He "borrowed" a cloak, and used the hood to hide his face. By now he knew the corridors well, and understood where to hide when he heard someone coming. At last he was able to knock softly on her door, and when she opened it, he slipped inside. Immediately, he drew her into his arms.

To his surprise, she melted against him, pulling his head down to kiss him. He froze, not sure if he understood what was happening. Even as his cock hardened and his brain grew fuzzy, he broke the kiss.

"Elizabeth, I heard what Bannaster plans to do. We have to go forward with my plan—"

She dropped the dressing gown that she was wearing to reveal her nudity. He lost his voice in confusion. He stared at her breasts that fit so perfectly in his hand and mouth, as he already well knew. He swallowed.

"No words, John," she whispered. "I've been thinking of this all day. I need you."

He pulled off his garments and picked her up off the floor as they kissed. She writhed in his arms and moaned, wrapping her legs about his waist. When he carried her to the bed, he turned and sat down with her in his lap, running his hands up her smooth back, gripping her shoulders to arch her away from him so that he could taste her breasts.

As their hips pressed even harder together, he groaned as his erection was trapped between them.

She suddenly straightened up, her arms about his shoulders. "We can make love like this?"

He nodded. "Think of me as your mount, my little captain."

He lay back and watched her expressions of wonder and expanding possibilities as she sat atop him. She slid her body along the length of his erection, and he closed his eyes on a groan. She played that game until he was mindless and trembling. When she licked his nipples, he finally had to stop her.

"I need you to take me," he whispered. "Just guide me inside you."

When she took him in her hand, he shuddered. As she impaled herself on him in a wet, hot slide into bliss, it took everything he had to control his need to pump inside her.

While everything else in her life was falling apart, he would give her this one thing to control.

"This feels wondrous," she whispered.

She leaned forward over him, her hands braced on either side. He lifted her hips and pressed her back down again, showing her the movement. As she experimented on her own, he caressed her breasts, molding and tugging, rubbing her nipples between his fingers. He watched the passion that lit her face, the intensity as she struggled for her own climax. He came up on his elbow to kiss her, and then gathered her breast like a ripe fruit to bring into his mouth.

With every stroke she grew bolder, and he arched his hips to thrust inside her ever deeper. When she found her release, he fell back on the bed, catching her hips to grind her against him as he came.

When she collapsed across his chest, he held her, fingering her wet hair aside so that he could press kisses to her forehead, her cheek, her ear. His cock still pulsed inside her, urging him to roll her onto her back and take her again.

"Thank you," she whispered.

Though he wanted to hold her, she moved off of him and seated herself beside him on the bed, using the sheet once again to hide herself from him. That didn't bode well.

"So you heard the news," she said softly.

He sat up beside her, his anger renewing. "Aye. I will not allow that bastard to usurp my place as your betrothed."

"John."

"How can he not wait for the king's decision?"

"John, please listen to me."

When she touched his arm, he finally looked down into her determined face. He didn't like what he saw there.

"I'm through fighting this, John."

Her quiet voice filled him with confusion.

"Elizabeth, what are you talking about? Of course we are going to fight this."

"Nay, I have been the source of too much pain. My steward died—"

"Through no fault of yours."

She continued as if he hadn't spoken. "Anne has been cruelly imprisoned for over a sennight now."

"She wanted to help you!"

"And you—John, you have risked your life for me over and over. You're a hunted man now. I cannot live with that."

She let out her breath with a shudder, and he realized that the fall of her hair had hidden her tears.

"It is my choice, Elizabeth. I am meant to marry you."

She glared at him wildly. "I cannot risk them killing you!"

"Elizabeth—"

"Don't you see, I thought I could be different

from other women, that I could make my own destiny. It's been a hard lesson, but I've learned that I am no better than anyone else. Too many people depend on me, and I couldn't bear it if anyone were killed defending me. I am going to marry Bannaster."

He inhaled quickly, struggling to control his anger. She would not respond to intimidation, but she was intelligent and logical. If only that tactic would work. "Elizabeth, it always comes back to control with you. You're doing all this to hold onto your power to choose, even if it is to choose a life sentence of misery."

"That's not true!"

"It is. Even tonight, you took control with sex, in desperation."

She shook her head, and though she was crying harder, he hardened himself against it.

"I am surrendering, don't you see?" she cried softly.

"But it's your choice, your power," he said. "You're not allowing me to choose. I have an army at my disposal."

"This is the only way to avoid bloodshed, John, can't you see that? How many more people have to have their lives disrupted so that I can have whatever I want? It's wrong! Every woman of wealth has to accept that her husband will be chosen for her— even you were chosen for me! Maybe I am exercising my last right to choose, but it is my right and responsibility."

"You had already decided on this foolish path before I arrived," he said in a low, angry voice.

She bit her lip and nodded.

"So you used this as a last farewell?"

She closed her eyes as more tears spilled down her cheeks.

He dressed quickly, while she kept her back to him and cried softly. He was too angry to sympathize and make this easier on her. She didn't trust him to work everything out.

A long time ago, he would have doubted his own abilities, but no more. He knew now that his father had believed in him. God's Blood, he'd even worded the contract so that John could inherit the chance to marry Elizabeth. His anger faded away as he felt a surge of grief for his dead family, whom he'd never properly mourned.

He didn't bother trying to persuade Elizabeth. He knew her too well—she would not change her mind. She thought she was doing the right thing, and who was he to tell her that she did not have the right to choose?

He was the man who loved her.

He would not give up on their betrothal, but if he told her that, she would only worry more. There was an army waiting to liberate her, and he would do his best to make sure that few people were hurt.

He stood over the bed, watching as she curled into a ball of misery. Her crying had stopped, but she quivered with each breath, as if it hurt to live. He gently touched her arm, and she flinched away from him. Distancing herself again, as if she were trying to make things easier on him. She sat up, wiping the last tears from her face, her expression at last stony and impassive.

She wanted him to hate her, so that he would go on with his life.

But she loved him; he knew it, although she would not admit it to him, and maybe not to herself. But in trying to save him, she was only proving her devotion.

"Good-bye, Elizabeth."

She finally met his gaze, and with a stubborn lift of her chin, she said, "Good-bye."

As Elizabeth watched John walk across the room, she found herself shaking. It began as little tremors, but turned into shudders of pain as he closed the door behind him.

Though her throat was tight from suppressing her tears, she would not cry again. It was time to grow up, to understand that responsibility and duty were what mattered. She could think of no other way to protect her people—to protect John—except by marrying Bannaster. Putting it off would serve no purpose.

But she felt as fragile as glass, ready to shatter if anyone touched her. John's last caress had almost sent her over the edge. She wanted to beg him to take her with him, but in the end, her resolve had held, and she could have some pride in that.

She knew she loved him; this was a real, adult love, not the girlhood fantasy she'd always imagined she'd wanted. It had to be real, because giving it up hurt like someone had plunged a sword into her heart. Not telling him of her love hurt the worst of all.

She washed herself with cold water, then dressed with deliberate care, wishing she could wear one of her own gowns. She had to look her best.

Because she knew what had to be done.

Chapter 24

❦

G etting out of the castle proved far easier than
getting in. The sun was setting; servants were
returning home to their villages. People streamed
out, and soldiers didn't bother to search them.

John wore his cloak and hunched his shoulders,
walking slower rather than quickly. Soon enough
he was out in the open countryside, where it was
easy to fade into a copse of trees and away from the
villagers.

He found his horse waiting for him in Rachel's
paddock, and he quietly saddled it and left. As true
night was descending, he reached the military encampment. Many fires dotted the meadow. On the
outskirts he gave the call of a skylark, and Ogden
and Parker appeared on either side of him.

They led him to where Philip was gnawing the last meat from a bone. He waved it jauntily.

John put his hands on his hips. "Elizabeth has decided to marry Bannaster."

Philip tossed the bone into the fire and rose to his feet. "That might mean taking your babe into the enemy's household."

John frowned.

Philip put up both hands. "As if I didn't notice the time you were spending alone with her? I could hardly think you would keep your hands to yourself."

John turned to Parker and Ogden. "Summon Sir Jasper and his soldiers immediately. The wedding is supposed to take place in the morning."

"You mean to attack?" Philip asked in disbelief. "Lady Elizabeth doesn't want—"

Grimly, John said, "For once, she's not the one in command."

Elizabeth knocked on Bannaster's door—the door to what had been her parents' suite. It was opened by the man's squire, who gaped at her, then stepped back so that Bannaster, lounging in a chair near the fire, could see her.

Bannaster gave her a slow grin. "You can tell your mistress that sending you here to plead for her will not work. The wedding will take place in the morning."

"I am here on my own behalf," she said simply, trusting in the mystery of her words.

Bannaster cocked his head. Then he nodded at his squire, who stepped out into the corridor, closing the door once Elizabeth had gone inside. She remained still, not even frightened, feeling calm—and in control. That was all she needed to get through each day.

Bannaster slowly rose to his feet and came toward her. He was not as tall as John, but he was formidable, a man used to power. Instead of stopping before her, he walked about her as if on an inspection.

Before her once again, he took her chin in his fingers and lifted it. She stepped back.

"No touching?" he said, wearing a half-smile. "Is that not what you came here for?"

She removed her wimple and his smile faded as her hair, which she'd brushed to a lustrous sheen, fell down in long curls about her body.

When Bannaster spoke again, his voice was husky. "Seducing me will not stop me from marrying your mistress either."

"I don't wish to stop the wedding," she said. "But you will not be marrying the woman in the tower. You'll be marrying me."

He started to laugh, but it faded away in his confusion. "Why would your mistress think I would accept a maidservant in the place of an heiress?"

"Because I am not a maidservant. I am Lady Elizabeth Hutton."

"Nicely done," he scoffed.

She went on as if she hadn't heard him. "I exchanged

places with my maidservant so that I could devise a method to thwart your plans. But I could not, so now I surrender to save my people."

He stared at her in disbelief. "Tell your mistress that I will not be tricked into marrying someone else."

"'Tis no trick, my lord. You have won; you have defeated me. Ask me any questions concerning my parents or the betrothal you are vowing to see nullified."

"You could have been taught what to say."

"Ask anyone, far and wide, about my identity. I have struggled every day to keep it from you and from your servants. My sisters even arrived while you were gone, and I had to send them away. Did you not say that your revelation about Lord Russell's identity came from Rodmarton Castle? And that day you drunkenly tried to force yourself on me—"

"I did not try to—"

"Did you not see how my people rallied to defend me? There was no fire in that kitchen, except the one started by my cook."

He looked confused and troubled.

"Did you never ask anyone what I looked like?" she asked.

"Lady Elizabeth has the reputation as a beautiful, fair-haired maiden."

"And what color hair has the woman in the tower? It is certainly not fair."

His eyes suddenly glittered as his face went pale. "If you are lying to me, I will discover it easily on the morrow, before the wedding."

He stalked toward her, and she moved, keeping furniture between them.

"It will be a relief for my people to cease pretending to ignore me."

She wasn't sure why he was so positive he would know the truth in the morning, but she didn't care. Now she had to stop what he might try in his anger.

He reached for her, but she danced aside, keeping away from the bed.

"You must stop this harassment at once, my lord," she said firmly.

"And why should I? I've been lied to, made a fool of. Those people down below have been laughing at me all along."

"They do not consider this a laughing matter, but one of life and death—mine, as well as theirs, should they be caught. They offered up their silence for me out of loyalty. And they will be loyal to you, if the king makes you earl."

"If?"

"There is no guarantee. The betrothal contract stipulates that the next earl will be the Russell heir."

"And I've proven how worthless he is. You should be glad I rid the castle of such a coward."

But it was obvious he didn't believe his own words. John had been the superior swordsman in their battle. Bannaster tossed aside the stool between them.

"I have conditions before I marry you, Lord Bannaster."

He threw back his head and laughed. "Ah, leave it to you to lighten the moment."

"I will make you an excellent wife. I will manage your castles, be devoted in public, and produce heirs."

"And my part will be . . . ?" he said sarcastically.

"That you do not touch me until our wedding night. And you must promise no retribution against my people, especially my maidservant and Lord Russell."

"They lied to me."

"*I* lied to you. If you cannot meet these conditions, I will make your life miserable. I will thwart you at every turn. If you think to show me off as your newest prize in London, I will make you the butt of jokes throughout the kingdom. I am quite the actor, as you've already seen."

He narrowed his eyes. "And all I have to do is promise to leave your servants and Russell alone."

"Aye, including the villagers. I made them part of my secrecy, and I can make them loyal to you."

"And if Russell returns for you?"

"I will already be married to you."

He turned away from her and went back to the chair before the fire. Only when he sat down did she let out a shaky breath.

"We have an agreement," he said finally. He looked her up and down. "I don't want a miserable marriage. I vowed to you that I would make you happy, and I will. Starting with our wedding night."

He smiled at her, and it took everything she had to nod and hold back her tears. Once she was out in the corridor, she leaned back against the wall and released a shuddering sigh. Bannaster had been surprisingly malleable, considering how she'd deceived him. The irony of it was, all she'd ever wanted was a husband she could make bow to her wishes.

But against John she'd had heated disagreements that somehow led to the greatest intimacy of her life. She had fallen in love with a strong, independent man, but now she would have to settle for her girlhood dreams of controlling a marriage.

It no longer held any appeal for her.

The challenge would be to see what Bannaster was hiding and thwart him if necessary. And if she bore a son quickly, her ultimate—but secret— triumph would be in knowing that John's child might be the next earl.

At the castle gatehouse just before dawn, John, wearing a hooded cloak, waited in the midst of a large crowd. He led the first wave of soldiers, who were dressed as farmers, as tradesmen, even a few *as* soldiers. Others would follow in groups over the next hour.

Luckily, Bannaster must have wanted many people in attendance, for half a hundred had waited since before dawn for the chance to see a noble wedding—or to see what happened when one was attempted. More people were slowly coming down the road. Plenty of wagers were being exchanged as to what Elizabeth would do. None of the possible scenarios considered by the villagers included the stealthy invasion by Alderley's own soldiers.

When the gates finally opened, there was a mad rush to enter, overwhelming the few soldiers stationed there to inspect the visitors. They made several random attempts to search satchels, but at last they decided to join the merriment and toast the bride and groom.

From his place near the stairs up to the great hall, John could see his soldiers spread out through the crowds and begin to hide themselves behind or inside all of the buildings. Over the next several hours, one by one, Bannaster's soldiers began to disappear. The skills in stealth that John's men had acquired from the League did them in good stead, because no one seemed to notice when a soldier was caught from behind and disposed of. The men were under orders to incapacitate rather than kill, but to do it all quickly.

The next morning, Elizabeth descended from the tower wearing the gold and white gown she'd had made for her wedding day. She let her hair flow freely as a maiden, and felt calm and full of purpose. She refused to dwell on what could not be changed, although Anne had wept and tried to talk her out of marriage.

Elizabeth knew she could not bear to consider what could never be—marriage to John, happiness with the man she loved.

Anne now walked sedately behind her as they entered the great hall, the first time she had left the tower in over a sennight. Bannaster was already waiting at the high table. He rose when he saw Elizabeth, and table after table went silent as well. Everywhere people gaped at her in shock. As she walked through the hall, people curtsied and bowed, their expressions changing into resignation. They understood what was happening.

Not so the soldiers, who talked among themselves in confusion. She hesitated for a moment at the table of the bearded soldier who'd once attacked her. After staring at her wide-eyed, he bowed to her and said nothing.

She walked on, smiling at her people, patting the head of Adalia's son, who came running up to her crying out her name in delight. Elizabeth did not bother to meet Bannaster's eyes at this further confirmation of her identity. He was no fool.

More people than normal crowded the great hall for the morning meal. Bannaster must have had couriers sent to the farthest villages in anticipation of the wedding, for people continued to stream in even as they all ate.

Elizabeth knew she should be greeting everyone, but on her wedding day, she felt almost numb . . . content to sit in solitude instead of making conversation. If she looked at too many people, she would be searching for John's beloved face. She prayed that he was gone, that he was not here to witness her ultimate surrender. And surely Bannaster's soldiers were still looking for him.

At last, Bannaster stood up and lifted his hands in the air. Voices died down instantly, as if they'd only been waiting for their cue.

Bannaster smiled. "Today is the perfect day for a

celebration. Today the priest will be joining the great houses of Bannaster and Alderley."

Only the soldiers cheered, and after a momentary look of impatience, Bannaster continued. "The truth has come out at last, and Lady Elizabeth has learned the errors of deception. Those of you who knew her true identity"—he paused, and there were low murmurs as people looked at one another—"your loyalty to her is commendable, but now that loyalty must extend to me, since we have agreed to marry." He tried to lighten the tone of his voice. "I have more good news. I have just received confirmation that King Henry will be here in time to bless this union. He is but an hour's journey away."

Elizabeth caught her breath, and she stared about her in growing awareness. She and Anne exchanged shocked looks. The king was coming? Surely Bannaster had known, but he had not told her the previous night.

Because it might have changed everything.

Elizabeth felt hot and cold and flustered. What should she do? Until now she'd been the one to decide her own course—posing as a maidservant, and then finally revealing herself, bargaining for her position as Bannaster's wife.

As if he recognized her conflicting thoughts, Bannaster suddenly became very attentive, and never left her side as the great hall was cleared of trestle tables. There was no room for all of these people to stand outside the chapel doors for the wedding, as was the custom.

"I wish you would have warned me of our royal guest," Elizabeth said to Bannaster. "I could have better prepared the castle."

"While you were a maidservant?" he asked with sarcasm.

She bowed her head. "I hope the condition of my home does not reflect poorly on you."

But Alderley was a jewel of a castle, one of the largest in the western half of the country, and they both knew it. Bannaster looked about with pride, as if he'd built it to what it was himself.

"The king will be pleased," he said. "And he'll be pleased with your acceptance of the inevitable."

Elizabeth bowed her head.

At last, a great horn was heard in the distance. People rushed out to the inner ward to watch the procession of soldiers and courtiers, and the king himself. Elizabeth stood beside Bannaster within the large double doors of the great hall, looking down at the joyous scene in the courtyard. King Henry, thin and blond, smiled and waved, and she knew he was a man courting his people, for he'd only won the crown from his cousin, Richard III, the previous year.

The king ascended the stairs to the great hall, and as Elizabeth curtsied, Bannaster bowed low.

The king took her hand and raised her to stand. "Lady Elizabeth, it is good to see you again. Our thanks for welcoming us to your home."

The last proof Bannaster might need of her true identity had now been supplied. Bannaster happily put her hand on his arm and followed the king indoors. The castle swelled as another contingent of soldiers merged with the crowd.

Elizabeth had never seen so many people, except in the streets of London. The hall grew overly warm before the ceremony could begin.

Though Bannaster obviously wanted to stay at the king's side, his captain of the guard came and pulled him aside to speak privately. Bannaster's expression remained impassive, but he glanced at the great double doors, then back to the king. He bowed and said something to his cousin, who waved him off and turned to speak to one of his councilors. Bannaster moved quickly through the crowd and left the hall. Elizabeth then considered King Henry.

At the last changing of the guard, the absences were finally noticed. John had been watching for the alert and the subsequent confusion. The captain of the guard was no fool, yet he had not shouted a warning, only gone quickly inside the castle.

Everything had become so much more confusing with the unexpected arrival of the king. John wished he could consider how this might affect him, but he was too busy leading the secret assault. The crowds in the inner ward had really begun to swell with the arrival of the king's party. Luckily, the royal soldiers had followed him inside.

Now that the captain of the guard had gone in to tell Bannaster what was happening, John knew he had to work quickly. He began to spread the word among the castle residents and the villagers to get out of harm's way, by either going inside or fleeing back to the village of Alderley. He hoped this would mollify Elizabeth when she learned what was happening.

The ward had begun to empty just as Bannaster came out the double doors, drawing his sword. As if a signal had been given, the remaining soldiers drew theirs and grouped themselves defensively, looking for the enemy.

Bannaster came running down the stairs, brandishing his sword against the first person who crossed his path. It was a woman, and she screamed as she froze in front of him. Though Bannaster waved her away, John could not risk harming Elizabeth's people. He came out from the shadow of the stairs, holding his sword aloft, throwing back his hood.

"For Alderley!" he cried in a loud voice.

A chorus of shouts and cheers answered him. Though John saw that Bannaster's soldiers turned to answer the charge, there were few enough left that Alderley's forces should win the day. But John concentrated on Bannaster, whose face had alighted with anger and determination at John's cry.

Bannaster came running at him, his sword upraised. Without a word, he slashed downward, and John parried the weapon away with his own. Bannaster then thrust at him, which John turned away with his shield.

"Give way, Bannaster," John shouted. "I am Elizabeth's legal betrothed. Just ask your cousin the king."

"You are not worthy of her!"

Bannaster unleashed several blows, which John countered. John had had enough of the man's arrogance. He went on his own offensive, driving Bannaster back to the stairs. Bannaster tripped and sprawled onto his back, and John had his sword at the man's throat.

"So you plan to kill me?" Bannaster demanded in a tight voice, lying still on the stairs.

"I would take great delight in it, after the way you've tortured Elizabeth," John said between gritted teeth.

"Elizabeth or Anne? Which one does either of us want?"

Angrily, John pressed the sword closer, where it grazed Bannaster's flesh.

"Halt!" shouted a commanding voice from above.

John did not look up; he stared his intentions into Bannaster's eyes. But he had recognized Milburn's voice, and allowed the steward to come down the stairs.

"No closer!" John commanded.

Milburn stopped just above them. "My lords, you must stop this! The king is growing anxious. Does either of you want to explain to him why one of his noblemen has been murdered?"

In that fraction of a moment, John played out every possible ending in his mind, but in none of them did he win Elizabeth. Killing Bannaster would just enrage the king, whose arrival had ruined all of John's plans to force Bannaster to relinquish Alderley.

John pulled his sword away and stepped back. Bannaster gingerly rubbed his neck as he sat up.

"There's no blood," John said. "If I would have cut you, you'd already know it."

Bannaster rose to his feet, glaring at John.

"My lord, the king waits!" Milburn said firmly.

"I've won, Russell," Bannaster said. "Guards, to me!"

But only two soldiers answered his call. Realizing the inevitable, Bannaster slowly backed up the stairs as Alderley's men gathered below to glare at him.

"The king will hear of this," Bannaster said as he reached the top.

"Go ahead and tell him," John taunted. "You don't have the courage to bring my name up."

Wearing a triumphant grin, Bannaster turned and went back inside.

When Bannaster returned, Elizabeth was staring at King Henry, the man who could decide her fate. Bannaster looked out of breath, but he was smiling as he put his arm around the king and turned him as if to speak alone—as alone as two men can be with various councilors present. Both men occasionally glanced at her, as if she were being discussed. King Henry frowned as he spoke to his cousin, and she knew Bannaster was fighting hard for this marriage.

Elizabeth's future was being decided for her; she'd always been an active participant in it. Even her decision to marry Bannaster had been her own.

Now the king might be able to help her, but she would have to risk anything he decided. The thought of baring her heart and soul, without knowing the result, was the most terrifying thing she'd ever faced.

But the risk was something she had to take. What good was control, if she was never going to be happy?

Slowly she walked toward the dais. The crowd parted for her, and whatever they saw on her face made a silence spread outward like waves in a pond. She saw Bannaster's expression change from curiosity to worry to outright fear. He tried to take the king's arm and lead him away, but too late—the king had seen her as well. He waited patiently until she came to a stop below them both.

And dropped to her knees. Her gown spread out about her, gleaming golden in the torchlight. The high stained-glass windows shown down on her as well; she'd chosen her position wisely.

It was the last thing she could control. Now her entire life rested in the hands of one man.

Chapter 25

John, now standing hidden within the crowd in the great hall, saw the moment that Elizabeth began her purposeful walk to the king. He felt like a failure. Elizabeth's people had *wanted* to fight for her, to win her freedom—and theirs. And John had been forced to back down.

When he had seen her in that golden gown, dressed as the heiress she was, his heart had almost stopped beating, so above him did she seem. Yet the woman who'd brazenly bedded him was there, too, trapped within the role she'd been given in life, the role she'd agreed to honor.

He'd almost wished she had seen his face, so she could decide between Bannaster and him one last time. Or was it at last time to declare himself?

When she dropped to her knees before the king, in a silent hall where even breathing had stopped, he felt himself caught in a strange moment in time.

Was he about to lose her to duty?

Or win her love?

"King Henry!" Elizabeth called in a strong, clear voice.

Bannaster tried to laugh. "My dear, if you're so impatient to begin the ceremony, there is no need for theatrics. I'm certain we can—"

"King Henry," she said again, "I have need of your help."

The king stepped forward, the tiny circlet of gold on his head glittering in the light. "I am sorry to hear that your betrothed has not arrived, Lady Elizabeth. But it is good that you wish to settle this great inheritance that you have borne with dignity."

"Your Majesty, I do not wish to be the bearer of unsettling news, but I can remain quiet no longer."

Bannaster tried to take the king's arm, but King Henry was now frowning at her. "What distresses you, lady?"

"Lord Bannaster claimed that in needing to protect me from the suitors who had begun to quarrel over my hand, he had to keep me secluded from my friends, from my people. He might have had the best motives, Your Majesty, but imprisonment is imprisonment."

A shocked gasp moved through the crowd, and John pushed closer to the center of the hall, his hand on the sword hidden beneath his cloak. Elizabeth risked much by speaking out against Bannaster.

"You were not imprisoned," Bannaster scoffed.

"Nay, but only because I switched places with my maidservant in a quest to free myself without bringing harm to my people. But Your Majesty, my betrothed is alive. I love him, and I wish to marry him."

John almost stumbled as her words shocked him. She was risking the king's censure, her own inheritance, everything—for him.

He wanted to swell his chest in pride—and tremble in panic at what the king would decide.

King Henry turned his formidable frown on his cousin. "You told me that Russell had not been found, that he was most likely dead."

"We all did assume that, Your Majesty," Bannaster quickly said. "He is an untrustworthy man, who even now has deserted Lady Elizabeth."

That was all John needed to hear. He threw off his cloak and strode forward, then knelt at Elizabeth's side. She looked up at him in shock and then wonder and then love, and he recognized the emotions on her face because they matched his own.

"King Henry," he said, "I am John Russell, ninth Baron Russell. I come to you to claim my bride."

He slipped his hand into Elizabeth's and squeezed. Her skin felt cold and moist, but the smile she gave him warmed him.

Before the king could speak, the great hall erupted in cheers that took several minutes to quiet. Bannaster had gone pale and angry, and the looks he cast at Elizabeth did not bode well for her happiness should John lose her hand.

King Henry lifted one hand, and the last excited voices faded away. He frowned at John. "Lord Russell, have you proof of your identity? You have been gone many a year, and although you resemble some of the Russell men I've known, I cannot accept merely that."

John held up his hand where the ancient ring now rested in its rightful place on his finger. He saw Bannaster's shoulders wilt, and then straighten. The fight was not over.

"And I vouch for him, Your Majesty," Elizabeth said. "I remember him well from my year fostering at Rame Castle. In our discussions, he has proven to me without a doubt to remember events that only a Russell would know."

The king frowned, and John felt despair begin to well within him. It wasn't enough proof.

Then one of the king's councilors stepped forward. He was a short man, with an oiled beard, but he looked on John with approval.

"Your Majesty, I was in Paris at this time last year, and I saw Lord Russell win a tournament with an impressive performance. This is the same man."

John bowed his head in acknowledgment.

"You have my gratitude, Lord Fogge." The king's brow cleared a bit, although he still spoke sternly. "Lord Russell, I have discovered that the prosperity of Rame Castle has faded in the last few years."

"Aye, it has, Your Majesty," John said. "I am dedicating my life to reestablishing the bond my family has always enjoyed with the land and its people."

"He only wants the heiress for her money," Bannaster said angrily.

The king arched a blond brow at him. "And money does not concern you, cousin?"

Bannaster flushed. "I am not desperate for it. This man has neglected his estate, siphoning off the profits to support his life in Europe."

"That is a lie, Your Majesty," John said firmly. "As the third son, I lived by what my sword arm could earn me. I only just discovered that, due to tragedy, I became the baron and inherited a bride."

"I have heard much of this sword arm of yours," King Henry said, glancing at Lord Fogge.

Even Bannaster could not have missed the interest in the king's voice.

John bowed his head. "You know it is in your service, Your Majesty. I will do as you wish." He met the king's stare once again. "But grant me my request; honor our parents' wishes. In the time I have been at Castle Alderley, I have grown to love Lady Elizabeth Hutton with a depth of feeling I would never have felt possible."

"He lied his way in here—" Bannaster began.

John interrupted. "Because I heard that my betrothed had been imprisoned, I felt the need for stealth, Your Majesty. I place myself on your mercy. I have learned much from my regrets of the past, my mistrust in my family, who only had the best motives for encouraging my stay in Europe. I have grown to understand the need for a father to teach his child to become a man. I never thought I would amount to much, but my father did. It is why he wrote that contract so that the Russell heir, and not one particular son, would marry Lady Elizabeth. I never understood what that meant."

"Cousin—" Bannaster began, with the first hint of desperation in his voice.

The king silenced him with a look. "Continue, Lord Russell."

"I am a changed man, Your Majesty," John said. He turned to gaze upon Elizabeth and took strength from the love shining in her eyes. "And it is because of this woman. Her courage humbles me. She risked her life for her people, where in the past I only risked my life for money. I thought adventure and travel could replace my family, could be my future, but she showed me how wrong I was. I have learned from my mistakes, and I need nothing more than her. She ran this entire castle and all of its many manors after her parents died, as she awaited me. It is my greatest regret that I could not arrive here in time to spare her the worry of imprisonment, her fear of the future. To earn her love is my goal in life. To stand at her side, her equal, is all I could ask for."

Elizabeth took his other hand, and kneeling, faced him. "Lord Russell, my betrothed, you have earned my love, and I regret I was too frightened of the future to offer it sooner."

He closed his eyes in gratitude. How had he deserved her—deserved her great love? He raised both her hands to his lips and kissed them with reverence. He had never hoped to touch her again, had never imagined she would offer herself to him so freely.

"Your Majesty," she said, her gaze never leaving John's face, "this man came to Alderley with no army and no resources, due to his brother's misfortunes. He risked his very life, even when we had only seen each other briefly as children. His honor and courage won my heart. Never did I think a man would deserve my devotion, but I gladly offer to John Russell my heart, my home, and my very life. I know he will care for it all."

The cheers were deafening, and King Henry had to raise both hands to quiet the crowd. Bannaster slumped back in a chair, his chin propped on his fist in dejection.

"I have had you investigated, Lord Russell, and your lack of blame in your brother's mistakes is recognized. The orders you gave to begin the restoration of Rame Castle were sound, and the prize money you offered was more than generous." He grinned. "Even enough to pay the taxes you owe to the crown."

Hardly daring to hope, John forced himself to grin in return. "Of course, Your Majesty."

"Your experience in Europe will only increase the prowess of my army, and having you in command of Alderley's troops seems like the perfect fit."

Elizabeth was squeezing his hands so tightly that surely her fingers must be cramped. Could it be true? Could they have won the king to their side?

King Henry's voice suddenly rose in volume. "I give my permission for the completion of the betrothal contract between Russell and Alderley. I commend my cousin for keeping a great heiress safe."

The last was said as he shot an amused look at Bannaster, who only gave a tight smile.

"Shall we have a wedding?" the king asked.

"But Your Majesty, the banns," John began.

"My cousin purchased a special license you may use. My signature will be enough to verify the change in the groom's name."

John drew Elizabeth to her feet. "You have my gratitude, King Henry."

"As long as I have your sword arm when I need it."

"Of course."

The king turned back to pat his cousin's shoulder, leaving John free to stare down at Elizabeth. All around them people prepared for the wedding. A lovely dark-haired woman smiled at Philip and they talked as old friends. She must be Elizabeth's maidservant Anne, who'd been so brave up in the tower. John wanted to meet her, but since for the moment, no one was bothering Elizabeth and him, he drew his betrothed into his arms.

He said, "That was a brave thing you did, confronting the king with the truth."

She shrugged. "No braver than you, sneaking back into this castle for—was it the third time? What did you plan to do?"

It was his turn to shrug. "To be honest, I wasn't alone. Your soldiers came back in disguise with me."

She gaped at him. "But I told you—"

"I know you wanted no violence, but the League of the Blade had helped us train them, and they wanted to be used. We removed many of Bannaster's soldiers before Bannaster himself came outside. I gave orders not to kill, if it could be helped."

Her eyes widened. "I remember when Bannaster left! But he returned and said nothing."

"That is because I had my sword at his throat before Milburn interrupted us. Perhaps he didn't want to admit his defeat. The plan was to make him see the futility of the fight. The king's arrival changed everything of course; how could I kill his cousin? Then I would never have the chance to win you."

"But would you have watched me marry him?" she asked softly.

He grinned. "I'm glad we won't ever have to know."

Philip cleared his throat behind them. "John, someone wants to see you."

John forced his gaze away from Elizabeth and frowned. "I don't—"

"The Bladesman is waiting for you both in your bedchamber."

John was about to tell Philip that the Bladesman could just wait, but his friend looked so solemn, so serious, an expression rare for him.

Elizabeth patted John's arm and smiled up at him. "We have a moment. Let's go before the king notices our absence."

How could John refuse her?

Philip accompanied them to the chamber, but only because John insisted. Inside, the Bladesman was waiting before the hearth, hands clasped behind his back. He gave Elizabeth a smile.

John looked down at her. "This is the man who helped train your soldiers. I wish I could introduce you, but he has never introduced himself."

The stranger kissed Elizabeth's hand, and she allowed it, saying, "You have my gratitude, kind sir."

"I fear we helped but little, as you both helped yourselves. Lord Russell, this situation could have led to bloodshed, yet between the two of you, a solution was found that satisfied all—except perhaps Lord Bannaster." His smile faded, and he regarded John with a solemn gaze. "Lord Russell, we are greatly impressed with you. We would like to make you an offer of membership in the League of the Blade."

Elizabeth gasped.

"Sir, I cannot accept your offer," John said.

"What?" Philip stepped forward. "Good God, man, are you a fool? They only offer this honor in the rarest of circumstances." Philip watched the stranger expectantly, and when the stranger said nothing to him, he gave a hearty sigh. "If it can't be me, I wish it to be you."

"But I will be married this day," John said. "I will not leave my wife."

The stranger said, "We only call members into service twice a year, for never more than a fortnight."

"I couldn't—"

"John." Elizabeth spoke his name. "You don't need to prove anything to me. I know I have your heart and your devotion. But this is a chance for you to help people, as you've helped me. You are a warrior for the king, and the League aids justice. Though they do not work for the king, he would not want you to refuse."

"Elizabeth, how can I leave you?" he whispered.

"The same way you'll leave when you have to attend Parliament and when I am too big with child to travel. We all take risks every day. You are a knight, better trained than most. I trust you to take care of yourself—and to claim the adventure you're due. 'Tis all right to want more from life than a satisfied marriage. I want you to be the man that you are."

"Take it," Philip urged.

John looked at the three people gathered around him, lastly at the stranger, who waited with infinite patience, as if he'd done this many times before.

"Very well, I accept your offer. But do not even think to come to me until at least six months have passed," he warned.

The man smiled. "And then your training begins." He allowed Philip to lead him out of the chamber, listening to Philip's questions while wearing an expression of great forbearance.

John hugged Elizabeth and kissed her brow. "I love you."

"And I love you." She cupped his face in her hands and tilted him lower. "That was not a proper kiss."

"You're already telling me what to do?" he said, laughing.

"About some things, perhaps," she said, and gave him a loving kiss. "I might as well have been trapped in that tower, my head above the clouds, but you brought me down to earth and showed me what real love is."

He grinned. "I am glad you think so, sweetling. But tonight you can order me about all you wish."

With a sigh, she murmured, "I will gladly let you take the lead."